THREATS

THREATS

BY

S. J. RITCHEY

Bookstand Publishing

http://www.bookstandpublishing.com

Published by
Bookstand Publishing
Morgan Hill, CA
3501_2

ISBN 978-1-61863-072-8

ACKNOWLEDGEMENTS

Sincere gratitude to members of Blue River Writers—Judy Beale, Carter Elliott, and Paul Poff for their helpful critiques and unwavering support. A special thanks is extended to my colleague, Joseph Maxwell, and to my wife, Elizabeth, for their review and helpful suggestions in bringing the manuscript to its final version.

Chapter 1

Intent on completing the daily task of approving the numerous documents that crossed his desk, Jason Spradlin glanced up in response to the knock on his office door. Audrey, the Biology departmental secretary, said, “Two men would like to see you for a few minutes. I told them you had a ten o’clock appointment.” She handed him business cards for James Feller and Ryan Sparks.

Jason stood to meet the men dressed in gray suits and somber ties. In an unusual move for a stranger, one closed the door to the outer suite. Each handed him a credential case with a badge and picture. Jason glanced at the documents that identified the visitors as agents of the Department of Homeland Security.

Trying to mask his wonderment and concern something had gone badly wrong around the university, Jason indicated cushioned, roll-out chairs around the small walnut conference table, feeling uncomfortable by the visitors he’d never seen before and whose blank and inscrutable facial expressions appeared threatening.

Feller, the taller of the two, spoke. “Dr. Spradlin, we won’t take much of your time, but wanted to meet you personally and relay a message from Dr. Brian Huffington, our Director.” His brown hair, light-brown eyes, and prominent chin matched the photo of his credentials. Sparks continued to survey the room as though looking for some danger or an escape route.

Still standing, Jason said, “How may I help you?”

Feller said, “We’re from the Department of Homeland Security and want to talk about a potential research project.” He pointed to the credential case in Jason’s hand as though to authenticate his authority to speak for a federal agency.

Jason glanced at the photo again, recorded the name of James Feller in his memory, nodded, and said, “Have a seat and tell me about this project.”

Feller began as they pulled out chairs and sat across from Jason. “We were assigned by the Director of the Agency for Biological Systems to investigate the feasibility of your participating in an effort to protect this country from biological weapons. We can’t tell you much about the actual research because we aren’t privy to that information, but arrangements will be made for you to come to Washington next week to meet the Director if our initial assessment proves satisfactory. He will reveal specific plans for the work at that time.”

Jason ignored the tone, implying an order rather than a request. “That’s not much to go on. I assume you know my background and the type of work I’ve been doing.”

“Correct. The Agency has done the usual background checks. The Director believes you could make a contribution or we wouldn’t be here.”

“Can you tell me anything?”

They looked at each other, weighing what to reveal to this young scientist in his tenth year at Missouri State University. Sparks, the non-talker, nodded, his face expressionless. Jason looked more closely at Sparks—black hair, dark eyes, a slight scar across one cheek.

Feller leaned forward and said, "No doubt you've learned through the news media that your government believes there is a growing threat to our national security by groups opposing this nation and our way of life. Our intelligence gathering has confirmed they are working diligently to develop biological weapons that could kill millions of Americans and disable our entire government. We must find counter measures if we are to survive. Scientists like yourself can play a vital role."

"It sounds like you're looking for someone to genetically manipulate organisms to impart resistance to foreign substances, or perhaps render them ineffective."

"Something like that," Feller said, "but we don't know the specifics. Only the Director and those close to him can tell you. That's why it's important you come next week."

"Will other scientists be involved?"

"We're not certain about that. Our assignment was directed toward you specifically."

Jason glanced at their business cards. "Why come this distance just to invite me to some meeting? A phone call would seem more expedient."

Feller said, "We wanted to meet you in person, ask some questions and look around this university and your laboratory. The fact is we've done a lot of investigating in the past two days and now we wish to clarify a couple of things."

He paused as though thinking about his questions, then asked,

"First, have you ever been a member of any organization other than those listed on your credentials filed with your previous grant applications to federal agencies?"

Jason said, "You probably know the answer if you did a thorough check of my background. But no, the only organizations I hold membership in are scientific ones." Jason realized they or some other agent had riffled through his applications to the National Institutes of Health and the Department of Agriculture. They could have contacted people who had known him in graduate school and in his post-doctoral stint in Boston, as well as key individuals at State University.

Ignoring Jason's obvious unease, Fellers asked, "Do you employ non- citizens or unregistered aliens in your laboratory?"

"Truthfully, I don't know. I have graduate assistants who are from other countries. I'm sure they've obtained student visas to enter the U.S. for the purpose of education, but the Office of International Students handles all of the paperwork and clears their status. We hear only if there's a problem at the time of their admission."

"Anyone from a Middle Eastern country in your lab at the present time?"

Jason hesitated, reluctant to focus the sights of these strangers on unsuspecting individuals. Then he decided Feller and Sparks knew already. "A young woman from Egypt is in her second year of a doctoral program with me. She has relatives in the U.S. and obtained her Master's degree at the University of Minnesota. I can't believe she's up to any clandestine stuff. She's too busy with her classes and research projects."

Feller and Sparks exchanged glances as though to communicate something to be checked out later.

Feller continued, "We have learned that you've been the department head for three years and have managed to maintain a research program along with the administrative responsibilities. Our review panel was impressed but wondered how much actual time you are able to devote to the research."

Still wary of these two government agents who'd appeared out of nowhere, Jason said, "Not as much as I like. I depend on post-doctoral fellows and graduate assistants for almost all of the laboratory work."

"So any new task you'd take on would involve others?"

"That's correct. I oversee the projects and try to help with any problems, but I don't have the time to do any actual analyses."

Without skipping a beat, Feller continued as though he'd committed to memory his list of questions. "One thing we've observed in our preliminary investigation is the lack of unused laboratory facilities on the campus. But would it be possible to convert other spaces, such as a classroom or conference space, into a secure laboratory for the work the Director might ask you to take on? Or could you take leave from the University and work in our labs near Washington for the next couple of years?"

Shaking his head, Jason said, "It would be very difficult for me to leave for any extended period of time. As for creating a new lab, I don't know. There's no room in Biology that's not being utilized to the fullest. I'd have to check with administrative offices about the availability of suitable space elsewhere on campus."

Feller nodded. "What about converting some off-campus facility into a research lab?"

"It's possible," Jason said, "but it could be expensive." He remembered a building vacated by a pharmaceutical company but had no idea of what had happened to the facility, but he saw no reason to recommend the agents search it out. He didn't know enough about the property to even place the possibility on the table.

"The Director would have to decide about any lab, on or off campus, if he concludes that you are the right person to take on this job. But I expect he has sufficient discretionary funds to accomplish any necessary upgrades of off-campus buildings." A slight grin, revealing a crooked tooth, broke across Feller's face for the first time.

Finally Sparks spoke. "Another item we need to ask regards faculty associates. Are there faculty in the department from other nations? Have they become U.S. citizens?"

Jason said, "We have a man from India and a woman from Canada, but I don't know about citizenship. They've been here several years but there's been no reason to question their status."

After glancing at his partner, Feller stood. "Someone from the Director's office will telephone you in the next couple of days to give you instructions about coming to Washington."

Irritated by the agent's approach throughout the session, Jason said, "I haven't committed to do that yet."

"We're certain you will after you understand the potential consequences of our government doing nothing in preparing to meet this threat," Feller said, opening the door. "The Director will make it clear."

Feller paused, as though thinking about his next statement. "And you must understand the Director has considerable influence with all the agencies supporting research."

The two walked quickly out the door and through the departmental suite, never looking back, as though the message from the Gods in D.C. had been delivered.

Jason felt threatened. Could these bastards walk in here and tell him his research grants with the National Institutes of Health and U.S. Department of Agriculture would not be renewed or cancelled? They hadn't said that, but the underlying implications were evident. He would be given no choice if some clown in Washington decided he should participate in the development of some yet-to-be determined biological weapons program. He didn't know how to find out how much influence these characters had. And he doubted anyone in the Research Office or the International Office could enlighten him. And it was possible he'd not understood fully the last comment from Feller. He could be a rogue agent throwing his weight around.

He walked to the large window and stared at the quadrangle in the middle of the State University campus. Masses of students were scurrying across the large grassy space with sidewalks arranged in convenient rectangles, huge trees providing intermittent areas of shade, on their way to ten o'clock classes. He stretched to his full height of almost six feet to ease a kink in his back and raked a hand through his unruly brown hair, his brain pondering the invasion of the Feds who could disrupt his entire career.

He remembered his meeting in five minutes with his research group and plans to meet his wife, Kathryn, for lunch. He grabbed a set of notes before heading to his research lab.

Jason waited two minutes in front of the Faculty Club, enjoying the bright sun and colorful leaves on the September morning. Among the horde of faculty and students leaving for lunch, he saw Kathryn coming along the walk, her heels clicking on the pavement, her green dress fitted perfectly, the hem wafted slightly in the gentle breeze. Most males stared at her. Jason had accepted she was going to be the center of attention because of her beauty and the way she dressed, always in stylish dresses or skirts that emphasized her figure. Her facial features and dark hair added to her attraction.

Nearing him, she smiled and reached for his hand. "Sorry I'm late. A student cornered me after class with questions about DNA replication. I had to show him sections in the text and explain some details."

They had been married for two years after Jason's first wife, Lucy Bacon, had been killed by a disgruntled faculty member intending to shoot Jason for denying his tenure request. Kathryn, a post-doctoral fellow in Preston King's lab at the time, and Jason had initially met during a fiasco involving accusations against King and his associates for manufacturing data.

As they walked, Jason recalled his first meeting with her. She'd come into his office to respond to his questions about the workings of King's lab. Her immediate impact had jarred his senses. He guessed she was five-five, but heels always confounded his speculation about height. Dressed in a white blouse, black skirt, with nylons and medium heels, he had difficulty not staring as she sat in the chair at the small conference table and crossed her legs, revealing her knees and flashes of thigh. Her dark eyes, almost black, bored into his face as though challenging his authority. Pushing aside his attraction to a beautiful female, Jason learned quickly that she was intelligent, intent on becoming a competent scientist, and irritated when others wanted to view her as only a pretty face. Now an Assistant Professor in the Biochemistry section of the Medical school, she had recently received a new NIH grant and continued to work with Preston King, a Professor in Biology, with whom she had served on a post-doctoral fellowship to investigate the implications of viral activities in cells.

Seated at a table and scanning the menu, Jason told her about the visit of Feller and Sparks. " I don't know where this is headed, but I'm wary. I'm not so sure I want to become involved in the development of agents that potentially kill millions of people."

They stopped their conversation as the waitress took their orders for salads and sandwiches and returned immediately with their drinks.

"Just say no if you're really uncomfortable."

"Their tone suggested my federal grants could be impacted if I decline."

Kathryn sipped her tea, replaced the cup on the saucer. "I doubt they'd throw their weight around to that extent." She smiled, touched his arm and added, "On the flip side, you might actually be saving lives of American citizens."

"We'll see what happens," Jason said, "but tell me about your meeting with your department head."

"It went well. I must submit my credentials for the three-year review by the end of November. Dr. Eggers thinks I'm in good position for a positive outcome."

"You should be with good teaching scores and a couple of research projects."

"I hope so. I was encouraged by his comments that the review will go well."

Forty-five minutes later Jason paid their check and they departed through the front door into the bright midday sun. Kathryn tucked her arm through his. "I'll walk with you to Quincy. I need to check on an analysis in King's lab." They mingled with the stream of students and faculty heading for afternoon classes.

"Is Preston planning to renew the grant you're working on?"

"We're drafting the proposal for continuation now. I've been working on sections as I can fit it around my other tasks. The second grant which I've been involved with will terminate next spring. Dr. King is not sure he wishes to continue that work, but we've done some preliminary brain-storming about possible thrusts."

"Could it be something you'd tackle on your own?"

"Maybe, but I have a lot going now and we're rather cramped in our labs. I won't do anything until Preston decides."

After a seven-minute walk they entered Quincy, the academic building housing Biology and other departments. Kathryn squeezed his hand. "See you tonight. Remember, Jennifer has a function at her school tonight."

"I recall, but thanks for reminding me."

The phone call came two days later as he organized a set of slides for a seminar he'd been invited to give at the University of Iowa. A brusque male voice said, "Dr. Spradlin, I'm representing the Director of the Agency for Biological Systems, a section of Homeland Security. We look forward to your visit next Monday to meet with the Director." Without interruption, as though reciting or reading a set of instructions, the voice continued, "Fly into Reagan National on Delta flight 948 leaving Spencerville at 7:30 a.m. You will need a passport to verify your identification to utilize the electronic tickets we've reserved for you. Someone will meet you at the gate upon your arrival. The person will have your name on a placard. We will pay all expenses. You will return on Delta 428 from Reagan at 8:15 that evening."

"Do I need to bring or prepare anything?"

"Everything will be provided. Have a safe trip." The line went dead.

Jason continued to hold the receiver for several seconds, not believing the conversation, or lack of one. Now he had to hustle to arrange for a replacement for his Monday lecture. He wanted to find out what biological agents were being used for weapons and read some background papers, but had nothing to go on. The possibilities were too numerous to start guessing. He could waste hours chasing details about irrelevant leads.

Nevertheless, he dialed the telephone in his research lab and asked to speak to Denise Harding, a post-doc from Washington State in her second year with Jason. When she responded, Jason said, "Denise, I need some help. Please run a search for any recent publications on biological agents being employed as weapons or threats against the U. S. or our friends. Then get me copies of the ones that appear well-founded."

"Would you like to see the list before I make copies of any?"

"No, use your good judgment."

He leaned back in the chair and surveyed the department head office, a space he'd occupied for three years, including the one in which he'd served as acting head after Henry Rogers, the person who'd hired him, had taken sick leave and died a week later.

Following a tumultuous year in which the search for a permanent replacement had gone on, Lucy's death and the resulting agony, his concern for his children, and marriage to Kathryn Helweg, he had settled into a busy and productive routine . He focused his energies on his work and family of a wife and two growing and happy children.

State University was a good place to work. From its early roots as a small academy started by a religious group, the institution had affiliated with the state when its founders could no longer support the original function. With support from the state, the school prospered, added new programs, brought in bright faculty, and created good facilities until it had attained full university status. Growing in numbers of students and in research funding, the university continued to gain prominence among its peer institutions around the nation. Jason seldom thought about leaving the place.

But was this demand from Washington bureaucrats destined to alter his life again?

Chapter 2

Dressed in suits either the same or quite similar to the ones they'd worn on their visit to State, Feller and Sparks stood waiting near the gangway from the plane when Jason arrived on Monday morning. They seemed more open today, shaking his hand and asking about the flight and the weather in Spencerville. They led him through the crowded terminal, dodging groups standing in the middle of the passageways, skirting around a beeping cart with two elderly riders, to a government sedan parked in a reserved slot in the front row of the adjacent parking lot. Washington weather, overcast and muggy, seemed to slow everyone's pace as soon as they exited the terminal. Sparks pulled off his sport coat as he prepared to drive. Jason was ushered into a rear seat. He had to place his legs across the middle hump to accommodate their length. He placed his small briefcase on the seat.

They eased along with the dense slow-moving traffic, dead stops at times as traffic signals seemed to take forever to change. Feller twisted to look at Jason. "The Director is pleased you're here. He believes it can be a productive session."

Jason leaned forward as much as the seat-belt would permit. "Are others coming also?" He had wondered if he knew other scientists to be invited After all, the world of those investigators doing similar work was not as large as the public sometimes believed.

Sparks spoke up. "Not today. He's meeting with several individuals, but at different dates and times."

Jason thought it was a strange approach since many ideas sprang from interactions between scientists focused on some common goal, but the Feds must have their reasons for maintaining a shroud of secrecy around the venture. He tried to give attention to their route so he'd know the general area in which they were heading and their final destination. After twisting and turning through the maze around the airport, they'd taken Highway 1 south, passing through Alexandria, going under the 495 Beltway and out of D. C. proper. As the traffic thinned and traffic controls became less frequent, Sparks increased their speed. The density of houses and businesses had thinned considerably. Several farms appeared, not yet taken over by the urban sprawl.

After forty-five minutes, they entered a small town, passed a six -store strip mall, turned onto a side street and pulled to a stop in an asphalt parking lot behind a non-descript two-story brick building surrounded by industrial warehouses and plants. A Shell station was in the next block. No identifying signs were apparent on the building. "Here we are," Sparks commented. He reached for his coat and stepped out. Jason wanted to pull off his jacket in the muggy conditions, but resisted the temptation.

Jason followed Sparks into the front entrance, evidence of air-conditioning immediately obvious. Feller lagged behind a few steps as he surveyed other vehicles parked in the space. At a desk in the foyer, Sparks stopped, showed his identification and said, "This is Dr. Jason Spradlin. He's meeting with the Director. His name should be on the visitors list for today."

The khaki-uniformed female ran a finger down a listing. "Yes, he's scheduled in ten minutes. And I assume he won't be wandering around on his own while in the building." Her eyes inventoried Jason's clothing and features as she talked.

Sparks nodded. "That's correct. Either Feller or I will be with him at all times except when he's in the Director's office."

Maintaining her stern demeanor, she said, "Dr. Spradlin, sign the register and follow Sparks."

Jason scribbled his signature on the appropriate line. Twelve feet down the hall Sparks punched an elevator button and waited for him to catch up.

To Jason's surprise, the elevator descended, passing two floors before stopping. After a quick glance at the indicator above the door, he realized there were two additional floors beneath them. He followed Sparks down a long well-lit hall to a suite of offices. Air moving equipment hummed, cutting through the eerie silence. A janitor emerged from a closet, rolling a large bin behind him.

Sparks pushed through a door and led Jason to a secretary almost hidden behind a computer monitor. Two other clerks were busy at computers; a third was bent over a low file drawer. The name plate on the desk identified her as Gwen Bloodworth. "This is Dr. Spradlin. He's to see Director Huffington."

Gwen swiveled her chair to look at Jason and Sparks, brushed strands of dark hair from her face, displayed bright teeth when she said, "I'm sorry, but the Director has been called to a meeting in the capitol. Deputy Director Johnson is taking his appointments." She pointed a red-nailed finger. “He’s in the next suite down the hall and is expecting Dr. Spradlin.”

They retreated into the hall, then walked thirty feet to another door. Sparks pushed it open and walked to the only desk visible in the area, although voices in the adjacent room suggested others were busy at work. He went through the same speech he’d given to Gwen. Beverly, the secretary, buzzed the intercom and motioned for them to proceed.

Ronald Johnson pushed out of his chair as they entered the office. An almost obese man with ruddy features and balding on top, Johnson seemed to examine Jason’s frame and said, “Dr. Spradlin, we’ve been expecting you.” Sparks nodded and exited, closing the door quietly behind him. The room was spartan with only a metal desk, a computer on a credenza, and two hard-backed chairs for visitors. The concrete-block walls were barren as though the occupant had recently moved in or planned for a brief stay.

“Before we start,” Johnson said, adjusting his frame into his desk chair, “would you like coffee or a soft drink? I know you’ve been on the go for several hours now.”

“Black coffee would be nice, “Jason responded. He settled into the chair in front of Johnson’s desk. Johnson buzzed the intercom, then said, “Beverly, two coffees, please.”

With a styrofoam cup in hand, Johnson said, “First, Director Huffington expresses his disappointment in not being able to meet with you, but he can’t ignore calls from the Secretary of Defense. “He paused, sipped his coffee. “We reviewed the report from Feller and Sparks and everything seems in order for your participation in our developing weapons program. But perhaps I should first explain Homeland Security's mission in all of this."

Johnson shifted in his chair, sipped from his coffee. "As you no doubt know, the Department of Homeland Security was created after the disaster with the twin towers in New York with the intent of focusing on the security of the U.S. population, including natural disasters such as hurricanes and earthquakes. The Department incorporates over twenty federal agencies—immigration, customs, border patrol, airport security, and others. As we developed our defenses against terrorist threats, the administration decided we should mount a small research facility with the focus on effective weapons against home-grown terrorists. This facility is the outcome of that decision.

"As you could surmise from our agent's visit with you, we're now looking for a group of scientists who can work independently in addition to our small group located here. Our goal is to have a stockpile of both weapons and defense mechanisms to combat the growing threat from terrorist organizations around the world, including those within our borders. At the present time we lag well behind our enemies in this arena and have been charged by the White House and the Defense Department to move forward as rapidly as possible. We've decided the best way to accomplish this is to enlist scientists who will work at their own institutions or companies, then we will take the basic concepts and employ some company to mass produce the most appropriate products."

Johnson finished his coffee, dropped the cup into a metal waste basket. "Our own scientists are examing the potential for both offensive and defensive approaches, including such things as ricin, malaria, respirable anthrax, and other biological agents. We will need to understand the best methods of combating pathogens exposed to large populations as well as how to utilize the same ones in an offensive manner. We have made good progress, but still have much to be done. And that's where you and others come into the picture. We hope you can take what we've learned and help us move to the next stage."

Jason broke into the monologue with the issue that plagued his thinking. "Does your plan include meetings of the involved investigators? Sometimes the best ideas are derived from the give and take among those directly involved."

"We considered that approach but came down on the side of maintaining as much secrecy as possible. We intend to have our own scientists review the progress of each participant on a regular basis to be certain we're on the right track and can meet our deadlines."

"I assume at some time you will conduct field trials to be certain the products will be effective?"

"That is in the planning stage still, but yes, we hope to do that. And as usual in these situations, trials with animals will precede any human exposure."

Jason decided it was time to tackle the key issue for him personally. "And if I choose to participate, will I be assigned a specific task?"

Johnson hesitated, stared at Jason as though the notion of not becoming involved was out of line. "Dr. Spradlin, we hope you will be interested enough in the security of this country to give this your best effort. We will be quite disappointed if you pass the opportunity to be of service. As to the other part of your question, we will assign a specific task, but will be flexible enough to be certain the researcher has the appropriate background, facilities and support to fulfill the mission in a timely fashion. And we will assign one of our own scientists as a liaison and advisor."

Almost without pause, Johnson continued, "The report form Feller and Sparks indicated a missing key in your situation is facilities."

Jason wanted to return to the question of participation, but felt that would be a waste of time. "That's correct. Since their visit I've investigated the possibilities and have concluded the better approach at State University is to upgrade an unused laboratory near the campus. This facility was constructed by an private organization hoping to enlist university scientists in the development of pharmaceutical products, but the operation never succeeded and they folded a year ago. It has chemical type laboratories including exhaust hoods, distilled water, the basic electrical and plumbing. The structure is sound but would require some renovations and perhaps special equipment depending upon the specific requirements. I don't know anything about the owner or his plans for the building although I'd guess it could be purchased or leased."

"Feller and Sparks didn't locate that facility. When the decision is made about the precise assignment for you, we will send a team to meet with you and analyze the possibility."

Johnson continued, apparently intent on completing the interview. "The other issue raised was your need for a support group, possibly including another established scientists or experienced post-doctoral type personnel."

"That's correct. I'm serving as department head and have limited time to devote to actual laboratory work. I don't wish to give up the administrative post at this point in my career."

Johnson eyed Jason for a few seconds. "I suspect we can work around that, but any personnel you propose will be submitted to the usual screening for security before engaging in the work. Dr. Spradlin, please understand that this is secret work, not to be published or shared in any way outside your small team and this Agency."

Jason twisted his empty cup, thinking about the paranoia about security. "The secrecy issue poses an obstacle for most working scientists and younger post-docs. They want and need to publish their findings as evidence of productivity. Their futures depend upon demonstration of solid work. In this case, we'd need to seek scientists who have most of their career behind them and no longer expect promotions or salary increases."

Johnson seemed to have not considered the implications. "We'll need to find a way around that, but your suggestion might be most appropriate."

Jason knew that most senior scientists had long ago lost their capacity to function in modern laboratories with all the high-tech gadgets, but he let the issue ride and moved on to another concern.

"What about finances? I assume all those details will be handled from here and will not involve any university people?"

Johnson hesitated, twisted a paper weight on the desk top as though looking for a flaw. "There's some debate on how best to handle finances and support. It's clear we can't advertise the actual goal of the contract. It stirs up too much opposition, especially among the local population who become jittery about the presence of dangerous materials that could contaminate the area. So, the prevailing idea at the moment seems to be that we establish a contract for an outside scientist to work on a project involving a contagious disease, but the real mission is the weapons development. In other words, set up a sham to provide additional secrecy. This, we believe, would serve as a cover for your activities and the renovation of a laboratory close to the population."

"So you're saying I would sign on for research on an infectious disease, but actually focus on development of a toxic weapon. And the finances would be shielded from university personnel."

"That's correct. We will provide a stipend, approximately twenty-five percent of your salary, to be paid directly to you and will pay all salaries and wages of your staff. We will supply all materials and equipment, travel and other necessary items required to complete the task. To the outsider, even to the purchasing agents and accountants working on the records in our offices, it would appear as a typical research contract with an outside scientist."

"Will I have the freedom to report to my immediate supervisor that I am spending time on this project? You understand, Director Johnson, universities must know what their employees are engaged in. They are accountable to the state."

"We will need to consider that further. But for the moment, let's take the position you may report the time you are utilizing on this project, but no details of the actual work may be shared. Understood?"

"Sure and my next question is about the specific assignment. When will I know that?"

"Probably within the next two weeks, but we'll send someone to visit that potential facility before we decide. We'll do that shortly and you should be prepared to go with our investigators. You may know more than they about the physical requirements for biological research and the maintenance of safety for both the personnel and the population residing near the facility."

A soft knock on the door interrupted the conversation. The secretary stuck her head in enough to indicate Johnson's next appointment was waiting. Johnson stood and came around the desk to shake Jason's hand. "Dr. Spradlin, we'll be in touch soon. One other thing, the Director wanted me to share with you is that your name was provided to us by Congressman Wilke from Maine. He recommended you based on some past interaction between the two of you."

Johnson glanced at his watch. "I believe you have ample time to make your return flight. Sparks and Feller will make sure you get back to the airport."

Feller was waiting in the outer office when Jason emerged. They began to move as another man was ushered in by Sparks. Jason had seen the other person at some national meeting but didn't know his name off the top of his head. No doubt another guinea pig dragged in to undergo the scrutiny of Johnson and others as the machinery of the federal government crept forward.

Jason had been surprised by Johnson's revelation that Wilke had recommended his participation in this clandestine operation. He'd met Wilke during Congressional hearings when Preston King and Kathryn had been called before the House Committee on Science and Technology to explain and defend a publication two other scientists had singled out as a fraud. Jason testified after he'd ferreted out the true motives of the two opposing scientists. Confronted with a civil suit, the two troublemakers had ended up paying King, Kathryn, two graduate assistants, and State University a substantial amount to settle out of court and avoid a public trial. Their patron, the Chair of the committee, had subsequently been charged with unethical behavior and resigned his Congressional seat. Wilke, regarded in high esteem by federal agencies dealing with science, had been a member of the committee and had made a point of congratulating Jason on his work in setting the record straight. But now Jason wasn't so certain Wilke had done him any favor by getting him involved with this secretive organization and potentially dangerous mission.

From the parking lot in the rear of the building, Sparks circled the facility to emerge on the side opposite to the entry. Jason estimated fifty or sixty cars were in the lot, giving him some idea of the number of employees in underground offices and laboratories, but to the typical passer-by, only a half-dozen vehicles would be obvious. He wondered if this facility was the headquarters for this effort to develop weapons and defenses. He could envision scientists toiling away in underground laboratories, exposed to the outside environment only before and after their work hours.

The drive back to the airport and the plane ride went without a hitch. Jason couldn't erase from his thinking all the information, plus the numerous holes yet to be filled, imparted by Johnson. After thinking more about the logistics, he thought about a couple of possible scientists who might be willing to work on the project. Both had recently retired, one from State, another from the University of Nebraska, and had solid records throughout their long careers. The unknown was whether they had settled into retirement and were no longer interested in the sometimes grueling tasks associated with a new research endeavor. He doubted either posed a security risk, but he didn't know their backgrounds well enough to be sure.

Dressed in her nightgown and robe, Kathryn was reading the most recent issue of *Time* in her favorite recliner when Jason arrived home near midnight. She closed the magazine, scrambled out of the chair, and led him to the couch.

"You want a drink or something to eat?" He looked tired, his brown eyes circled in deep rings. Sometimes she expressed concern about his work habits, always on the go, facing critical decisions each day, although he never seemed to tire or complain.

"I don't think so. Had a glass of wine on the plane along with the semblance of a meal. How'd your day go?" He ruffled her short black hair and rested his fingers on the back of her neck.

"The usual. Had a lecture and a lab session, then worked on the proposal with King, had dinner with the kids and Mrs. Carter, read them a story and helped Tony with a homework assignment."

Mrs. Lillian Carter had entered Jàson's life after Lucy's death when he needed help with his two young children. The recently widowed sixty-five year old Carter had agreed to take care of most household chores, make sure the kids were ready for school, and prepare breakfast and the evening meal. Jason provided her with a small apartment and a monthly stipend. She disappeared after dinner each evening and gave Jason time with his children, Jennifer, now eight, and Tony, now six. The arrangement had worked well and Carter had become another member of the family in many respects. But after four years and the entrance of Kathryn into the mix, Jason detected signs she was slowing and prepared himself for the day when she announced she wanted to move on.

Kathryn nestled closer to him. "Jennifer wanted to talk about new clothes but I put her off by saying you needed to be involved."

"But you know that's not true." He slipped his arm around her shoulders and pulled her close, feeling her warmth.

"I know, but I worry she's wanting outfits meant for girls older than she and hoped to delay the discussion for another time."

He turned her head kissed her. "You ready for bed?"

She smiled. "Sure, but first tell me about your visit to the Feds."

He told her quickly about the discussion with Johnson, the unique building that masked the activities that went on inside. "I still have misgivings about this whole deal, but it has its intriguing elements. It's difficult to turn down your own government if you think you can be useful, even when their approach seems sinister and threatening."

Kathryn stood and pulled him up. "You up to jogging in the

morning?" On most days they ran about three miles through the city park or around the campus before work. They missed the ritual when they couldn't do it and tried to avoid any interferences with the routine.

"Unless you need to sleep later." He slipped his arm around her shoulders and under her legs and picked her up. Her mouth found his as they eased up the stairs toward the bedroom.

Chapter 3

After stewing for two days about the secrecy of the pending contract with the feds, Jason decided he should confide in David Hawthorne, the Dean of Arts and Sciences, and his immediate supervisor. When he broached the subject with Hawthorne, the Dean insisted they discuss the potential fallout with the President of State University, thus they were now seated in Snyder's plush office in the administration building. Paintings of various university scenes adorned the walls. Through the large windows the main quadrangle of State ringed with the academic buildings and the main library presented a wonderful view marred temporarily by two large cranes at the construction site of a new dormitory. Jason wondered if Snyder ever took the time to enjoy the vista.

Snyder, always affable and smiling, leaned forward in one of the plush chairs arranged in a semi-circle around a glass-top coffee table, "Well, Dr. Spradlin, I haven't seen you in a while but understand you're confronting a serious issue."

Jason outlined the sessions with the federal agency representatives then added, "I'm not certain about the actual project yet, but should know within the next few weeks. In the meantime, two facility management people are coming tomorrow from the General Services Administration to assess the potential of a building on 29th Street. If this facility is okayed by them, there will be some renovation in preparation for the actual experiments. The bottom line is I'll be doing some work related to biological weapons and the Director of Biological Systems has made it clear it's all to be secret. In fact, I've been reluctant to share anything, but concluded Dean Hawthorne should know since this will consume some of my time."

Snyder said, "I'm glad he brought you to my office. I like to know these things in case there's some political fall-out and the Governor or a legislator hear rumors. At this point I won't alert his office and will keep it to myself. But you should know, the Secretary of HS called me about the pending contract about a week ago, but he didn't reveal any details about the actual research. And he may have communicated with the Governor, but he didn't indicate he intended to do that."

"I didn't know that," Jason said. "But it makes me feel better about coming in today. I was concerned about breaking the order to keep everything secret."

Wanting every aspect of the federal contract to be clear to the upper administration, he added, "Nothing will show on the records of the university about my salary. I'm to be paid a stipend directly and all expenses for any other scientists, technicians, supplies, travel and miscellaneous operating expenses will be paid directly from the federal offices. I haven't broached the subject of a reimbursement to State for my time or for the usual overhead associated with grants and contracts."

Snyder broke in. "Let's agree to allow your time to be part of State's support of a national effort. If we worry about those things, accountants get involved and it escalates from there. Soon some energetic reporter gets wind of your activity and it's beyond control."

Jason said, “Just so the two of you know, I will be able to employ another scientist and one or more technical staff, but those will be treated as federal employees and their salaries and benefits will be paid from the agency.”

Snyder stood, signaling the end of the conversation. “Dr. Spradlin, I’m pleased you’ve confided in us and rest assured the matter will stay confidential. However, if there are problems, let me know.”

Jason stood to follow Snyder’s lead. “If other issues arise that I believe may impact the university, I’ll talk to Dean Hawthorne, but I believe I’ve conveyed the essence of the deal.” Jason moved his folder from one hand to the other in order to shake the President’s hand.

Standing closer to Snyder as they moved from the chairs, Jason realized the President was showing his age. His once thick black hair had grayed and thinned. An obvious paunch couldn’t be hidden beneath the suit jacket. But he departed the administrative office, relieved Snyder had understood and accepted the limitations demanded by the government without a lot of details and repeated assurances all would go okay.

Jim Feller and the two facility experts flew into the Spencerville airport two days later, called Jason’s office to let him know of their arrival and their plan to rent a car and meet him at the building to be inspected. Jason called the representative of the owner who agreed to meet them at 864 29th Street within minutes, no doubt eager to have an interested potential user of a defunct and decaying building.

As they assembled in front of the one-story brick building with the name Ozark Pharmaceuticals mounted on a large wooden board above the entrance, Feller introduced him to Joseph Higgins and Roger Nevers and explained they were from the General Services Administration, the agency that dealt with building and facilities for all the federal agencies. Both were dressed in suits, carried briefcases and clipboards, and smiled and nodded as Jason shook their hands.

Feller continued without pause, "Dr. Spradlin, I appreciate your setting this up and would like you to accompany us through the facility. You may have ideas about the lab layouts we wouldn't understand." Jason had arranged his schedule to do that in case the feds asked. In addition, he wanted another look at the future lab for himself.

Inside the front door, they were met by a local real estate agent, Joe Burris, who shook all their hands and led them on a tour of the building. Higgins and Nevers switched on lights and fume hoods, tested the water faucets, opened cabinet doors, looked under the sinks, checked windows and doors, asked about the electrical current, inquired about the distilled water system. They moved from one thing to another in a methodical way as though they did this every day.

Nevers asked Burris if the building had an attic and was reassured there was none, only a small crawl space above the paneled ceilings with utilities lines running through the area. Then he asked about trash removal to be told the city would start regular visits when they were alerted to the occupancy. They could arrange for pickup either on the street in front or at the loading dock at one end of the building.

Jason was impressed with the condition of the facilities that had sat idle for two years. The chemistry type labs had good work space with counters resistant to acids and other harsh chemicals, fume hoods that functioned, the latest safety features, including an eye-wash station that could be started with a foot or knee, a plethora of electrical outlets, and sufficient aisle space for easy working and moving carts loaded with small equipment or supplies. The section for housing animals contained all the essentials, including metal racks for housing mice, rats or guinea pigs. An adjacent room served as a washing facility with steam lines and large tanks. All the overhead lights worked and it was obvious the owner had maintained the structure in prime condition. The slight odor of cleaning solution suggested the building had recently been cleaned. Near the entrance a reception area fronted two offices and a small conference room. A couple of oak desks and three metal file cabinets had been left. It was obvious from the quality of the construction and maintenance the owner had intended to utilize the building for an extended period of time.

Burris pointed to the various features, indicating the electrical and plumbing systems had recently been checked to make certain they were working properly. He noted the owner would be open to either selling or leasing the facility. He handed Feller a folder that Jason suspected provided a breakdown of the prices and conditions of both options.

While Jason waited in the parking area with Feller and Burris, the two inspectors circled the building. They returned and nodded their okay to Feller. Higgins said, "It's in good condition. I believe it will meet our purposes." Nevers nodded agreement.

Burris asked, "Will there be alterations to the labs?"

Feller nodded. "We'll convert a lab to serve a different function and alter the air-handling system for that space, but the Agency will pay for that conversion. We will provide all the essential furnishings and equipment for both labs and office spaces. Beyond that, I can't say more at this time. In addition, we may wish to install a fence around the building. And we'll change all the locks and perhaps install other security devices. But anything we do won't alter the essential features of the facility."

He glanced at the others, including Jason and asked, "Any other items you can think of at the moment?"

When no one volunteered an idea, he reached to shake Burris' hand and waved the folder. "I'll run these numbers by our Deputy Director and get back to you within a week, but from our perspective, everything seems good. I think this will work out fine."

Jason and Burris watched the group leave for the airport. Burris commented, "They're the most efficient group I've dealt with, but I'm curious. Can you tell me anything about their plans for the use of the facility?"

Jason grinned. "I'd rather not if you can be satisfied with that response."

Before Burris could respond, he asked, "What happened to the owner? The company seems to have folded pretty quickly."

"I wasn't privy to the details but from what I've deduced, he got in over his head. He'd dreamed of producing new pharmaceuticals but couldn't cope with the competition from the huge established organizations. Truth is, he never got it off the ground and learned quickly that the research involved to concoct some new drug could take years. He didn't have the resources to support that and apparently couldn't interest other investors."

Jason turned toward his aging Accord, a twelve year old vehicle that continued to serve him well. "Thanks for your help with this. We'll know what the feds will do soon."

As had been their custom for several years, Peter Townsend and Greg Harris, two professors in Biology, met each Friday after working hours at the Campus Bar and Grill near the campus to review the events of the week, speculate about coming events and observe the students and other faculty who habited the establishment while they enjoyed a draft beer. The sessions had originally been organized by Hugh Riley, a third biologist with the reputation for doing everything within reason, and some beyond the usual boundaries of acceptable behavior, to undermine the leadership of the department. During Jason's first year as department head, Riley had been forced to accept a buyout and left the university under a cloud of suspicion related to stalking Kathryn Helweg. The stalking had led to a two-year suspended jail sentence but with a court order to stay off the campus and away from Helweg. At times Harris and Townsend had invited other faculty to join them, but there had not been a regular participant.

With draft beers before them, they observed the crowd for a couple of minutes. Townsend got his pipe going and blew smoke into the atmosphere. Harris, ever aware of good-looking females, gave attention to two women whom he believed to be faculty in Sociology, as they found chairs at a table across the room.

Through the haze of smoke from his pipe, Townsend recognized Riley as soon as he entered the door. Pushing aside his surprise, he stood and waved to gain Riley's attention. Riley waved back in recognition and weaved through the crowd. He'd gained weight and lost hair since his last visit. He looked his age of sixty or above.

They stood and shook Riley's hand. Harris said, "It's good to see you but what brings you around? It's been what, over two years since we saw you?"

After hailing a passing waitress and ordering a draft, Riley said, "I had a free afternoon from teaching and decided to see if you guys still got together."

"So how is life at a community college?" Riley had landed a teaching position at Webster Community College after being forced out at State. Webster had been a prominent citizen who'd pushed the legislative branch of the state to establish a group of institutions devoted to serving those who intended to work in the trades or use the two-year program to prepare themselves for the university.

"Actually it's good. No demands to do research, very few committee assignments, meet my scheduled courses, may do a bit of advising." He shrugged to indicate the easy life he'd experienced since leaving the stress of a faculty position filled with demands to obtain grants, publish papers, and work with graduate students.

Riley sipped his beer. "So tell me, how is life under Spradlin?

Harris and Townsend looked at each other acknowledging Riley's obsession bordering on hatred with Jason. Harris said, "From my perspective, he's been a good department head. He leaves you alone to do your work without looking over your shoulder about every little event that goes on."

Townsend chimed in. "The truth is he's helped me get back on track after several unproductive years. He challenges you to do better without nagging and helps you locate resources. For example, he helped me obtain a small starter grant through the Research Office that enabled me to do some preliminary tests as a basis for a successful proposal to a federal agency. I would never have made that effort on my own."

Riley drank from his stein. "I heard he married Kathryn Helweg after his first wife was killed by that idiot Boseman."

Townsend banged his pipe on the table leg. "They've been together a couple of years. I understand she has an appointment in the biochemistry section of the Medical School and I believe she has a project still going with Preston King. I see her in Quincy once in a while but haven't talked to her."

"I'd like to see her again," Riley said. "I still remember her as the most beautiful, sexiest female I've ever known."

Townsend and Harris exchanged glances. Then his tone gruff as though admonishing a small child, Harris said, "Hugh, don't go there. Remember you got in big trouble for following her around before the authorities charged you with stalking."

"I'm past that. All I want to do is see her one more time."

"Remember you've been warned and it could be worse if you're caught around her again. You'll do jail time." Townsend placed his pipe in a holder he carried everywhere he went. "We have guests for dinner tonight so I'd better get going. Greg, see you in the hallways. Hugh, come again, we‘ve missed you. We’re here every week at the same time.”

Harris stood. “I’m going to introduce myself to those two women. I know one of them, but she may not remember where we met.”

Riley remained in his seat, his mind focused on Kathryn and the effect she had on him. He twirled his mug as he thought about her perfect facial features, her shape that attracted everyone around her, and the manner in which she dressed that seemed designed to drive him crazy. He determined, in spite of his buddies’ warnings, to seek her out and watch her for a while. He wondered what it would be like to actually touch her, just to feel her skin.

Chapter 4

On Tuesday of the following week, Jason received a call from Feller who started immediately. "Dr. Spradlin, our Deputy Director has authorized moving ahead with the building we looked at last week. We're sending facility management representatives, probably Joe Higgins and maybe a second person, to line up a construction firm to do the necessary upgrades and changes, but you should be involved to be sure the labs will function properly. For your information we intend to lease the facility for a three-year period with the possibility of extending the lease for another period."

"Do I need to contact the real estate agency or anything else?"

Feller hesitated for a beat. "I don't think so. I've notified Burris to get the leasing documents prepared and our representative will review and approve the lease while he's there. Burris is to bring you the keys, but we'll change the locks as soon as we get started. You may wish to walk through again to be certain we have everything in order for the actual research to progress."

Feller continued. "One more thing. Deputy Director Johnson would like you to come to Washington on Monday of next week. At that time, he plans to outline your specific assignment and work through all the details of reimbursements. Either Sparks or I will meet you at Reagan and we'll set up the ticket as before. But be prepared to spend at least two days, maybe three, if you can spare the time this trip. We'll leave the ticket flexible and arrange for housing while you're here."

"I'll come prepared for the three days," Jason said, thinking about the things to be accomplished and agreed upon while there. A major hurdle yet to be crossed was that of locating an experienced scientist to join him on the project, but he couldn't begin on that until he knew the parameters of the work to be done.

Jason replaced the receiver, his thoughts reviewing the messages from Feller. He took his desk calendar to Audrey, the department secretary, to rearrange several appointments on the days he'd be away.

But his immediate focus was the presence of Roy Blount, a young faculty member who'd begun with Jason as a post-doctoral fellow and had worked on the project with Redlake Industries to produce pork products by reproducing pigs through an artificial approach. The scientific phase of the project had moved to a successful completion and they'd actually marketed a limited number of products from the process.

The lanky red-head dropped into the chair by Jason's desk. A grin broke across his face. "We finally have Food and Drug's approval to move to full-scale production. Redlake has pressured the commissioners to get off the fence and act one way or the other. Cynthia called a few minutes ago to let me know they'd agreed to support Redlake, but she's holding her breath the Commissioner won't cave in to the right wing types who believe every animal must be derived by natural means."

"Does she think he might reverse himself?"

"Apparently that's a possibility and he's done it before with other projects."

"Are they doing anything to support him? You know some of these Congressmen are going to lobby him on behalf of those constituents regardless of how silly their case."

Roy nodded. "Yeah, the President of Redlake is lining up the Illinois delegation and any of their colleagues they can influence just in case the Commissioner wavers. Redlake believes it's now a matter of days before there's an administrative sign-off."

"Do you need to go to Chicago or is the process set?"

"I wouldn't think I need to go. We've refined the methodology of culturing the embryos, so the process goes without a hitch. We have skilled people ready to do implants and have growers lined up to provide sows. The only obstacle has been the bureaucracy."

"Keep me in the loop and how's the General Biology section this fall?"

"Filled to capacity. Maybe I've gained the reputation as an easy grader."

"I doubt that. More likely, the kids find your lectures understandable." Jason had received good reports from students about the class. Students appreciated Roy's style and easygoing manner, plus they learned the material.

Jason grinned at his young colleague. "How's your relationship with Cynthia or should I not ask about personal issues?"

As usual, Roy blushed a bit when Cynthia's name came up, his face almost matching his hair. "It's good, but distance is a problem. At the present, neither of us wants to give up our position and move." He shrugged. "So long-term is hard to predict." He stood and eased toward the door.

As Roy left, he turned his attention to the ever-present stack of forms to be approved. He had come to regard the necessary chore as mindless work, a term he'd learned from his predecessor. But he paid attention to the various requests to avoid approving some outlandish travel by a faculty with no specific mission in mind or one that seemed on the fringe of what the department was trying to accomplish. One purchase order concerned him as he wasn't certain the piece of equipment would fill the purpose intended. Remembering how young faculty could be pressured by salesmen to buy some new apparatus, he set it aside to ask questions before approving.

Feller was waiting when Jason arrived fifteen minutes behind schedule at the gate on Monday morning. He shook Jason's hand and led him through the crowded terminal to the spot reserved for government vehicles. He pulled into the flow of traffic exiting the lot and looked at Jason. "You need to settle into your motel before we meet with the Deputy Director?"

"No, I'm okay to get started if I can leave my gear in the trunk."

Forty minutes later they pulled into the rear of the two-story brick building he'd visited before. Three minutes later he was ushered into Johnson's office and handed coffee.

Johnson seemed more amiable this time, smiling and asking about the flight. Settling his overweight frame behind his desk, he said, "Feller and his cohorts gave a good report for the facility you found for the work, although there'll be some modifications required. Not unexpected I might add. You wouldn't believe some of the buildings we're shown. It'd take a year to renovate and repair those, but the one in Spencerville will require only modest upgrades and security measures. Plus, the price is right."

Jason said, "I suspect we were lucky with the timing. Not often do buildings sit idle around the university always short of space."

A soft rap on the door preceded the secretary's voice. "Director Johnson, Dr. Walcott is here if you're ready for him."

Johnson struggled to his feet and took a couple of steps toward the door. "Come in, Fred. I'd like you to meet Dr. Jason Spradlin who will be the chief investigator for our project." Swiveling his head toward Jason, he added, "And Dr. Walcott is going to assist in outlining your assignment and serve as your liaison with the Agency. He's been involved with this type research for many years and has led several of our efforts to create defense mechanisms against bioterrorists."

Walcott, a lanky skeleton of a figure capped with a full head of white hair, shook Jason's hand. They found chairs in front of Johnson's desk and waited for him to settle in and open a folder.

"Now let's discuss your specific assignment," Johnson started. "What we hope to accomplish with this project is to develop a new weapon for our arsenal. Most of the ones we now have at our disposal have been around for several years and are commonly found in the stocks of almost everyone working with these systems. We want something new and different, an unknown so-to-speak, that could become our primary weapon against terrorist groups and populations intent on destroying us."

As on a prearranged cue, Walcott spoke. "As you may know, we have a number of disease producing agents, including botulism, tularemia, malaria, and others, but so does most everyone else. We know how to counteract these with minimum loss of life and only scant ripples in the daily lives of our people. Now we hope to take some seemingly benign organism and genetically modify it to be lethal with no known anecdotes. And it must be in a form that is easily deliverable to a target group."

Jason placed his coffee mug on the corner of Johnson's desk. "You hope to kill millions of people with this thing."

Johnson broke in. "We hope to not kill anyone, but we wish to let our enemies know of the possibilities if they attack us. And it's only a matter of time before they do. We need to be ready."

Jason had wrestled with his reservations, discussed his concerns with Kathryn, and he'd wanted to share his worries with a couple of trusted colleagues, but had refrained because of the security issue. He'd stopped looking for an escape and decided to give the Agency his best effort. He said. "So where do we start?"

Walcott said, "That's what I hope we can decide in the next couple of days. I'm going to show you several possibilities and, between us, reach a conclusion about the most expeditious process to take from here." He stood as he concluded.

As though they had rehearsed the actions, Johnson stood behind his desk. "Dr. Spradlin, go with Walcott and the two of you, and perhaps others, wrestle with this dilemma. If you would, check back with me at the end of the day."

In the hall, Walcott said, "Let's find lunch before we get started. There's a small cafeteria in the building that I utilize most days or we can go out if you prefer."

"I'll follow your lead." Jason thought he remembered seeing Walcott at a scientific meeting in the past five years, but wasn't certain and didn't wish to ask at this juncture of the orientation. They went through a door on the same floor, passed a couple of suites before approaching the cafeteria which seemed to occupy the end of the building farthest away from the street.

Then Walcott confirmed his suspicion about seeing him previously as they entered the cafeteria. "I've heard several of the papers presented by you or your students. I've been impressed, especially the work on Wilson's disease. That has improved the lives of numerous people, including one family I know personally."

"I thought I'd seen you, probably at the FASEB meetings if you heard those papers."

"Several of us go each year. Sometimes we get ideas that move our projects along. And we attend other meetings as well, anything that seems appropriate to our ongoing research. Of course, we're never able to present any of our work except on the rare occasion when we've discovered something of a basic nature that could apply to the field generally." He grinned and added, "And getting approval to present anything takes months."

Walcott led him to a small counter and they made selections from a limited menu posted on a board behind the servers. Jason choose a

Reuben sandwich and soft drink. They found a table for two along one wall. Twenty people were seated in clusters, engrossed in their private conversations. Fluorescent lights illuminated the otherwise sterile place. No pictures or plants were evident. As expected, aromas of food permeated the air reminding Jason it had been several hours since his early morning breakfast.

Walcott resumed the conversation. “To reiterate what Johnson said, we’re modifying our thinking about weapons. Rather than focusing on a population as a whole, we’re beginning to consider toxins that can be lethal to a small group. Terrorists are not operating as a national effort anywhere in the world, but are functioning as small cells. They hit targets then hide out and plan for the next raid, usually on an innocent group to spread fear among the masses. They’re like those suicide bombers who are brain-washed to sacrifice themselves, sometimes at a very early age, to kill and maim innocent bystanders. We want to hit those organized clusters before they act, especially when their focus is on American citizens and targets.”

Jason wiped his mouth on a paper napkin. “You mean insert a weapon into a house or a compound with the intent of killing everyone inside.”

“Exactly and with such effectiveness no one survives within the narrow confines of the place. Then over a number of minutes or a couple of hours the toxin becomes inactive and dissipates. Likely no one could determine what had occurred but we would have sent a message to other such groups. You know, Dr. Spradlin, nothing is more fearful than an unknown. And another plus in this approach, we’d kill fewer innocents, often just in the wrong place at the wrong time with no ties at all to the terrorists."

"And this is the type of thing the Agency wishes me to tackle?"

"You and a couple of others around the nation while we maintain our focus here on the more traditional types of biological agents."

"That was a good sandwich," Jason said, pushing the plate aside and sipping the soft drink. "Tell me, has anyone done any preliminary work on this new approach."

"Not really, other than to begin a list of potential microbes that could be the basis of the approach." Walcott stood, saying, "Let's drop by a rest room then I'd like to show you our facilities here and introduce you to some of my colleagues. We'll give you some background material for overnight reading, then have a brain-storming session tomorrow morning with the goal of coming to a conclusion about the initial steps." Jason was surprised by the potential involvement of others given the previous message from Johnson, but he'd reserve judgment until the afternoon unfolded.

He followed Walcott through the entire building, peeking through glass windows at a white-coated scientist or a technician leaning over rows of vials or a petri dish or in front of a safety hood, their hands covered with gloves and working an instrument inside the controlled space. Walcott gave him a broad picture of the particular research, but nothing specific enough to understand the actual project going on behind the closed doors. It seemed at every turn and on every door signs of danger jumped out. On the floors below ground, Jason estimated there were a dozen small labs interspersed with offices and meeting rooms. A constant was the steady drone of air moving equipment interrupting the almost eerie quiet.

An hour later Walcott led him into a seminar room on the upper floor of the structure where he had assembled a group of four other science types. He introduced Jason and led them through a lengthy discussion of the goals of the Agency, then homed in on future endeavors, including the idea of a extremely lethal toxin with limited half-life. Each of his colleagues injected ideas and suggestions when called upon but there never was a free exchange of ideas or debates about the most appropriate technique. At the end of the two hour session, Walcott handed Jason a thick folder with background materials.

Jason asked several questions and received concise answers. Finally, he voiced his need to locate a scientist with some experience in the development of toxins. No one volunteered, although one man indicated he would provide a name by the next morning.

Walcott led Jason back to the main office and reminded him of the focus of tomorrow morning. Then he said, "I can give you a name for your position. She retired from the Agency six months ago and I suspect would like to continue working somewhere."

"Is she up to date with all the techniques I'll need?"

"She is. You will find her very capable."

Walcott tore off the top sheet of a note pad on the secretary's desk and scribbled on it for a bit. Jason could read the name and address of the person. He stuck the note in his coat pocket.

Walcott said, "I'll meet you here tomorrow morning. They'll have you here by eight-thirty and we should be able to complete our assignment by noon."

Walcott turned to leave, then said, "Maybe Johnson didn't say, but I'm to serve as your liaison on the project. I look forward to working with you."

After Walcott left, Beverly, the secretary, said, "Mr. Feller will be here shortly and you have a telephone message from Congressman Wilke. He'd like you to come by his office tomorrow afternoon. I've told Feller you need to leave here in time to do that before your flight. And Dr. Johnson had to leave for a meeting in case you were to report back to him."

As he waited, Beverly smiled at him and said, "I understand we'll be seeing you more often. I look forward to helping when I can."

"Thanks. However, I hope not to be here much. In fact here's my ride now."

Feller dropped him at a quaint motel about a mile from the government building. "We've reserved a room for you here and they have a decent restaurant. We use the place often for guests so they'll know to bill us directly. And I'll pick you up at eight tomorrow morning.'

Jason responded, trying to break the ice and learn more about these guys who chauffeured him around. "Can you stay long enough to have a drink before taking off?"

Feller looked like he'd been asked the impossible. He stuttered for a moment, then said, "I'd better keep moving. Johnson doesn't like us to interact unnecessarily with visitors. But thanks for asking."

Jason said as he opened the door, "We'll do it in Spencerville when you're there next time."

Checked into a quiet room at the far end of the motel, Jason pulled out the note from Walcott and decided he'd make contact with Helga Grimes at her address near the research laboratory. She answered on the third ring.

Jason identified himself and told her about his mission of finding an experienced scientist to help with the assignment given him by the Agency.

For several seconds she remained silent, then said, "I could be interested but am surprised Walcott gave you my name. If you are free for a while this evening, I'd like to meet with you and discuss the potential."

"I'm at the Norris Motel, but don't know the address. If you could come here, we might have dinner and talk."

"I know the place and will be there at six-thirty. And, Dr. Spradlin, thanks for calling."

Jason tried to read some of the materials given by Walcott but his mind kept wandering back to the conversation with Grimes and the surreptitious method of Walcott passing her name to him, as though there was some hidden agenda involved or some issue that had driven Grimes from the Agency. He'd find out soon.

He called Kathryn to hear her voice, tell her he missed her and he loved her, asked about the children, and how her day went. She seemed reluctant to tell him something but he didn't press. He'd learned to detect certain signals in her voice when she wanted to reveal something, but waited until an appropriate time. Likely something to do with one of the kids or her upcoming review.

Chapter 5

As Jason sat on a couch in the lobby and watched through the front window of the motel, a woman appeared precisely at six-thirty, parked in a visitor's slot near the entrance, and entered the front door. Brown hair with tints of gray parted in the middle and falling to the level of her ears, rather square body build, competent expression on her face, she was dressed in a tan pantsuit, white blouse and low heels. Assuming she was the person he'd called, Jason approached. "Dr. Grimes?"

She smiled and stuck out a hand, her grip firm. "And you're Dr. Spradlin." A slight trace of a European accent surprised him. He'd not detected the slight difference over the telephone.

"Thanks for coming. Shall we locate the dining area?"

Walking by his side, the top of her head level with his eyes, she said, "I assume this is your first time here."

"It is. A man by the name of Jim Feller dropped me after I'd met all day with Dr. Walcott and others at the Agency. As you might guess, they've asked me to take on a job for them and today was my initial orientation to the task."

A young woman dressed in a black pantsuit led them to a table in one corner of the modest dining area, handed them menus, and asked about drinks. After scanning the list, they both ordered the house Merlot wine.

Grimes said, “I’ve eaten here on several occasions with visitors to the Agency and have found the food quite palatable. I think you won’t go wrong with anything on the menu. And their wines are good.”

Placing the menu on the table, she said, “I’m surprised in a way that Walcott recommended you meet with me. But in all fairness I feel I must make you aware of my situation. I don’t want you to discover later and believe I’ve not been forthright.”

She waited until wines had been served and orders taken. “I worked at various federal facilities for twelve years and received promotions and merit raises on a regular basis. The powers in charge seemed to appreciate my work, although there were several changes in the leadership. When Homeland Security was created and they initiated a research arm, I transferred there because it fit better my training and experience.” She sipped the wine and smiled, obviously pleased with the drink.

“A year ago Mr. Johnson assumed the Deputy Director’s position. At the time I was working on a project to perfect a different method of delivering anthrax. We were experimenting with a new type of capsule that would disintegrate when released and allow the toxin to spread through the air. After numerous attempts I decided the capsule wouldn’t be suitable because of some inherent flaw. It was too fragile and continued to come apart well before we could reach our destination for the test runs. Even under controlled laboratory conditions it just didn’t function up to the specifications required for actual use. And because of its fragility it posed dangers to the technical staff and would have been extremely hazardous to operators in the field. In short, I decided we should attempt another model."

She paused as their salads and a tray of bread were placed and they both ate a few bites. She wiped her mouth with the cloth napkin. "At that point, I went to Johnson and recommended we ask the manufacturer of the capsule to modify the composition to make it more resistant but still come apart when released into the environment. He suggested I hadn't used it correctly and should continue to work out the bugs.

"So I did as he asked and in frustration and against all the rules of the place brought in a couple of colleagues to observe and discover if I had missed some key element in loading the capsule. To this point we'd used only harmless agents but with the same characteristics as anthrax. Neither of them could find a problem with my approach. Nevertheless, I tried several different techniques that they thought might possibly work, but none did."

They focused on their salads and shoved the plates aside when the entrees appeared. Jason cut into his steak and watched as Grimes took the first bite of her pork chop.

Jason interrupted his chewing to ask. "Then what happened? Were you able to get the thing to function properly?"

Finishing her bite, Grimes said, "I gave up and went back to Johnson. He became irate, accused me of incompetence. That's when I told him I'd enlisted advice from co-workers, although I knew that had gone against policy. I refused to give him their names although he pressed me hard for them. I knew if I did they'd be in trouble.

"Two weeks later I was told my employment would be terminated at the end of the fiscal year. The usual litany of reasons was given but the bottom line is I'd violated a cardinal regulation. That was three months ago. I was devastated. I'd given this Agency my best for all those years only to be kicked out by an administrator who knew nothing about the products or processes we were working on. Even more frustrating, he didn't trust the judgment of the scientists working there."

"Did Johnson have some vested interest in the company providing the capsule?"

Her eyes brightened at the idea. Then she shook her head. "That possibility never arose and I truly don't know if that were the reason for his stance with me. I'm more inclined to believe he was just throwing his weight around to establish his authority. "

"Have you sought other positions?"

"I'm just beginning that process but once you've been fired from a secretive agency, it is difficult to explain why you're suddenly on the market as you reach middle-age. At any rate I thought you should know this in case Johnson raises a fuss with you."

They ate for several minutes. Jason thought about Grimes' story and wondered if she'd been completely honest and why Walcott had recommended her. But she'd been right about the food. It was excellent and the wine complemented the steak very nicely.

Jason asked, "Was Walcott one of those colleagues you asked for advice?"

She didn't respond immediately but stirred a few remaining pieces of potato around on her plate. "He was but you must never let Johnson know that. Walcott will get the same treatment as I. He believed I was right about those capsules but couldn't go to bat for me or he'd risk losing his position. I understood that and didn't pressure him in any way, although I knew he felt badly for what happened to me."

"Obviously Dr. Walcott thought your work was good or he wouldn't go out on a limb to suggest I give you a call. But tell me a bit about your educational background."

Grimes seemed to organize her response while she sipped the last of her wine. "I was raised in Austria and attended schools there. I received two degrees or the U.S. equivalent of a Master of Science in microbiology. I was employed by a private firm in Vienna for four years, then met my husband, an officer in the U.S. Army. We married and I emigrated to this country as the wife of a citizen. Through his connections I was employed by the Food and Drug Administration in their test laboratory. Then later I moved to a facility under the Defense Department. That led to Homeland Security and the Agency when they were established."

Her expression turned dour as she continued. "Jim was killed on a training exercise in Kuwait."

A deep frown covered her face for a moment. "For a time I was at a loss as to what to do. All my family were in Europe and I had very few friends in this country. Maybe as a way of breaking out of my lethargy, I enrolled in graduate school at Johns Hopkins and obtained a doctoral degree in genetics. The Agency offered me a position upon graduation and I was happy there until Johnson forced me out."

"So you've retained your married name?"

"Yes, I had become known professionally as Grimes and thought changing would only confuse those who knew me, although as you can tell, I haven't completely lost my accent." She smiled and added. "Neither have I sought another companion, although there have been a few overtures from male acquaintances."

Jason asked, "How long have you been a widow?"

"Soon to be six years. My life has changed a lot in that time."

Jason pondered his next move, not absolutely certain of the boundaries under which he was operating but decided to push ahead. "If this works out and I'm given the flexibility to employ individuals for the position I'm allocated, would you consider moving to Spencerville? My initial contract will be for three years or until the task is completed. Beyond that, I don't know what might happen." He told her about Spencerville and about State University, the predominant presence in the medium size city.

Grimes twirled her spoon and examined Jason's face. "I know State University by reputation and have heard papers given by scientists from the institution. I would take the chance. I'm in a rut here and must break out soon. I suspect Johnson has contaminated any job possibilities I might have in this area, but I'm guessing. And he will likely object to your bringing me onto this project."

"Was Johnson a political appointee?"

She nodded. "As best I have figured out, he has no experience in the sciences underlying our work. He talks a different language than the investigators at the Agency. We never know some things but I'd suspect he worked on some Senator's last campaign and was rewarded with a cushy appointment."

"Is there a legitimate reason for all the secrecy? I have been flabbergasted that scientists are unable to confer with each other. In my experience, some of the best ideas are derived from those interactions."

"I understand what you mean. But the Agency desires to keep as many people as possible from knowing what goes on in those individual laboratories. It's an extreme form of paranoia in my thinking but it's prevalent throughout this Agency and perhaps others."

Jason retrieved his wallet from his pocket and pulled out a business card. "If you are interested, send me a resume at this address within the next week or ten days. Include names of references I might contact."

He explained the provisions attached to the position, including the manner in which salaries would be paid. Then he told her about his position at State University and the limited time he could give to the federal project. "I'm looking for an experienced person who can work independently with minimum supervision or backup, but with the assistance of one or more technicians. And I'd think your salary could be the same as you had with the Agency."

He laughed and finished his wine. "And that would actually turn out to be a raise because Spencerville is much less expensive than the D.C. area."

Grimes smiled. "Dr. Spradlin, this sounds perfect. I would be doing essentially the same kind of work I did for the Agency but out of sight of the Washington bureaucrats."

Jason said, "Send me your credentials and let's see how it goes from there. Now, would you be interested in dessert and coffee?"

"That would be nice."

Jason waved to gain the waitress' attention.

The next morning went quickly as Walcott, Dr. Edwards and Dr. Hastings briefed Jason on the background materials he'd spent two hours reading last night. Much of the information dealt with the basic stuff associated with the spread of toxins into a population and the manner in which terrorist groups were identified. None of their individual projects was ever mentioned.

Jason wanted to ask Walcott about Grimes, but the opportunity never seemed correct. They all went to the cafeteria together and discussed the pending World Series and the beginning of the Redskins season. After lunch, Jason was shown the accounting offices on the top floor. He received the necessary forms and instructions to have monthly stipends sent directly to his checking account. The accountant concluded, "And there are extra forms for anyone you employ on this project." He grinned. "If you have difficulties, let me know and I'll try to solve the problem for you. My card is stapled to one of the forms."

"I haven't yet been told the details of my stipend nor the parameters for those I'm permitted to employ."

"Mr. Johnson will send those contracts to you when the time is right. You'll be treated well. My guess is the Agency will match twenty-five percent of your salary." If the accountant's estimate proved correct, it would be much more than he'd anticipated in his wildest guesses and confirmed Johnson's earlier statement.

Sparks appeared on cue to transport Jason to his session with Congressman Wilke. The traffic downtown was jammed, cars creeping along the streets, horns blasting at the least provocation, pedestrians packed at each corner waiting for lights to give them the signal to cross, others ignoring the crossing signals and dashing through the four lanes of slow moving vehicles. Sparks seemed to take it all in stride, cutting through some side streets that most didn't know about or were wary of traversing.

At the main entrance to the Rayburn building, Sparks pulled into a space by a fire hydrant. "Dr. Spradlin, if you don't mind, we'll let you get to the airport by the Metro. That'll be faster than my driving you. Or if you're reluctant to do that, a cab would be another option."

Jason shook his hand and pulled his small bag and briefcase from the rear seat. "I can find my way via the subway. Thanks for getting me here."

After passing through the guards at the entrance, utilizing a restroom, and getting directions from a woman walking rapidly along the hall, Jason found his way to the third floor offices of Wilke, the senior Congressman from Maine. As he'd anticipated, there'd be a delay while Wilke completed a session with constituents from his home state. The receptionist offered him coffee while he waited. He accepted, unsure of how quickly this meeting would end and he could be on his way.

Twenty minutes later, three people left Wilke's office and Jason was shown in by a secretary.

Wilke came around his huge desk filled with stacks of papers to meet Jason. "Dr. Spradlin, it's good to see you again. Thanks for coming in. I know it was another hassle you didn't need."

They expended five minutes discussing the hearings involving Preston King and Kathryn. Wilke asked about them and seemed pleased they were doing well and had obtained a solid settlement from the group who accused them of publishing a fraudulent paper. Jason added little to the conversation as he waited for the real purpose of Wilke's request to appear.

Wilke got around to the issue by saying, "The reason I wanted to see you was I've heard you're being courted by the Biological Division of Homeland Security to do some work for them." He paused as though gathering his thoughts and continued. "As you know I'm now the Chairman of the House Committee for Science and Technology and while Homeland Security doesn't fall under our bailiwick, some members of the committee have become concerned about their efforts to coerce leading scientists into doing research for them. Based on our past interactions, I believe I can depend on your judgment to let me in on those type activities. If I've read you wrong, I'll apologize and let you be on your way."

Jason shifted in the chair and leaned forward. "Congressman, I can't speak for others but my initial meeting led me to believe any grants I had with other federal agencies could be jeopardized if I refused to take on the task they wanted me to do. That threat, presented in a rather mild form, appeared a couple of times. I didn't press them or attempt to clarify what they meant in a precise way, but it was there."

"How did the warning come?"

"At the first meeting with two representatives who came to State University and my office, I was told the Director planned for me to come to their offices for a briefing. When I suggested I might not be interested, one of the reps responded by saying the Director had considerable influence with all federal agencies and my present and future grants could be jeopardized. So yes, I felt some pressure. But admittedly I didn't push back as I thought I might be able to accomplish something for national defense."

"How do you feel now? Any change of heart?"

"I've been here for a session outlining my specific job. It's something I believe I can accomplish and if it helps in our defense against terror groups, I'll be pleased to have contributed. But if the product is used to kill innocent people, I'll no doubt wish I'd backed away at the first opportunity."

"You may not wish to respond to this, but what was your impression of the group in those labs outside of Washington?"

"I've had limited exposure at this time. But my initial impression is there are several excellent scientists working there under highly secret conditions. One has no idea what the other is doing and apparently all are forbidden to discuss their specific project with any other colleague. Of course, that's a polar opposite environment of that at a university where ideas and results of experiments are shared openly and discussion is invited."

"Would they be more effective if they were less focused on security and secrecy?"

"I expect so. I've said several times in meetings with

representatives of the Agency, the sharing of ideas between scientists usually leads to improved methods and a better product. I'm sure the Agency has it reasons for their approach, but it goes against everything I've encountered in the academic world."

A secretary opened the door to the outer office. "Congressman, your schedule calls for you to be on the House floor for that vote on the NIH budget in ten minutes."

Wilke stood. "Then I'd better get going. Dr. Spradlin, thanks for your insights and call on me anytime I can assist you."

Jason stood to shake Wilke's hand. The Congressman rushed out the door, leaving Jason alone in the large office before he gathered his wits and followed. One of the secretaries in the office gave him directions to the nearest Metro stop. The short walk to the escalator leading to the underground stop took less than ten minutes. Three minutes later the train he needed roared into the station, a loudspeaker announcing the destination.

As he sat at the rear of the car, watched the commuters enter and exit, and listened to announcements of next stations, his mind remained on Wilke's probe and he hoped he'd not stumbled into a hornet's nest of power grabs between the Congressman and the Agency. And Wilke had not revealed why he'd recommended Jason to the Agency. Was he to become Wilke's inside person or was there some other motive? And he heard about the competition among federal departments and wondered if Homeland Security, the new player in the system, was resented by others who'd been forced to yield resources. He had no interest in becoming embroiled in those mini-wars.

Kathryn was focused on the computer in their upstairs office when he arrived home shortly before eleven. He felt drained after the whirlwind trip, but he leaned over to kiss her and caress her back. She saved her work to the hard drive and stood to stand against him.

"I always miss you and am glad you're back. You want a drink or something to eat?"

"Let's have a drink and watch the late news."

At the first commercial break in the newscast, Kathryn took his hand and said, "I want to tell you something, but didn't want to over the phone. I didn't want you to worry while you were involved with those spooky people in D.C."

She twisted on the sofa to look at his face. "I saw Hugh Riley the day you left for Washington. He was loitering near the back entrance to Quincy. He didn't say anything, but I was aware of his staring at me as I walked toward the quadrangle."

Chapter 6

As soon as he got into his office the next morning, Jason called Tom O'Hare, the Chief Detective for campus security. "Tom, how are you? I haven't had the need for your advice for quite some time."

O'Hare laughed and broke in. "But something has come up, I take it. You wouldn't call an old friend just to pass the time of a busy morning. And I haven't talked to you since you and Kathryn married. Congratulations."

"Thanks and you're correct. There may be a problem. Kathryn saw Hugh Riley on the campus yesterday. We're concerned he's stalking her again, although this was the first time she's been aware of him nearby."

O'Hare said, "Hold a minute while I look at a record." Jason heard the phone being placed on a wooden surface. As he waited, he began pulling papers given to him by Walcott and the Agency accountant from his briefcase.

Back on line, O'Hare said, "I scanned Riley's plea agreement with the City Attorney. According to the copies I have, he has completed his bargain to stay away from the campus for two years. I can't bring him in for violating that agreement."

O'Hare continued. "But if he shows again under strange circumstances, we'll bring him in for questioning. If you remember from three years ago, I told you that stalkers seem never to get past their obsession with their target and eventually harm them in some way. So let's keep alert to Riley's presence. Kathryn should not be alone in places he might show."

"We'll keep you up to date if he's around again. It could just be a random crossing on a busy campus although Riley has no business here now."

"Don't assume it's random until we know better."

Jason didn't look forward to passing this warning to Kathryn but she needed to understand the potential threat from Riley. She hated to be always on the lookout and not be able to move about freely. But he'd insist she take the essential precautions.

Jason had continued to peruse the materials given to him by Walcott and to think about his specific task. Three days after he'd returned from D.C., Joe Higgins appeared at Jason's office. He waited by Audrey's desk until a graduate student had left with corrections to a paper he'd prepared and Jason had critiqued.

Jason stood when Higgins entered and walked to shake his hand. "To remind you I'm from the GSA with the task to oversee the updates to that building you're going to use. We've employed a contractor who started with a bit of preliminary work yesterday and is continuing today. If you'd like to be involved, meet me and the contractor at the building at eight tomorrow morning. Johnson is eager to get the changes completed, so the sooner we can complete the scut work, the faster you guys can move ahead."

Jason was impressed they'd acted so rapidly, especially in lining up the contractor. "I think things were clear enough based on your visit before, but I'll come by sometime tomorrow to check on progress. I can't make eight because of another commitment, but maybe early afternoon."

Higgins stood. "I'd appreciate that. To be honest, I'm not very familiar with research labs and would hate to screw up." He grinned. "And I'd hate it more to get on Johnson's bad side even if I don't report to him directly."

"I assume you found housing okay. Sometimes Spencerville is overrun with university events and all the motels, hotels are filled."

Higgins grinned. "Actually, I'm staying at that small army base in Crews. They had a vacancy in the Bachelor Officers Quarters and will permit other federal employees use of the facility. It's only a fifteen minute drive from here. So I can get an early breakfast, drive here, grab a bite at noon at some fast food place, and get back to the base in time for the evening mess. It's a lot less expensive than a motel and the per diem I'm getting is not great."

Jason walked to the door with him. "I'll get by around two-thirty." Although he wasn't certain he could give Higgins any advice, he'd stick with his promise.

When Jason arrived at the 29th Street building, two workers were busy on the outside. The sign for the previous company had been taken down. Inside he found Higgins who had spread plans on one of the desks left by the owner and was engaged in conversation with a foreman, clipboard in hand and wearing the usual hard hat.

When he saw Jason at the door, Higgins stepped toward him.

"Thanks for coming. I have a question about the hood to be reconfigured in the safety lab. Let's walk there and I'll show you what I mean."

In the lab Higgins pointed to the hood in question. "As I understand the plans, the air flow needs to be reversed here so there's pressure being placed inside the hood rather than feeding to the outside. And the entire structure is to be surrounded with a tightly sealed glass wall with a secure doorway equipped with a combination lock."

"That's correct," Jason said. "That's to prevent toxins from being exhausted into the atmosphere. It's the reverse of the typical system, but it prevents contamination of the environment and avoids the problem of local citizens becoming infected. And the wall protects other workers in the facility. Those using the hood will wear protective clothing while inside and rinse off immediately in the shower being placed here." He pointed to the spot.

Jason followed Higgins to a corner of the larger lab. Higgins pointed to marks on the floor. "Now here, as I understand, is to be a small space walled off from everything else."

"Correct. A solid wall, with one door. Good lighting but with controls so the intensity can be varied. This is for sensitive instruments we need to protect from dust and grime that naturally builds up when people are working. And an exhaust system to clear the room." Higgins made notes on his clipboard and turned to another page.

"Another issue I'd like your opinion about is signs on the outside. Typically we put up signs denoting the facility as Homeland Security property, but Johnson alerted me to the issue of secrecy and security.

I'm of the opinion we should just skip the signs. No reason to call attention to the facility."

Jason nodded his head in agreement. "I'd rather not get the locals concerned about the work. And the press will push to discover why Homeland Security is suddenly active in the area. Let's leave it unidentified."

Higgins nodded understanding and checked a note on his list. "I think those are the only questions I have to this point, but I have two sets of keys for you. If you need additional sets for the workers, let me know." He handed Jason a key ring with four keys attached. "One fits the front entrance; the second one is for the doors onto the loading dock."

"You're moving quickly. I'm impressed."

"The contractor knows what he's doing and seems to have good workers. For him, time is money and for me, I just want to get it done and back home."

Jason turned toward the front entrance. "I'll get out of your way, but give me a call if I'm needed."

Jason had not looked forward to telling Kathryn about O'Hare's warning. But he had to do it and soon. That evening after dinner and the kids had enjoyed their usual down time with their Dad, he tackled the unpleasant task. He took her hand and led her to the couch. "I called O'Hare about Riley. As you might guess, he can't arrest Riley, but he reminded me of the dangers posed by characters like him. You know as well as I that stalkers become dangerous and more often than not damage the person they've been following. The short version is you need to stay on the alert and not get into isolated places where he can confront you."

Her face broke into a deep frown, nodding in understanding. "It's scary. But I hate to live like that."

"It's best we give attention to O'Hare's advice. If for no other reason than my peace of mind, promise you won't get into situations where you are by yourself. If you have to go to the lab at night, make sure someone else is there or I'll go with you." He leaned over to kiss her on the cheek.

She smiled. "I'll pay attention until we know he's disappeared again. Now, I want to raise another matter with you. See what you think."

She twisted on the couch and brought her legs under her, revealing nylon covered knees, her eyes on his face. "I've thought about this a long time and decided I'd delay until after my three-year review."

She paused, as though considering the issue or how to phrase it. Then she blurted. "I want to have a child before my biological clock ticks down to zero. I love Jennifer and Tony, but I've always dreamed of having one of my own. I think it's every woman's dream and I'd love to do that." She seemed to bore into his eyes, looking for reactions.

Jason was not completely surprised. She'd hinted at her desire before. "That would mean taking leave from your job for a time unless we're lucky with the timing."

"I've thought about that too. What I've considered is going on half-time after the baby is born and give more time to all the kids. You know, Mrs. Carter has hinted at leaving at the end of the school year and we'll need to alter our living style anyway."

"Have you talked with your section leader about this?"

"Not yet. I wanted your reaction first." She giggled and added, "And I may not be able to get pregnant anyway."

"No reason to think you couldn't. You're healthy, never have physical problems."

They both became silent, thinking about the implications of another small child in the house and the demands that could be placed on both of them. Jason pulled her closer, one hand caressing her knees. "If you want this, I'll do whatever we must do to make it work. We're okay financially so we don't need your income, but you may miss the excitement of work. You seem to have enjoyed your job in spite of the demands."

"I have, but it's the dilemma every professional woman confronts. I'd like to discuss the idea with my leader and suggest I revert to half-time at the time the baby is due with the option of going full time again when the time seems right for us. Maybe when the youngster is ready for a child care program. By then Jennifer and Tony can probably get into after school programs or I could arrange my work to be free when they're home after school."

"Okay with me. I wouldn't mind being a father of a newborn again."

She kissed him, her lips parting as she pulled his head toward hers. He moved his hand up her legs, shoving her skirt higher on her thighs. She slipped off her blouse and pulled his head to her breast. He kissed her neck and caressed her breast. Fully aroused, he muttered. "Maybe we should get started on this project."

"Not yet. I must see my gynecologist and get rid of birth control devices first. But call this practice." She unbuttoned his shirt and ran her hand across his chest.

Jason received a resume from Helga Grimes and a letter from the Agency scientist who'd promised the name of a possible person to work on the project. The scientist had contacted his friend who declined any future work, indicating retirement was working out well for him.

He was impressed with Grimes' credentials. She'd been unable to publish routinely because of the Agency restrictions associated with the secretive requirements but she'd contributed several papers to microbiology journals focused on projects indirectly related to the mission of concocting toxic substances for the Agency's war on terror. There'd also been a couple of publications based on her dissertation.

Wanting to move forward as expeditiously as possible, he called the three references she'd listed. Each had good things to say about her intelligence, drive and work habits. One summed up his thinking by saying Jason probably couldn't find anyone better than Helga Grimes for a three year assignment or as a permanent appointment to the faculty.

Not wanting to ignore the other possible candidate, Jason called Homer Chichester at his home phone in Lincoln, Nebraska. He explained in general terms the nature of the proposed work and the projected length of time to be committed. Without hesitation,

Chichester indicated he wouldn't be interested. "Dr. Spradlin, thanks for your interest, but I've settled into a good retirement and have found things I enjoy doing. I'm not dedicated enough to get back into the hassle of a full time position. Plus, I don't want to uproot my wife and move very far away from our grandchildren."

Unsure of how much leeway he had in filling the scientist position, Jason called Johnson. As he anticipated, he bumped against the first snag in the progress toward getting started.

When he revealed to Johnson he intended to offer the position to Helga Grimes, Johnson responded gruffly, "That's not a good idea. You know we let her go from here for going around an important policy."

Remembering Wilke's concern about the Agency and suspecting the Congressman would go to bat for him if asked, Jason pushed his case. "She told me the circumstances under which she was terminated. But she seems the ideal fit for what we want to do. And she'll work for the same salary she had at the Agency."

"And if I won't approve?"

Jason wasn't certain of his authority but had been led to believe he had flexibility in hiring, he responded by suggesting he might go over Johnson's head, then tempered his argument. "Mr. Johnson, from my perspective Dr. Grimes has all the qualifications and experience required to move this idea forward. She can do this more expeditiously than bringing in someone who has no knowledge of the Agency's goals. She knows the essential laboratory techniques and the expectations. And she's been cleared for security. I trust you won't let a minor discrepancy on her part cloud your vision for this endeavor."

Johnson wavered. "I take it you've looked widely for another candidate."

"I've talked with another retiree referred to me, but he's no longer interested in working. And as I said previously, younger people aren't likely to take this on with no potential for publications and recognition, particularly for the short period of time that can be guaranteed."

Johnson took several seconds before growling, "Okay, go ahead with Grimes and hope this doesn't lead to problems down the road."

"Thanks and I don't know if you've been kept up to date on the renovations of the facility but in another week or ten days we'll be ready to move equipment in and prepare for the experimentation."

"Faster than I thought possible," Johnson said. "Keep me in the loop."

Jason asked. "May I assume responsibility for the purchase of equipment?"

"Yes. Send the invoices to our accounting group. And we'll begin your stipend immediately. Let accounting know the date of Grimes' start."

Jason said, "I won't know all the equipment requirements until I know the specific task, but I'm assuming there will be need to manipulate the genetics of organisms. To do that we'll need a high-powered electron microscope. If that becomes a reality, I'd like to suggest we purchase time on State University's rather than bringing one into the lab. There should be no problem of secrecy. In fact, they may be amenable to allowing our own technician to utilize the equipment with minimum oversight. Doing that would be much less expensive and save installation time."

Johnson said, "Let me pass this by Walcott, but your idea seems feasible and could save us money. Anything else I need to think about?"

"That's it today," Jason responded. He heard the click of Johnson replacing the telephone in its cradle.

He called Grimes immediately and offered her the slot. "I trust you are still interested and can move to Spencerville in a couple of weeks. I know that's not much notice but I'd like your input into the purchase of equipment and supplies."

"That's wonderful news, Dr. Spradlin. I believe I can sublease my apartment quickly and move there. In fact, I've talked with a real estate agent in Spencerville to get some feel for the cost of housing. And you were correct. It'll be less expensive than the D.C. area. Now I'll call him back to begin looking for a furnished place or one that requires little of my own things until we see how this all goes."

Jason said, "I've advertised for a technician but will not make that decision until we both interview the people who apply."

"Dr. Spradlin, I'm looking forward to getting back to work. And if it would help, I can send a list of essential equipment."

"Do that. It might move things a bit faster." He gave her his e-mail address at the office.

Riley had established a routine after his first sighting of Kathryn near Quincy. Based on the remarks of his drinking buddies, he'd learned she came into Quincy and worked in King's lab but he didn't know if she was on a regular schedule or came when needed by the graduate students. And he didn't dare ask anyone in the lab about her. Tipping her off would be a huge setback. And he couldn't afford to advertise his interest by alerting others and have the cops after him again.

But the day he'd inadvertently spotted her had whetted his appetite to be near her as often as possible. She looked stunning in the green dress, black heels and nylons showing off her perfect legs and body shape. Just touching her would be heavenly. Going beyond the slightest physical contact could drive him out of his mind.

After years of working in Quincy and sneaking around the halls to observe the activities of others, always hoping to find something about which to spread rumors, he knew the places he could wait unobserved by those in the hallways and class rooms. Now he had to be patient and bide his time.

An opportunity to corner her came three days later when he saw her enter Quincy a bit past eight in the evening while he was parked in the faculty lot. He congratulated himself. His three day vigil had paid off. He waited until she had time to settle into the task that brought her into the building after hours. He climbed the two flights of stairs. He eased the door to the third floor open and seeing no one, moved as quietly as possible along the hall until he could see into King's lab. He decided to give her time to become immersed in the work and ducked into a tiny closet he'd used on numerous occasions before.

After fifteen minutes, Riley walked toward the door of the lab. Kathryn was busy with a set of vials arranged in a rack and so intent on the work, she didn't hear any noise or detect any movement. Riley's heart jumped. His opportunity had arrived much sooner than he'd expected.

But as he prepared to open the door, two graduate students emerged from the elevator a few doors down the hall. Talking to each other, they ignored Riley. He scurried back to his den. The students went into King's lab. He heard them talking to Kathryn and accepted he's missed his chance. But other opportunities would arise.

Chapter 7

Significant progress occurred during the following three weeks. Construction in the laboratory facility neared completion, the final installation delayed for ten days waiting on a back order of special glass for the safety hood. The six-car parking lot had been graded and graveled then topped with asphalt on the west side of the building with an entrance from 29th Street. Helga Grimes visited Spencerville to check out apartments, and after viewing four in the company of Joe Burris, signed a three-year lease for a partially furnished unit located within a large complex only six blocks from the laboratory. She indicated to Jason she planned to walk to work except in lousy weather.

She and Jason interviewed a half-dozen applicants for the technician position and opted for a single woman in her mid-thirties who'd had experience in a microbiology laboratory prior to moving to Spencerville. They submitted her credentials to obtain security clearance to the Agency in Washington. They ordered essential equipment, including a large freezer/refrigerator, a small bench centrifuge, balances, a pH meter, a small but powerful computer, supplies for gel staining, and other pieces required for the type of work to be done. They visited the electron microscope unit located in the basement of an academic building on the campus and discussed with the director the potential for leasing time on the microscope. They purchased necessary glassware and expendable supplies through a reputable laboratory equipment company that sent representatives to campus on a regular basis. Jason had utilized their services throughout his time at State, knew most of their sales reps, and had faith in their products.

Jason tried to give the federal lab some time each day among the mix of faculty meetings, the required sessions with the dean and other administrators, a graduate seminar, advising his cadre of six graduate students and conferring with two post-docs. He had little time to stand back and consider the future of either the department or his own research projects.

Roy Blount kept him up to date on the Redlake project. The FDA Commissioner had given final approval allowing the project to clear the last hurdle within the bureaucracy. On his last visit, two days ago, Roy had given him a document outlining the procedure Redlake would follow in paying royalties to both State and Jason. While Jason's percentage of net profits would be low, there promised to be a huge payout if the products took off as the organization projected. Early signs from the market suggested consumer acceptance and return purchasers. The long-term looked bright. Jason could likely count on a steady income for a long time for his efforts and the university would benefit as well, giving the Research Office discretionary funds to benefit young investigators.

On the home front Kathryn had been given a clean bill of health by her physician and she and Jason hoped to succeed in having the desired child be born during mid-summer. That would give Kathryn sufficient time to become acclimated to the baby's whims and get things in order for half-time work in the fall semester. Jason realized a new youngster in the household would impact his habits as well. He recalled with no great fondness the late night and early morning feedings and the changing of diapers at critical moments but he looked forward to cuddling a tiny child again, feeling its softness and knowing its dependence upon the parents was a vital element in its development. During those few moments he gave in to retrospection, he recalled the struggles he and Lucy had experienced with their two children. And in those times he remembered her smile and their good times together.

Riley had become frustrated. His plan to wait for Kathryn's appearance in Quincy had not worked out as he'd hoped. He'd seen her a couple of times in King's lab but in the company of other faculty or graduate students. He decided he should try a new tactic.

In the central library where no one would recognize him he used an available university telephone directory and found Kathryn's office number in the Medical buildings. With that information in hand he meandered through the large complex of hallways on the third floor of the teaching hospital, feeling vulnerable among the white-coated medical types as they hurried along, dodging each other and carts filled with trays guided by young orderlies who often appeared to be in a trance as they pushed by others. No one gave him undue attention but nevertheless he felt out of place in an alien environment. And he acknowledged he would be challenged by some one with authority if he continued to lurk in the halls. He was well aware he could not dawdle or he'd be confronted by some authority or reported to the campus security by a worker who knew most of the regulars. He hurried along as though with some purpose and clear destination in mind, hoping no one stopped him to ask if he required assistance.

He passed Room 327 without noticing and had to double back. The door was ajar enough he could see Kathryn at her desk talking on the telephone. He searched for a hiding place but in the unfamiliar surroundings didn't see anything accessible. He tugged at a closet door only to find it locked. Rather then loitering and calling attention to his presence, he went to the nearest stairwell and waited for a few minutes, hoping no one came along to query him about his presence.

He cracked the door to the third floor and, seeing no one, walked quickly along the hall and past 327. The door was closed and the lights were out. He kept moving, turned a corner and found himself near a group of laboratories, exhaust hoods humming and technicians intent on some task, discussing their problems or the outcome of an experiment with each other. To his surprise and delight he saw Kathryn and another woman huddled over a microscope in the second lab. They alternated taking turns peering through the lens at some specimen, conferring about their observations, making notes on a clipboard. Just seeing her caused his heart to race and he determined to attain his goal of holding her close. From that his fantasies grew.

Kathryn handed the clipboard to her colleague and said something beyond his range of hearing. Riley stopped to stare at her and attempted to overhear the conversation, but lost his nerve when a young man shoved past him and into the lab. Riley had learned her location and felt rewarded, but he'd rather confront her in the more familiar confines of

Quincy.

Leaving the Medical building, Riley remembered the cops questioning him until he thought he would pass out after the earlier stalking charge. He didn't want to go through that again. But he couldn't shove aside this overwhelming desire to do intimate things with Kathryn. His urges deepened each time he saw her and, although he realized he could be headed for trouble with the authorities, he could not resist.

As furnishings and equipment arrived, Helga Grimes began the task of setting up the laboratories and an office. She brought in reference books and arranged them on bookshelves. She tested the telephones. In the laboratories she unpacked and sorted the glassware into drawers under the benches. She tried out the equipment as it was delivered to be certain it functioned properly.

Then with only twenty-four hours notice, Johnson and Walcott appeared in Spencerville to check out the facility and decide if they were ready to move to the next stage. As scheduled, they arrived at the 29th Street address under the guidance of Higgins who had met them at the airport.

Walcott greeted Helga and Jason warmly, shaking hands and asking about their welfare. Johnson was much more reserved, especially with Helga. He could hardly look her in the eye, not yet willing to admit he'd made a mistake in firing her. Or he still held to his initial reaction to her breaking a rule, but hadn't the courage to refuse Jason's hard sell and underlying threat to go above his head to bring Grimes onto the project.

Higgins led the tour of the building. Grimes explained the various features as Jason tagged along prepared to respond to any questions and to gauge their reactions. Walcott gave close attention to the laboratory with the biosafety features, nodding his approval. They completed the inspection by assembling in the conference room using chairs dragged in by Jason and Higgins.

Helga apologized for not having coffee available. "It's something that hasn't seemed important among the rush of more critical tasks."

As they settled into chairs in the small conference room, Walcott said, "The deal looks good to me. I like the set-up and the lack of identification on the outside. I believe you're ready if all the equipment functions as you've stated."

Johnson chimed in. "Let's be absolutely certain of the safety of this operation. We can't afford to contaminate the civilian population. The Congressional oversight committee will close us down on the slightest pretext."

Jason said, "We've checked everything several times and are confident of the safety."

Johnson persevered. "What about possible break-ins and destruction of the facility? There are crazies in our society who see Armageddon in every government activity."

"Higgins and I have discussed the situation," Jason said. "We think we've taken sufficient precautions. We've tried to avoid calling attention to the facility during the renovation and there's not been publicity about it or our work inside. You probably noticed we've not erected a sign. Nor have we installed a fence, believing that would raise questions about the facility."

Jason left his chair to find his briefcase and pull out a section of the local newspaper. On an inside page, the *Herald* had published a short article about the new lab on 29th and a research award to Dr. Spradlin to conduct cutting edge research on infectious diseases. The article described the potential for the genetic modification of toxins to render them harmless.

He handed this to Johnson. "As we discussed, we've tried to construct some camouflage story to head off undue speculation." He didn't relate the details of how he convinced the media people at State to release this to the papers.

Johnson scanned the short article and nodded. "This should work okay. Now the locals will understand the rationale for those signs about hazards associated with the building."

Walcott nodded agreement. "I think we're ready to provide you the organism on which to initiate the development of the weapon. We'll send this by a military plane to Spencerville. One of you can meet the crew and bring the package to the lab." Walcott stopped, paused a moment as though thinking about his next comment, then continued, "The beginning point is an unknown organism, harmless to other living creatures in its present form. Your goal is to modify or add to its genetic structure to make it as lethal as possible in a very short period of time following exposure. We want to produce something so that a minimum number of the organisms will shut down a vital system and culminate in almost instant death. Then it should disintegrate within minutes in room air so that it cannot be detected by any means. We believe delivery by an aerosol method would be most effective but we'll leave that to your judgment after you understand the characteristics of the product."

Jason nodded understanding then asked, "Any known models?"

"Not to our knowledge," Walcott responded. "And we explored widely. Our intelligence people have been unable to uncover anything approaching what we hope will evolve from your efforts. It will be a unique approach to terrorizing the terrorists. And we hope it will tamp down their desire to do us damage."

Jason probed for a starting point. "Has anyone tried this before?"

"Not to our knowledge. But there are hints of how to approach the problem in the scientific literature related to known toxins. Although the focus of those reports is geared more to either rendering the organism harmless or the development of antidotes, there are clues about manipulation of the basic structures of the toxin."

Walcott continued after a short pause. "And this will take time. It will be a trial and error approach. Modify the genome of the organism and test it on either mature rats or guinea pigs. If that doesn't succeed, modify again and test until you've succeeded."

Johnson cut in. "That's why we've left the contract for the building rather open-ended. We don't expect a quick fix." But the manner of his staring at them left no doubt he wanted something as soon as possible. He was no doubt under pressure to produce during his appointment which could be short-lived in the helter-skelter of the federal bureaucracy exacerbated by the changing of administrations and the subsequent payoff to political cronies associated with the majority party.

Johnson stood and moved toward the door signaling the termination of the visit. Walcott tarried long enough to say. “You’ve done a good job. I’ll call you when we’re ready to ship the organism.” He shook their hands and hurried to catch up with Johnson and Higgins.

After the car had left, Jason asked, “What’s Walcott’s title and role in all of this? He told me he’d act as liaison to the project, but beyond that?”

Helga grinned, creating creases in her face. “Fred is the stable science advisor to these administrators who come and go. He’s been there a long time and in many respects is the guiding force behind all of these developments.”

Jason touched her arm as he asked, “Were you uncomfortable in dealing with Johnson after his previous actions toward you?”

“Not really and I personally dislike him. He has no idea of what goes on in those D.C. labs and relies on Walcott to keep him up to date and out of trouble. Then he throws his weight around to remind people who’s really in charge.”

Jason laughed. “Universities are not immune to the problems of bloated egos and incompetence. The worst is when the two show up in the same individual.”

Grimes glanced at her watch. “I need to get going. The movers are due in thirty minutes to deliver those furnishings from D. C. to my apartment. By next week I should be established and through with that ordeal.”

Jason said, “Go ahead. I’ll lock the doors.”

Kathryn and Jason had started a routine early in their marriage they had dubbed "date night." Once each month they did something together with no one else involved. Sometimes it was nothing more than a movie and a snack at some small café. They discounted events to which they were expected to appear because of their ties to the university community. Jason called those overtime work and after attending several she agreed with his description. A couple of times each year they had dressed in their best clothes and dined at an upscale restaurant.

Now early in November, they were in the rooftop restaurant of the downtown Marriott, a recent development in Spencerville and a testament to the continued growth of both the city and State University. Executives and their staff often visited State to confer with those faculty on the cutting edge of their discipline as a way of maintaining their business on the forefront of technology. These company big-wigs expected, almost demanded, upscale accommodations. Marriott had set its target on meeting that market and seemed to be succeeding with crowded dining facilities and delays in obtaining room reservations.

Jason and Kathryn were impressed with the facility and the service. Lights of the city and surrounding area were clearly visible on a cloudless evening. Headlights of cars and other vehicles moved along the street below giving an eerie feeling of invading aliens.

The dessert plates were removed and they leaned back in satisfaction. Jason asked, "You too stuffed to dance one time? The music seems slow enough for me to manage."

"I'd like that if this dress doesn't pop apart at critical places."

He led her to the dance floor occupied by three other couples. "I haven't seen this dress before or have I neglected to give proper notice?" They settled into the beat of the small band.

"It arrived yesterday, another reminder from my father to maintain a proper attire in this backward community. But this time he gave some attention to my request to scale down the gifts by including two sets of slacks and matching blouses." Her father, the owner of a large department store in downtown Minneapolis, sent on a regular basis the most recent designs for her use. And at irregular intervals he included a suit for Jason and outfits for Jennifer and Tony now that they had begun to participate in affairs beyond the normal school day activities.

"You look beautiful as always," Jason said. When he'd seen her in the living room of their home, he almost gawked at the black and white sheath that seemed to scream sophistication and sexuality. He'd realized every eye was on her as they were escorted to their table in the restaurant.

She seemed to get closer to him. "I have news for you that will change the manner in which I dress in the next months. My physician confirmed this afternoon I am pregnant and should deliver next August if all goes well. He thinks there's no reason to be concerned."

Jason tightened his arm around her waist and touched her lips with his. "Wonderful. Almost like we planned. And it happened more quickly than I anticipated. Maybe all that practice paid off."

Back at their table, Jason asked, "I dislike bringing up a distasteful subject tonight but I assume you haven't encountered Riley recently? You haven't said anything."

“Nothing to report. Maybe he gave up his goal, whatever that was, other than gawk like a teen-ager seeing his first attractive woman after his hormones kicked in.”

“I suspect he’s still around and waiting for the right moment to confront you. So stay alert.”

She changed the subject. “You can likely guess from my questions and reactions, but I worry you’ve taken on too much with this federal contract. Other administrators steer clear of any involvement beyond their normal responsibilities.”

“It takes some time but Helga has done most of the work thus far. I don’t want to go into details if you can accept that.”

“I understand the secrecy involved. Now could we forget work and Riley and dance one more time. This may be my last chance before none of my decent dresses fit.”

Jason stood and took her hand. “You’ll always turn on my juices.”

She edged closer. “That’s my plan.”

Chapter 8

Jason was signing purchase orders when the phone rang ten minutes before eight. “Dr. Spradlin, this is Fred Walcott. We’re sending the organism today by a small military cargo plane. They will leave Fort Myers soon and should be at your airport by ten or soon afterwards.”

“Either Dr. Grimes or I will meet it,” Jason said, beginning to turn the page of his desk calendar to review his schedule for the day. “Any particular instructions about handling?”

“Other than it’s an anaerobic type, sealed in a closed container with nitrogen gas, and must be protected from oxygen, nothing else. Grimes will know how to deal with it.”

“We’ll let you know when we have it to the lab, “Jason said.

Expecting Walcott to sign off, Jason almost dropped the receiver into the cradle, but Walcott continued, “I just wanted to say I’m pleased you were able to interest Helga in the project. Between the two of us, she got a raw deal here and I hope this will help her recover and get her career back on track.”

“She seems quite capable and is eager to get going on the project.”

“Good. Talk to you later.”

Jason called Helga at the lab and they agreed he’d pick her up and they’d go together to meet the plane. Now at the airport they watched as the clearly identified plane landed and taxied toward the cargo terminal utilized by transports for loading and unloading goods. A large Fed Ex plane moved slowly as it left the gate headed for the runway and its destination. The clear blue sky and slight wind promised a great day for flying and outdoor activities before the winter season changed for the worse. A couple of private planes were being released from their moorings in preparation for some recreational jaunts.

As soon as the military aircraft stopped moving, two men emerged from the compartment in the middle of the plane. One lugged a small package while the other seemed to be surveying the surroundings as though expecting hijackers or another threat. Jason and Helga hurried out of the terminal to meet them. Both were prepared to show identification, knowing the military would expect such under the conditions of security involving the project.

While she held the package, Jason signed a form accepting delivery. The pilots turned immediately and by the time Jason had stowed the package in the rear seat of his car the plane departed Spencerville with a roar of engines and emission of vapor.

"What we have," Helga said, pointing toward the tightly wrapped container, "is the organism sealed in liquid nitrogen. That's the typical manner of transporting and storing potential dangerous organisms. In this case we have just the backbone of what we hope will evolve into a toxin but it's another way to protect it from the air."

"So our first step will be to reproduce the bug to be certain of an ample supply, then begin unraveling its genome."

"Correct. I see you've been doing your homework." She laughed as Jason parked near the front door of the lab. "And that may be the easy part. Altering the basic structure to produce a lethal organism will tax our skills and push our luck."

"How may I help you best? Jason asked. He unlocked the door and they entered the front of the facility.

She placed the vital cargo on a desk. "I can get the reproduction started and let you know how that went. Then we can confer about decoding the structure. I have ideas, but you probably know more about that than I."

Helga continued as she thought about the process and the challenges ahead, "You might schedule some time on the University electron microscope. Maybe early next week."

"I'll take care of that," Jason said. "By the way, when does our technician begin?"

"Tomorrow morning. Just in time for the real work."

"No problem with her security clearance?"

"Johnson pushed it through. That's what he's good at doing, skirting the bureaucracy. Another thing I've thought we should do is put up the international symbol for biological hazards near both entrances. I don't want somebody to push into the facility without some warning of the potential dangers. And you know we'll get visitors as soon as salesmen realize we're running a laboratory."

"Should we check with Walcott? I don't want to advertise our activity if we don't need to do it, but I agree we'll have people come in. The only way to avoid it is to keep the door locked at all times, then that in itself elevates the curiosity of some people. The reason I say that is because there are a few labs on campus with those warnings. Passer-bys always stop to peer in."

Helga said, "I'll call Fred in the next few minutes. He'll want to know we received the organism in good condition."

"Good. I promised him we'd confirm receipt."

When Jason approached the door to the lab the next morning, the warning symbol jumped out at him. Although he acknowledged the need to alert visitors, he worried the sign represented a form of advertising they should avoid. But he'd trust Walcott's and Helga's opinion. However, the sign made him stop and consider again the neighborhood in which they were located. Next to them was a vacant lot grown high with weeds and turning brown. Then a warehouse used by a local manufacturer. An Exxon station occupied the corner. Across the street, another warehouse owned by a furniture dealer flanked by vacant spaces. He acknowledged that at times they would be the only structure with activity, like an island in a sea. He thought about the possibility of a fence again and then dismissed the idea as another red light calling attention to them.

Inside the lab Helga introduced him to Ingrid Crain, the technician who'd been on the job for only a few minutes. The thirty-fivish, brunette, round-face Crain smiled and shook Jason's hand. "I'm glad to be here and Dr. Grimes has already lined out some tasks for me."

"She's an organized soul," Jason said. "It's good to have you with us."

Helga led Jason into the safety lab area. "When we have sufficient organism, I'll freeze-dry a portion. I thought that'd be a good form for us to work on the genome."

"Any idea of how large it is, probably one of the smaller in terms of base pairs?"

"I'd guess two hundred thousand or fewer base nucleotides. It can't be too large or we'll have trouble with packaging it when we're sure of its lethality."

"Characteristics?"

Helga shrugged. "My speculation is Walcott either chose or had someone select a benign organism which in itself is harmless, although I doubt they know much about its characteristics. There are thousands of these things which should serve our purpose splendidly because no one will think to look at any single type when they attempt to develop a protective agent."

Jason turned toward the door. "I just wanted to check. Now I need to get back to a meeting with the dean and other department heads. He doesn't like us to miss."

Almost out the door, Jason turned back. "Helga, if you don't have plans, we'd like you to have Thanksgiving dinner with us."

"Thanks, that's nice of you. I'll look forward to the occasion."

"We usually eat around four, but come early and spend time with my wife and children."

"May I bring something?"

"Not necessary. Just come and dress causally."

The downtime around the university meant that most buildings were not occupied or there were very few people around after normal working hours, if any at all. But Riley remembered how some of the diehard scientists took advantage of the break from classes and committee meetings to accomplish things they'd let slide during the rush toward the holiday or were so intent on their research projects they ignored the holidays. He didn't know enough about Kathryn's habits to know if she'd continue coming into the lab late afternoon or evenings that had been her usual pattern since he'd started watching her or if she would alter her schedule for the holiday period.

On Monday evening of Thanksgiving week, Riley chanced he'd find her and more likely alone with all the graduate students away for the holiday. He parked toward the rear of the faculty lot near Quincy just after dusk and waited, thinking he'd give her until eight or eight-thirty to show. And if his plan worked, he'd need only enough time to grab her and manhandle her into an empty classroom, certain to be vacant. Only two other vehicles were in the lot, one of those a university truck left there by workers. At intervals he ran the motor and heater of his car to ward off the cold.

His luck and perseverance paid off. At eight-fifteen Kathryn parked as close to the entrance as possible and hurried from her car to the building. Tamping down his anticipation, Riley waited five minutes and followed, going up the stairs rather then use the noisy elevator. He eased through the third floor doorway and walked quietly toward King's lab.

The lights were on but the door had been locked. Frustrated for a moment before he recalled he'd stolen a key to King's lab as well as others during his time on the faculty. He retreated to his car and opened the trunk where he'd stored miscellaneous items over the years. After a few minutes of rustling through the horde, he found what he was searching for—a metal ring with a group of keys he'd labeled "Quincy labs." Now, if the locks hadn't been changed, he was in luck.

As he climbed the stairs again, he stopped on a landing to catch his breath and to sort through the keys. He found the one to King's lab fairly quickly, then resumed his ascent. Outside the lab door, he stopped to listen for sounds. For a moment he detected nothing, then the scrape of a stool being pushed away from a desk or lab bench. He inserted the key and to his delight, the lock turned and he eased in, gently closing the door behind him. He shoved the keys back into his pocket, careful not to rattle them.

Kathryn was in front of an incubator with her back to his position, intent on her work. He watched her for a moment as she placed a rack of tubes into the device and closed the door. Beneath the ever-present lab coat, she had on brown slacks and a matching blouse, the color neither obvious nor important to him. Scanning the layout quickly, he realized he could block her in the aisle between benches, the perfect location for his plan. He eased toward her, hoping he could wrap his arms around her before she saw him. He couldn't take his eyes off her, his mind racing with the next stages of his conquest.

Riley's foot scraped against a waste basket that had been left partially in the aisle and in his focus on her, he'd not noticed. The noise grabbed her attention. She jerked at the sound and turned toward it. Riley was standing ten feet away from her.

Kathryn recovered from the shock of seeing him almost

immediately. Without moving, she said, "Dr. Riley, what are you doing here? You have no business in this lab."

Riley took steps toward her, his eyes surveying her body and face, his heart racing with eagerness of what was about to happen after all his planning and waiting for the right moment. He reached for her, but without any warning, she kicked him in the groin. Pain shot throughout his frame. He doubled over, grabbed his midsection, and dropped to his knees. She kicked under the chin, slamming his head against the metal cabinets under the bench tops. He passed out as the pain shot through his cranium.

His next sensation was water being dumped into his face and cascading onto his chest, soaking his jacket and shirt. He attempted to move, but his hands were bound to some immovable object. He shifted his head enough to see his wrists had been tied together with duct tape and then lashed to a drain pipe. Shifting as much as he could, he saw Kathryn standing a few feet from his prostrate form.

"No reason to struggle, Riley. The cops will be here soon. They'll release you. You should know I thought about dumping a bottle of nitric acid on your lousy head. That'd give you something to think about in the next few years."

Riley couldn't move enough to do anything while she stood there cool and collected as though she did this every day. There'd not been a scream as he'd expected when he approached her. It was almost as though he'd been set up by this not-so-frail female. And her veiled threat about dumping acid on him scared him badly.

Two minutes later the cops arrived. Two uniformed campus

security patrolmen surveyed the situation for a brief moment. Then Jason rushed in. He surveyed the scene and moved to Kathryn. "Are you okay?"

She nodded and leaned into him. "It was scary, but I'm fine."

At the request of the officers, Kathryn described what had happened. "I didn't know how long he'd be out, so I tied his arms to the drain. I didn't want him to come at me again. Then I called you and my husband."

Jason spoke up. "Riley has been stalking her for weeks. And if you go back into the records, you'll find he was put on probation two years ago for the same thing. Detective O'Hare can confirm this. Now we hope you can get Riley out of our lives forever."

The officers released Riley from his bonds and pulled him erect, handcuffed his hands behind his back. Riley moaned and tried to say something, but grimaced with pain.

Then one officer asked, "You think he needs the hospital. His jaw looks like it might be broken."

They stopped moving and the second uniform examined Riley's face. He brushed Riley's jaw and asked, "Are you hurting?"

Riley nodded and mumbled, "Jaw hurts like hell. The bitch kicked me full on."

"We'll run you by the emergency room just in case. Don't want a moaning prisoner in our lock-up all night."

Thirty minutes later at home, sitting on the couch with drinks in hand, Kathryn said, "I guess I should tell you how I knew to defend myself." She sipped the soft drink and shook the glass to loosen the ice. Her hand was shaking slightly as she placed the tumbler on the coffee table.

Jason noticed, realized she was unnerved still by the events with Riley. "You can wait until another time."

She smiled at his understanding and shook her head. "No, I need to tell you this and it will help me get past the last couple of hours. Actually, it's more scary now in retrospect than when it happened. It went so fast, I didn't have time to think about what might have been."

She paused, thinking about where to begin. "When I was fourteen or fifteen, my father insisted my sister and I learn to defend ourselves. He warned us males would always be accosting us and forcing us to do things we didn't want to do. We had some inkling of what he meant because of minor clashes with our male classmates at high school."

"He enrolled us in a karate school and in a couple of years we became reasonably proficient at the craft. But I've never used it since I've known you. And you know I don't work at maintaining the skills"

Jason took her hand. "Did you ever feel the need to defend yourself?" The slight quiver was still evident.

She bobbed her head and squeezed his hand. "Once in university. I'd been dating this fraternity boy, Justin, whom I thought was truly interested in me for all the right reasons. We'd had three or four dates and he'd never pushed me to do anything beyond the usual petting that went on between the genders. Then at a frat party toward the middle of my junior year something happened to change my opinion. The fact is, it altered my outlook about men in a profound way—be very careful whom you trust."

She swiveled on the couch to assume her favorite position, legs pulled under her. She straightened the crease in her slacks. "At this party, Justin suggested I might wish to talk with his buddy, Pierce, in a side room that turned out to be a bedroom. I had no idea what was going on, but as soon as Pierce and I were alone, he grabbed me, pulled me against him and began to fondle my hips, trying to pull my dress up. I shoved him away, although he was much bigger than I. He grinned and reached for me again.

"I said no. This wasn't going to happen. At that point I realized the whole deal was a scheme hatched up by Justin and Pierce, maybe even others were in on it.

"He either didn't believe me or was determined to have his way, telling me Justin had promised I'd have sex with him, then he would get his turn. I couldn't believe him and started out of the room.

"He grabbed me by a shoulder and spun me around. I shoved him away, but then he came toward me again. That's when I kicked him in the balls. While he was groaning and holding his middle, I walked out.

"I went directly to Justin who was grinning like a cat who'd eaten a mouse. I slapped him across the face, called a cab and left the place. I never heard from him again."

Jason grasped her hand. "Women go through some agonizing events, don't they. Especially those who are beautiful."

"I suspect all of us do, although I never talk to others about their problems. But I've always appreciated my father's insisting we enroll in those defensive oriented classes.

"While I'm telling you this," Kathryn continued, "I came close to using that same technique on Greg Harris, one of your faculty members. For a while after I first came to State on the post-doc, he followed me around Quincy, insisting we meet for a drink after work. He wouldn't take no for an answer until one day I told him the next time he tried to come on to me, I would go to the department head."

"He has the reputation of philandering," Jason said. "I'm not surprised at his actions."

Kathryn became quiet but Jason knew she wanted to tell him something more. He turned her hand and meshed his fingers into hers.

She smiled at him, her dark eyes on his face. "You know the reason I became attracted to you so quickly was the manner you treated me in those interviews about the problems in King's lab. You approached me as a professional with a brain rather than as a nice looking female and the possibility of getting her into the sack. I appreciated that more than you know. I knew you were married and from all accounts from your graduate students wouldn't stray from your vows. Then the thing with Lucy, as tragic as that was and as deeply I felt for you during that time, I realized the opportunity of our getting together had changed dramatically. Truth is, I fell in love with you the first time I saw you."

Jason touched her cheek with his fingers. "I thought we'd rushed into our relationship too soon after Lucy's death, but in retrospect, I'm glad we did it the way we did. I've been blessed. And now we're going to add another dimension to our lives." He pulled her close and kissed her.

She stood and tugged at his hand. "Come on. We won't be able to do this much longer."

"You're sure you're okay?"

"I want to be held by someone I love and trust beyond any doubt."

Chapter 9

Although most university offices were closed during the Thanksgiving week, Jason went in as usual the Tuesday morning after the Riley conflict. The office was eerily quiet without the hustle and bustle of secretaries, telephones ringing, students coming for a signature or advice. Even the custodians were away. As he settled in with a draft of a paper prepared by one of the graduate students, O'Hare telephoned. "I was expecting you," Jason said, "but I thought you might call Kathryn instead."

"We have her version of what went on last night. I wanted to be sure she's okay and decided you'd more likely tell me how she really is than she would."

"She was more shaken than your officers suspected, but she's fine this morning. She planned to work in her lab in the Med school and come to Quincy around eleven to check on the experiment she started last night."

"Just so you know, Riley was admitted to the hospital last night with a fractured jaw. I anticipate he'll remain there a few days. He's being fed through tubes at present and that may continue for a while."

"Then what?"

"We're charging him with stalking with the intent to sexually assault. And we're fining him for illegal use and possession of unauthorized keys to university property. The City Prosecutor is meeting with us later this morning. If he doesn't go along with our recommendation, I'll be surprised and will let you know."

"As I told the officers last night, we want Riley out of our lives. He's plagued us too long."

"I understand how you feel and think it will happen this time."

"Tom, thanks for keeping me informed."

After the call ended, Jason walked to the window overlooking a large quadrangle and thought about the conversation after they stopped. He hoped O'Hare was correct but he had qualms. Riley seemed to have a way of escaping when all the odds were against him. He'd devise some tale that led people to believe he was innocent and that Kathryn had indeed attacked him without provocation.

No one was out on the cold morning to hold his attention. The sidewalks were empty, an unusual occurrence around the huge university. He turned back to the paper with the goal of completing his review and necessary modifications by the time he was to meet Kathryn for lunch.

Thanksgiving morning dawned bright and clear. Only a few high clouds remained from the Wednesday storm that had covered the ground with five or six inches of powdery snow. Jason came awake when the plow growled along their street. He lay in the semi-darkness for a while thinking about the various projects he'd gotten involved with and the pending Riley indictment.

Fifteen minutes later Kathryn stirred and turned toward him. She touched his cheek and ruffled his hair. "Are the kids up yet? You know they'll expect you to go sledding in the park. Jennifer was reminding Tony last night."

"Are you coming with us?" A lark in the snow had become a Thanksgiving tradition although the year before had been a huge disappointment when the ground remained brown and bare. Jason didn't know if he or the kids looked forward more to sledding down the huge hill than coming home to the fireplace and hot chocolate.

"I probably should skip. The last couple of mornings I've been a bit queasy. I'd hate to become ill and scare the kids while they're having such fun."

He shoved the covers aside. "I'll roust them out and give you some time alone after breakfast."

"That'd be nice and I can get some of the dinner things going."

"Remember Helga is coming around four."

After two hours of sledding in the park, Jason decided to drive by the 29th Street lab, concerns about security nagging at his psyche. He dropped the kids at home and wound his way past piles of snow left by the plows on all the streets. He slowed as he approached the lab, then, concerned about getting stuck in the snow, pulled into the driveway just far enough to be off the street. He walked near the loading dock, inspected the heavy doors, and continued around the facility.

Footprints in the snow revealed at least two people had walked around the entire building late yesterday or last evening. Around one window, they had tromped in the powder indicating they'd tried to look in, shifting positions to obtain a view of the inside. Drifts on the window sill had been disturbed. It could be nothing more than a couple of curious teens or homeless people seeking shelter from the cold. But it could also be a couple of hoodlums scouting out the building. He doubted teens would make the effort to circle the facility under the weather conditions. His uneasy conclusion came down to the likely possibility that the pair were attempting to scope out the building and its contents.

Wanting a better feel of the surroundings, he left the lot and drove out 29th, passing the Exxon station, a strip mall of small businesses, and a bar and grill that, based on the traffic patterns in the snow in their lot, had enjoyed heavy patronage the evening before. Crossing a railroad, he realized the spur ran behind the lab and the warehouses adjacent to it. Three blocks farther both sides of the street turned residential in nature, narrow lots occupied by modest homes, some in poor repair. A small church with a sizable parking area took several spaces. Jason slowed but couldn't determine the name of the religion.

He turned around in the church lot and reversed his route. He'd learned little or nothing that would support his suspicions about the foot traffic around the lab. He couldn't imagine why people were interested is this rather isolated lab, other than looking for items they could grab and sell on the street for a few dollars. He hoped it was nothing more than curiosity about a building coming into use after sitting vacant for two years. Nevertheless, the feeling of unease refused to be tamped down. He determined to talk with Helga about the worry, but he'd wait until a work day rather than broach the subject during the Thanksgiving period. Plus he didn't want Kathryn to confront another concern. She wouldn't admit it but she harbored reservoirs of unease from the ordeal with Riley. He'd noticed her staring into space on occasions when the turmoil created by active children subsided for those rare moments.

The campus came alive again on Monday following the break. Faculty returned to offices. Students filled the classrooms anticipating the approaching end of the fall term and cramming to do all the assignments they'd procrastinated about for the past several weeks. Everyone hurried from building to building as a cold wind swept across the open spaces. Piles of snow had frozen where the plows and custodians had left them.

Mid-afternoon Jason drove out to the federal lab. Helga hovered over a chromatogram while Ingrid prepared a gel plate for another run. Helga motioned for Jason to look at the images. "That is most of the nucleotides that make up the genome of the organism. It's fallen into place very nicely." She pointed along the strip.

"That's great progress," Jason said. "Now the difficult phase."

"I suggest we try moving these four pieces from this end to the other and see what happens." Helga pointed to the present location of the four fragments representing sizable components of the genome then to the position she proposed. "I'd read in a recent publication that moving nucleotides could alter the actions of the entire genome. Doing that with the one we have here seemed like a good place to start."

"I don't have a better idea," Jason said. "If that works, great. If it doesn't, we'll try something else. But to shift topics, let's go to the office. I want to run a concern by you."

Helga preceded him and offered coffee as they sat at the small conference table. "I finally got around to setting up the coffee pot.

Ingrid and I usually stop for a break mid-morning and enjoy a bit of down time."

Sipping the brew and twisting the mug, Jason said, "I've become more concerned about the security issue." He told her about his inspection on Thanksgiving morning.

"Should we talk to Walcott or Johnson?" Helga asked, her features becoming creased with lines he'd not seen before.

"Frankly, I don't know. Those tracks could be nothing more than kids roaming around with nothing to do on their holiday break."

"But you don't think so, do you?"

"I have this strange feeling that someone is interested in what goes on here and I don't know how to get a grip on it. I don't want to get the local police involved on a visible scale. That'll only call more attention and likely bring out some reporter who follows the cops around looking for a juicy story."

Helga said, "Let's watch more carefully for a few days and then decide. If someone comes around on a regular basis, I think there's cause for concern. Both Ingrid and I will pay more attention to outsiders coming on to the property than we have previously. We get busy with our work and pay little heed, but we are aware when the garbage truck picks up at the street level. We'll try to be more alert."

Jason nodded. "Do that. And I'll drive by at odd times after work hours. That's more likely the period someone will try to force their way inside." Jason stood and reached for his heavy coat draped across another chair. He added another thought for consideration. "We could install video cameras at critical spaces around the building, but that could call attention also."

Helga thought about the idea, then said, "Let's try the old-fashioned approach first. Smart intruders would smash the equipment before it caught their image."

"I'm probably being paranoid about the entire issue." Jason pulled on his coat. "Or I could run the notion by some of the university security types who may know the limitations and advantages of the cameras."

Helga stood. "I enjoyed spending Thanksgiving with your family. You have a beautiful wife and lovely children."

"They can be a bit lively at times."

She said, "That's the nature of the young, but they were well behaved youngsters."

Jason drove by the lab on Wednesday evening after he'd spent two hours in the office working through the budget submission for the coming fiscal year. Meeting the guidelines provided from the Dean had proved more than the usual challenge this year with the state facing a budget shortfall and all agencies were being asked to reduce spending by five percent. Universities were expected to accomplish the same level of productivity they'd done previously but with less support from state government.

Not expecting any activity around the dark premises, Jason drove slowly past, trying to see any movement around the structure. To his surprise he spied two figures busy at some task near a window on one end of the building, well shielded from passing vehicles unless the driver happened to look back. Jason veered through the Exxon station and stopped on the street across from the lab. He eased out of his car, waited for a city bus to roar pass, and walked toward the two individuals. Nearing them he could hear talking and a tool being scraped around a window. The trespassers were so intent on their mission they didn't realize another presence was closing in.

From twenty feet away, Jason yelled, "What the hell are you doing?"

The two jumped, startled by the voice out of the darkness, but they inadvertently turned to look, dropped a tool into the residual snow, and scurried away. Jason had not gotten a clean vision of their faces and couldn't with any degree of certainty identify them. But they were not teenagers. One stood well over six feet. His companion was shorter by four or five inches but much stockier. Jason's first instinct was to chase them, but better judgment prevailed. He may not catch them and if he did, he'd lose any physical struggle with the two.

He went to the window, stepped on a crowbar they'd dropped in their surprise and haste to escape. The window sill had been scraped as they obviously intended to pry it open and enter the lab. He had no idea of their intentions—check out the interior, wreck equipment, just satisfy their nosiness, or all of the above. But he knew he had to make the lab more secure if they were to succeed with their mission. And not infect some idiot with a potent toxin.

The following morning Jason did two things as soon as he got to the office. First, he called Walcott and explained the situation around the lab. Walcott listened then said, "I'm going to send Joe Higgins to check it out. He'll know what to do."

Concerned Higgins would take days to get there, Jason called O'Hare, although campus security had no jurisdiction in the city itself. But he needed advice and knew Tom would help if possible. O'Hare responded as predicted. He agreed to go with Jason for a meeting with the Spencerville Chief of Police.

Two hours later and three adjustments to his schedule for the day, Jason followed O'Hare into Chief Durwood Hayden's office in the downtown headquarters. As they drove together from campus, Jason attempted to gain some feel for Hayden's relationship with campus groups.

O'Hare stopped at a traffic signal. "I've found Hayden to be a straight-shooter. He tries to understand the behaviors of both our students and faculty." He laughed. "And he does it better than I on many occasions when our responsibilities seem to overlap."

Hayden was a big man. Tall, heavy-set, his hair cut short, his uniform spotless, he eyed Jason with curiosity. He invited them to chairs in front of his desk and asked, "Tom, what's on your agenda today. The dispatcher said it was about security around a building on 29th Street."

O'Hare said, "That's correct. This is Dr. Jason Spradlin, Head of Biology, and responsible for the facility. I'll let him explain the situation."

Jason revealed that he'd taken on a federal project and in the absence of usable space on campus, they had leased the building from the owner of the defunct pharmaceutical company. He'd become concerned about the security when he'd seen two guys trying to break in and hoped the city police could run patrols by as often as possible.

Hayden surprised him. "We've been aware of the renovations going on there and the use of the space for research and development by university personnel. We were alerted by the contractor who tries to keep us abreast of changes in buildings around the city. And I saw the article in the newspaper."

Jason decided to tell Hayden the facts rather than shade the truth and make matters even more suspect. And again bend the mandate to maintain as much secrecy as possible. "Chief Hayden, I'm going to level with you and trust you are able to maintain what I tell you in confidence."

He paused and looked at O'Hare who nodded. "The news article about research on infectious diseases was intended to cover what is actually going on. The actual project is one supported by Homeland Security with the goal of developing a biological weapon to confront terrorist groups. I have a contract as the lead investigator for the agency. We intend to accomplish the work with as much secrecy as possible, thus we've not erected signs identifying the lab as one being operated by the federal government, nor have we put up a secure fence to keep out interlopers. We believed the less advertised, the less attention it would generate. But if we are successful in moving the project along, soon there will be dangerous toxins within the lab. For that reason we put up that sign about biological hazards."

"And you trust me to keep a damper on this while providing security?" A sly smile broke across Hayden's broad face.

Jason nodded. "I hope you will support our efforts to maintain as much secrecy as possible. I'm concerned if the press begins to search for information, the word will be out. That in my mind has the potential of attracting splinter groups who oppose everything the federal government tries to do."

Hayden shifted his weight in the chair causing it to squeak in protest. He leaned forward to put his arms on the desk. "Who knows about this development?"

Jason said, "At the present time, Dr. Snyder, the President, Dean Hawthorne, and three of us working on the project. Now you and Tom have some idea about the work."

"I'm sympathetic, Dr. Spradlin, and will do my best to maintain the present status. I worry about these terrorist groups more than you might think. There are a couple of splinter cells in the area who harbor hopes of disrupting our society. We keep an eye on them but can't do anything until they commit a criminal act. So, I'm willing to maintain as much surveillance as we can afford on your laboratory, but that may not be sufficient because of our limited manpower."

Jason asked. "Would it make sense from your perspective to put up a fence around the lab? If nothing else, that would make it more difficult to break in."

"I'd recommend that. Make sure it's high enough to dissuade the curious. But regardless of the measures you take, someone who really wants in, can find a way."

Jason stood. "Thanks, Chief Hayden. I'll talk to the Agency about a fence and perhaps other measures of security." He shrugged, "And hope the press doesn't become overly interested."

Hayden stood and reached to shake Jason's hand. "Those are the choices our society gives us. We have to figure out how best to work around them."

"Thanks for your understanding the issue," Jason said. "I'll let you know what the Agency decides."

Three days later Higgins appeared and after talking with Jason and Helga called the contractor who'd done the renovations. With the cold weather firmly in control the contractor was looking for jobs and in five days had erected a heavy wire mesh fence around the building, installed a gate that could be opened using a pass card, and put up a sign on the building warning trespassers of potential prosecution if found on the property.

Higgins and the contractor agreed that video equipment might be another safeguard, but both suggested waiting. Higgins summed up their thoughts, "It's too easily circumvented once the intruders realize cameras are focused on certain and often predictable positions. They move out of the line of sight without any detection at all."

Chapter 10

Helga called Jason three days after the contractor had left the premises. "I wanted to let you know, I've been able to modify the organism as we discussed and have impacted it into a nitrogen aerosol. If you can bring those rats, we're ready to test the lethality." Several days earlier they'd considered purchasing a group of laboratory rats for the purpose of checking out their modifications of the organism they'd begun to label 'Factor Q'. But Jason had volunteered to take animals from his stock in Biology. From several experiments he'd accumulated a sizeable number of male rats that were not going to be used except for the occasional demonstration of taking blood samples for an uninitiated graduate student. In the meantime it cost money to feed and care for them. Using them as test models would be a better use than euthanizing them.

"That's great progress. I'll bring the animals this afternoon and perhaps we can check it out together." Hanging up the phone, Jason realized he'd become dependent on Helga and now had significant confidence in her ability. She moved the experiments forward with little supervision or input from him.

Helga and Ingrid were ready when Jason brought in the half-dozen adult rats at two-thirty. They removed each one from the holding cage Jason had used to transport them from the campus vivarium and put the animals in individual cages then placed all of them in the safety hood.

They decided to delay for an hour to permit the nervous critters to settle down in this new environment. Checking them in forty-five minutes, Jason saw each resting peacefully inside their new place. He called to Helga, "It's okay to go ahead. They're no longer skittish from the move."

Making certain everything was air tight and properly closed, Helga released the aerosol into the hood. Looking closely they could see a fine mist floating through the hood. The animals stirred from their slumber at the sound of the release, sniffed the air as the foreign substance contaminated the air, paced the cage for a couple of minutes, then returned to their previous positions. Fifteen minutes passed before the investigators acknowledged the test had failed, but they left the test mechanism intact just in case there was a slow response time and to allow the toxin to dissipate.

Jason said, "Obviously it didn't affect the animals as quickly as we want, but let's check them again in the morning. If they respond overnight, it will give us a clue about the next step."

Helga volunteered, "I'll check them every hour until we leave today in case the reaction was delayed."

Ingrid giggled as she stripped off her protective gown outside the lab. "I think they loved the stuff. You could see them perk up for a bit then it became a bore."

Jason and Helga smiled at her humor, then Jason said, "Assuming this approach failed, where do we go next."

When she looked blank as she thought about the possibilities, Jason said, "I've thought about it some. Maybe we should transpose ends of the genome. I mean, take about two hundred nucleotides at one end, move them to the opposite end and do the same for the opposite end. As I recall, the components were not the same so we'd modify the organism a lot."

"I'll check the printout from the computer to be certain they were different, then if so, make the switch as fast as possible. I don't know how long that will take but not over a week, I'd think." On the advice and guidance of a technician in the electron microscope facility, they'd been able to transfer the output from the scan directly into their computer, thus saving hours of labor intensive entry by manual methods.

Jason said, "Give me a call in the morning if the rats in the test exhibit any unusual behaviors. If they don't, we can house them here until we're ready for the next trial. I brought sufficient lab chow for several days, and remember to add fresh water to their bottles."

At the door he stopped. "Any sign of people snooping around?"

Helga shook her head. "No, but we haven't checked the fence around the property. I'll have Ingrid make a quick walk around before we leave for the day."

The next morning went quickly for Jason. He gave a brief lecture about phenylketonuria followed by a report based on a recent publication presented by a student in his graduate seminar group focused this term on genetically based diseases in humans. Then he met with four faculty who were serving as a search committee for the vacancy coming with the retirement of George Stuart, a long-time member of the department who would be missed by everyone. They had narrowed their search to four candidates and in the hour session, Jason and his colleagues discussed each resume and scanned the recommendations for each, then decided to bring in two for interviews. From Jason's perspective, either would be a solid addition to the department but one would likely impress the committee during the visit to campus to make that individual the heir to Stuart.

As planned Kathryn rapped on his door just before noon. Preparing to walk to a downtown café for lunch, Jason grabbed his heavy coat from the closet. He took her gloved hand as they exited Quincy.

As they walked quickly, Kathryn said, "I had my conference with the section head this morning. He's recommending I be awarded tenure at the end of this cycle. Then I raised the issue about my appointment after the baby comes. Of course, he was surprised at my revelation and hadn't really had time to consider the possibilities."

"So he thought half-time would be okay?" They circled around a series of cones put up by a maintenance crew on the street. Two men watched, hands in their pockets, while another wrestled an iron cover over a manhole.

"He suggested I consider taking a years leave, then come back full-time. He told me about his wife who was on the faculty in Geology. She'd tried the half-time approach and found it very difficult trying to juggle her work, the baby's schedule, plus her slow recovery from the delivery. She finally took a year off to gain some control of her life."

"And that worked for her?"

"Actually, she never returned to work and they had another child two years later."

"So what do you think?"

"I wanted to talk with you first, but I'm leaning toward the year-off approach. Our household is facing major changes with Mrs. Carter leaving at the end of the school year and the baby coming in late July or early August. I can manage a year of taking care of all the kids, then we can find a sitter for the young one and enroll Jennifer and Tony in after school programs."

"Or we could look for another live-in nanny type. It's worked out well with Carter."

"That'd be another possibility but let's face it. Carter was unique and we're not likely to find her clone." He held the door for her as they entered the restaurant. They unbuttoned their coats in the warm waiting area. Aromas of food stimulated their appetites further.

They stood for a couple of minutes until a waiter led them to a table. Jason lifted her coat from her shoulders and piled both hers and his on a vacant chair at the table. Menus were placed before them and they scanned the offerings for a minute.

Kathryn said, "You haven't responded to my dilemma."

"I'd be in favor of the year off. But you'll need to keep reading the literature, maybe going to seminars just to keep your thinking alert to your field." He grinned at her. "And keep thinking it's our problem together."

She smiled and touched his hand. "Then let's do that. I'll maybe volunteer to be in charge of the section seminar. That would take a minimum of effort and time but keep me connected to the field and to my colleagues. If I had time, I could continue to work some on the research projects. I can't just let them idle for a year."

"We don't have to decide now, but lets exert our best effort in locating a live-in nanny," Jason said. "Then you could opt for half-time. Keeping up with the research will require time in the lab, reading background papers, working with technicians and graduate students. It all adds up."

"You're right, but Dr. Eggers will have to agree with either scheme."

Their orders were taken and coffee brought to both. "I'm going to run with you in the morning. I haven't had nausea for a couple of days and need to stay in condition. And my physician recommended I keep in shape as much as possible."

"See how it goes. If it's too tiring or you feel some twinge, you could double back and maybe go only half the usual distance."

In mid-afternoon Helga called. "Ingrid walked around the outside of the fence this morning. She's reasonably certain there was one spot where people had paced for a while. The dead grass and weeds had been trampled and she thought the top of the wire had been bent as though someone attempted to climb over. But there's no sign of anyone's being inside the fence. I thought it might be nothing more than evidence left by the construction guys. You know how they stop working and stand around for a bit, but she could be correct about prowlers looking for a way in."

Jason said, "Let's not take chances. I'll call the City police and ask that they patrol for the next several nights."

Jason asked about the rats and if there had been any different response overnight.

Helga laughed. "I think Ingrid had it right. They paid little attention to the stuff floating around them and it certainly didn't affect their appetite. They gobbled up everything we gave them and emptied their water bottles. We returned them to the animal room just before noon."

After everyone had left the office for the day, Jason decided to examine the fence line to satisfy his own concerns vandals were looking for an entrance to the lab. With the sun setting and the darkness and cold settling in as the days shortened, he parked outside the lot, grabbed a flashlight from the car pocket and started around the outer boundary of the property.

In his thinking, Ingrid's observations were correct. A couple of places the dead grass and weeds had been trampled. At one spot, the mesh wire had been bent with fresh marks on some strands as though some sort of clipper had been tried. He reckoned they'd misjudged the gauge of the wire and would return with a more suitable apparatus. Now he wished the contractor had installed a heavy steel fence, one that would resist almost any tool. But, remembering Chief Hayden's comment, if the individuals persisted in wanting to cross the barrier, they'd find a way regardless of the impediments.

Harris, Townsend and Bob Pierson, a second-year faculty in

Biology and a recent recruit to their weekly beer social, met on the Friday after classes had resumed. They arrived separately, stomping snow off their shoes and shaking heavy coats outside the door of the bar and grill. Harris, the first to arrive, grabbed a booth as four students were leaving. He stood to attract his buddies when he saw them enter.

With mugs in front of them and news exchanged about their holidays, Townsend said, "I visited Riley in the hospital during his brief stay. He could hardly talk with his jaw wired closed and tubes running everywhere."

Harris chimed in. "I heard he had an altercation with Kathryn Helweg and came up on the short end of the deal. In fact, there was a short article on an inside page of the paper about his arrest and the pending charges."

Townsend filled his pipe from a pouch of aromatic smelling tobacco. "My wife and Riley's wife are good friends. Goes back to our early years in the department. She alerted us to Riley's hospitalization or I would not have known. She gave us more information than Riley was able or willing to convey. Seems like Riley followed Helweg into King's lab during one evening over the holidays. When he accosted her, she kicked him in the balls and then in the chin. Either the kick or his being rammed against the metal cabinets fractured his jaw."

Pierson, not yet fully engaged in their exchange of tidbits of information about others, said, "I met Helweg with Dr. Spradlin at one of those functions for new faculty my first year, but I wouldn't think she'd have the strength to harm anyone. She's such a small person," he grinned, "but beautiful and sexy."

“That’s what Riley believed,” Harris said, “and he got his ass kicked by what sounds like karate or another of those martial arts a lot of women are learning these days. So I assume the cops are on his case again.”

Townsend puffed, sending smoke spiraling around their heads. “They’ve charged him with stalking with intent to sexually assault. According to Riley’s wife, he was going to sue her for assault, but when the cops discovered he’d been following her for days and had somehow ripped off keys to most of the labs and offices in Quincy, including one to King’s lab, coupled with the previous penalty for the same crime, he caved in and is now trying to reach a bargain with the prosecutor.”

“How’d they know about the keys?” Pierson asked.

“Riley had a ring of keys in his pocket when they searched him at the lab. All had identifying numbers connected to rooms in Quincy.”

“It won’t go easy this time,” Harris said. “He got off light before because it was his first offense and he’d never been arrested before, but not this round. He’ll do jail time then be monitored for the rest of his life unless they quietly move from Spencerville.”

“The final straw for Riley is his wife is seeking a divorce. She’s had enough of his antics.” Townsend continued, “And I can’t blame her. Riley has been a pain in the butt for a lot of people for years, all the way back to Henry Rogers’ time as department head. Most of their friends have given up on them rather than be associated with Riley. So it’s been tough for his wife and I’ve been surprised she’s tolerated his perverse behavior as long as she has.”

“I need to get going,” Townsend said, after glancing at his watch.

"My son is playing basketball for the high school team this year. He hopes to get some playing time tonight." He finished his beer and collected his coat.

Harris drained his mug. "Remember, we warned Riley more than once."

"But his obsession overwhelmed any advice we could give him," Townsend said, turning away and heading for the exit.

Harris touched Pierson on the arm. "See those two women at the corner table. They're faculty in Sociology, both single and you're single. Come on, I'll introduce you."

Pierson asked, "You sure it's okay. I've heard you're pretty close with the brunette."

Harris grinned. "But the brown-haired one is available and I think she'd be interested in you, if you get my meaning."

Two days after talking to Walcott, Joe Higgins returned to Spencerville. He called Jason from the lab. "If you can work it in, I'd like to walk the fence with you and then let's figure out the best strategy. Walcott and Johnson have given me freedom to do what I believe will protect this work."

"Give me thirty minutes," Jason said, knowing he'd have to rearrange a meeting with a faculty complaining about student noise in the hall near his office while they waited for class. Jason would hear the complaint knowing there was little he could do about controlling students quietly talking in the hall.

Higgins was ready when Jason arrived. They skirted the fence line.

Jason showed him the spots he thought had been tampered with and the foliage trampled. Higgins fingered the wire. “You’re right. Someone tried to cut through, but didn’t have the proper tool or was interrupted by something going on along the street.”

“Maybe the city patrol came along and he thought better of proceeding. Wait for another time.”

“That’d be a reasonable guess.” Higgins moved along, turning the corner next to the warehouse. “Are these places busy at night?”

“I couldn’t tell you with any certainty,” Jason said. “I’ve never seen anyone around or trucks moving during those times I’ve been here after normal work hours. My guess is no one is around after five or six in the evening. But there’s steady activity during the day.”

Back in the building, Higgins said, “I’m going to recommend we mount a guard for this building. I think someone patrolling each night would be sufficient. They could be based over at Crews and come here around six in the evening and remain on duty until your staff arrives the next morning. We might, if manpower can be found, rotate those guys so they can remain fresh and alert. It’s hard to keep on your toes for twelve or fourteen hours. You can get bored out of your mind.”

Jason shook his hand. “Let’s us know what’s decided. And thanks for coming. It must wear you out with all this coming and going.”

Higgins grinned. “That’s why they pay me big bucks.”

Chapter 11

As the Christmas holidays and the end of the fall semester approached, the pace around the university accelerated. Students scurried to complete assignments, faculty prepared for the giving and grading of final exams, and plans were made for all to vacate the campus for almost two weeks. Jason and Kathryn had discussed traveling to her parents in Minnesota for the holiday, but decided the kids would enjoy Christmas more in the closeness of their family and known surroundings. Mrs. Carter planned to spend ten days with her daughter in Arizona, leaving Jason's family for the first prolonged period since she'd joined them over three years ago. Her absence would be a good test for the family functioning without the numerous tasks she accomplished daily and now were taken for granted.

Jason met with Helga to evaluate their progress with the potential toxin. She had worked diligently at moving nucleotides to swap ends on the primary genome. Then she'd encapsulated the organism into an aerosol spray ready for another trial with the rats.

Deciding to move ahead as rapidly as possible, they set up the test system as before and released the aerosol into the sealed chamber. Within three minutes two animals collapsed in their cages as though struck in the head with a blunt object. Four minutes into the test run all had dropped onto their sides. Peering through the glass and the mist, they were unable to tell if the animals were breathing. Jason shook

Helga's hand and they prepared to celebrate a major victory.

Then to their surprise, disappointment, and frustration, the animals began to rouse themselves and within another five minutes, all had regained their bearings and were pacing around the boundaries of their cages, noses sniffing the air as the foreign substance slowly dissipated. No permanent damage had been evident. The toxin had apparently functioned as a mild anesthetic. They talked for a minute about having a pathologist examine a couple of the animals, but backed off not wanting to describe to an outsider what they'd administered to bring about the short term collapse.

Leaving the test unit in place for overnight, they discussed next steps while sipping coffee in the small conference room. Helga expressed the most disappointment as she had been the primary worker in rearranging the genome. Neither had a good idea about the next possible approach. They thought about calling Walcott to obtain his view then knowing the secrecy cover under which the Agency operated, they decided against the call.

Jason suggested. "I think we're almost there and perhaps the shuffling of another group of units will do the trick. The problem is knowing which."

Helga sipped from her coffee mug. "Perhaps if we shifted an additional set of a hundred from each end or moved only a set of fifty from each end. It's a trial and error approach. Nothing seems logical."

To move the decision forward, Jason said, "Let's try interchanging only a set of fifty from each end."

Helga nodded in agreement, turned her coffee mug to scan some inscription. "I'm thinking about the timing. I'd like to go to Jim's family for the Christmas holiday and Ingrid wants a few days off with her family. If you don't object, we'll move forward with the shifting as quickly as possible, then take a break for a week. We'll start again just after New Year's Day. If it goes okay, we likely could test again in mid-January."

"Let's do it that way then," Jason said as he drained his mug and took it toward the lab and a sink. "Return the rats to the animal room and I'll check on them during the time you're away. I'll bring the kids to help me feed and change water bottles. It'll be a new experience for them."

"Have you heard from Higgins since he was here?"

"No. I assume he's run into snags with the bureaucracy or they haven't shifted troops to Crews to take over the guard duty here. Thanks for reminding me though. I'll check with him the next couple of days."

Helga leaned against the lab bench. "Working with two federal departments is always a problem. Defense wouldn't want to divert their forces for such a small operation as ours and Homeland Security may not have the resources." She continued, "One thing I learned working for federal agencies is we always believe they have unlimited resources, but the fact is they're often struggling to meet their basic mission."

"Not unlike universities," Jason added.

Jason's plan to complete a host of administrative tasks two days before the holiday was interrupted by the appearance of a reporter from the local paper, *The Herald,* that circulated in Spencerville and the surrounding counties. Often news from the university appeared there first, then was picked up by the wire services and larger newspapers. Audrey, the secretary, accompanied the reporter in and offered coffee. Susan Randolph had been around the community and the university for several years and Jason had interacted with her on a few occasions. He'd found her sensible and not overly aggressive in trying to generate a story out of rumors and innuendos. Nevertheless, he was always on the defensive when talking with the media. And the work with the toxin, the likely issue that brought her to his office, exacerbated his caution.

Seated across in front of Jason's desk, she said, "I've been assigned the job of reporting about this laboratory on 29th Street. I know it used to belong to a pharmaceutical company that went under, but in checking around as the renovation has occurred and those warnings erected, there seems to be little knowledge of what goes on there. My editor wanted me to check and university public relations sent me to your office." She crossed her legs and straightened the crease of her slacks.

Jason had dreaded the day he'd be asked to explain the situation. He'd thought some about his response, knowing it would not be satisfactory. "Miss Randolph, I can't tell you much except the lab was established for the purpose of working on a contract for the federal government. In fact, an earlier release described generally the basis for the contract. There was not suitable space on the campus and we were fortunate in being able to lease the facility on 29th."

Looking up from her writing in a notepad, Randolph asked, "What, if any, is the significance of the signs warning people about biological hazards? The primary reason I'm here this morning is the paper has received three or four calls from citizens suggesting the facility is not what it's purported to be because of those signs, thus we thought we should come to the person who really knows."

Jason didn't want to appear on the defensive, but the notion that outsiders were raising questions about the real mission of the lab was disquieting. He decided quickly to talk around the question. "If you walk through the science buildings on campus you will see that same sign. It's an international signal or symbol alerting people to danger and for them to keep a safe distance and don't enter those areas without a knowledgeable expert."

"Can you tell me about the contract? What is the purpose of the work?"

Jason sought appropriate hedge phrases. "I'm the investigator of record and have two other people working in the building. As for the actual mission, I'm not at liberty to reveal other than to suggest you review the article published some time ago."

"You mean it's a secret known only to you and those working there." Randolph's question suggested that she suspected the news release was a cover for something more sinister. And those anonymous calls had triggered her curiosity, a trait seemingly ingrained in reporters.

"Correct, along with a few people in the federal system who contracted with me to do the work."

"Can you tell me the agency with whom you have the contract?"

Jason thought about his response, knowing if he told her the truth, only more questions would arise. "I'd rather not reveal that at this time."

She smiled and pressed on. "Why the fence around the property?"

"We put that up after we found evidence of vandals snooping around the facility. It's for their protection as much as it is for security of the laboratory and the equipment."

Randolph smiled again and fingered her pencil. "The truth is, Dr. Spradlin, you'd rather not have any more publicity about this project or this lab. Correct?"

Jason returned her smile. "I'd appreciate having nothing appear publicly at this time. Perhaps in the future we can release information that will satisfy those who are curious."

Randolph placed her pad and pencil into a small case. "I'm going to tell my editor essentially what you've told me and recommend we not publish anything. However, when you're ready to release information, I'd appreciate having the first shot at the story."

Jason stood and walked toward the door with her. "You have my promise to do that." He shook her hand and watched her leave through the suite into the hall. But her revelation about outsiders calling the paper caused him to consider other possible issues, none of which were comforting.

Christmas day broke bright and clear following a four-inch snowfall the evening before. The kids were up early, excited at the couple of gifts they were allowed to see before their parents came downstairs, but eager and prepared to open the others. Soon they were climbing into Jason's and Kathryn's bed, urging them to get moving.

They spent the day in a typical fashion, opening presents, trying on new clothes given to each other or sent by Kathryn's father, consuming a big meal, playing games, and sorting through all the boxes and wrappings to be sure a gift had not been discarded. Jason and Kathryn spent time assembling a couple of toys for Tony and dressing a new doll for Jennifer. Jason had logs burning in the fireplace for the first time since last Christmas. He watched the interactions between the kids and Kathryn, recognizing they'd meshed as a family much more quickly than he'd dreamed. Kathryn seemed to have as much fun out of all the activity as the children. They exhibited no reservation in hugging her or sitting on her lap. Neither Jennifer nor Tony rarely mentioned their mother as their memories of Lucy faded. Jason experienced relief along with a bit of nostalgia that they'd moved forward, remembering the adage that time heals many problems.

At the urging of Jennifer and Tony, the family walked to the park for a sledding outing on the afternoon of the day after Christmas. Kathryn, reluctant to participate for fear of damaging the fetus, pushed aside her nerves and scooted down the steep slope several times, but Jason intervened when she started dragging the sled up the hill with Tony perched on top.

He took the rope from her and grasped her hand. "Don't overdo this. Let me or perhaps we should force the kids to retrieve their sleds."

At the bottom again and the kids showing some boredom in doing the same thing over and over, Jason led them toward the car parked in the large lot at one end of the park. "I want you to help me with a chore at the new lab." He'd gone each day during the break to feed and care for the animals there and had thought the children would enjoy feeding the rats when no one else was around. On a previous occasion he'd shown them the animal lab in Quincy and they begged to go in and pet the animals. Jason had told them they could spread disease to the entire colony and no one other than researchers and technicians were allowed. If the animals in the federal lab came down with some malady, he'd replace them without any loss and no costly experiment would be damaged.

He pulled through the gate after inserting his pass card in the slot and the gate opened. He led them through the lab into the animal room. "Now, first thing we'll remove their feeding dishes from the cages and clean them a bit."

"Will they bite?" Tony asked, the one who usually was more skittish about new ventures.

"Not unless you hurt them, but let's not touch them today," Jason said, "and remember don't leave the cage open or we'll be chasing rats all over the place."

Placing a replenished dish in a cage, Jennifer said, "Look, he's eating fast. He must have been hungry."

"Now the next thing," Jason said, "is to change the water bottles hanging from the side of each cage. We'll pull them off, like this," as he demonstrated removing the container from hooks placed through the wire mesh with the spout pushed through at some point convenient for the animal. "Then we'll dump the remaining water and put in new. Then hang the bottle back. Be careful and don't drop it." He showed them how to check the bottle to make certain an air bubble hadn't disrupted the flow.

Jennifer watched closely as she put a bottle in place and the animal began to obtain fluid by licking at the spout inside the cage. "He's thirsty too."

Jason said, "They always like the fresh water even though their bottles still were half-full."

Kathryn paced around the lab while the rats were being fed. "You have a lot of expensive equipment in here. Must have cost a fortune."

"They're sparing no expenses," Jason said "But they will demand a product soon."

Security on his mind, he said to her, "Watch the kids for a minute, I'm going to walk around the outside."

"Is there a problem?"

"I'll explain later," Jason said, going through the outer door. He walked rapidly around the inside of the fence, paying closer attention to the area hidden behind the building and away from the street. At one place, the wire had been cut sufficiently to allow an intruder to crawl through. The snow had covered any signs of entry or footprints leading toward the building. Thinking they'd go to the nearest window, Jason examined closely the three windows on the rear. One had been tampered with. The sash had been raised. Scrapings along the sill suggested someone had scrambled through.

He trotted around the building to the front and reentered the lab. Kathryn was explaining to the kids how some apparatus worked and how you could determine the composition of a compound in a solution. Near the window Jason could detect faint footprints, dirt covered from the thawing earth prior to the last snow. The prints faded within a couple of steps, but he guessed the intruder had wandered around the entire facility, then escaped back through the entry point.

Concerned about damaged equipment, he walked along the aisles, looking at each of the pieces, but detected nothing awry. Touching Kathryn on the arm, he said, "Someone has broken in but I don't see any damage."

Her eyes widened. "I looked at most everything. I didn't see any problems, but I wasn't looking for any, so I wouldn't have noticed minor alterations."

Jason shrugged at another mystery. "It's strange someone would go the trouble of breaking in just to walk around and see what's here."

"You're thinking some crank is trying to sabotage this effort?" Kathryn moved along an aisle, looking at the floor and bench tops. She examined the door to the safety lab and shook her head.

"Someone has been more than curious since the day we began renovation. You'd think though if they got in, they'd break up equipment. Maybe steal something."

"When is Helga back?"

"Both she and Ingrid return to work on Monday. But they never notice anyone around during working hours. I'm going to call Chief Hayden and ask him to increase his patrols but it'll be hard for him. I'd guess he has reduced manpower during the holidays with some people off duty. And I'll get the contractor to repair the fence and install more secure locks on the windows."

Jason dropped the family off at their house and went to the office. He called Walcott and was surprised when he answered on the second ring. He told him about the break in and the inquiries to the paper then asked if Higgins had been able to secure personnel to guard the facility.

Walcott said, "Dr. Spradlin, Higgins' request was denied by a higher up in the Pentagon. They're so short of troops for the conflicts in Iraq and Afghanistan, they're pulling everyone possible out of other duties to give more support to those units fighting the wars. He likely forgot to communicate with you in the rush of the holidays, maybe thinking it wouldn't make any difference for the short term."

Jason decided to share a concern that had been nagging him for several days. "I believe some group knows what we're trying to do here and is planning to do something destructive to undermine or stop our efforts. These break ins and scouting around the building have been their way of determining how to do the most damage without being caught."

Walcott remained silent for several seconds as though thinking Jason's worry had little merit or no solid basis for his conclusion. "You haven't had information leakage there have you?"

"No. At the local level only the three of us know what's going on. And the technician may not fully comprehend our ultimate goal. And you know both Helga and Ingrid were cleared by security checks. But someone has suggested to the local paper the lab is not what we‘ve advertised it to be."

"Could someone working with the contractor have figured out what kind of research was being planned?"

"I wouldn't think so. I didn't give much attention to those workers and assumed they were the typical crew used by local contractors and would care little about the function. Just do their jobs, collect their pay and move on to the next one."

"The reason I asked is we've had one experience where a group opposing the federal government infiltrated the work force and gained access to the building. A month after we started, experiments were wrecked. We never could pinpoint the actual perpetrator, but always suspected someone from the builders."

Jason admitted he'd not considered that potential source of trouble, then said, "If that happened here, we'd never find out who. But there's been suspicious interest in the building since the day we started work there."

Walcott said, "I'll discuss the situation with Johnson and Higgins next week when they return from the holidays and get back to you."

Jason replaced the receiver, frustrated by the failure to obtain a reliable guard for the facility, and worried the work would be wrecked at some vital point or worse, some group would be exposed to a deadly toxin and he'd spend the rest of his career dealing with law suits. He recalled his reluctance to become involved with this venture and, in retrospect, he wished he'd taken the chance the Agency couldn't harm his federal contracts and he'd have bypassed this worry. But he'd hadn't and now he was responsible and would see it through to a logical conclusion.

The ringing telephone snapped Jason and Kathryn awake at four on Sunday morning, the day before classes were to resume at State and faculty were to return for the beginning of the spring term. Jason grabbed the instrument hoping it hadn't wakened the children.

Chief Hayden was on the line. "Dr. Spradlin, there's been a fire in your building on 29th. The fire department crashed through the gate and the front door and are working to put out the flames. The damage seems to have been confined to the office section, but you'll have to check to be certain."

"I'll go there now," Jason said, struggling out of the covers and standing. Rubbing his eyes, he told Kathryn about the problem, then said, "I'm going there. Go back to sleep if you can. I'll be sure to get back in time to get the kids up."

Chapter 12

In the early morning darkness, Jason parked across the street from the 29th Street building. Wisps of light fog dotted the lower elevations, street lights provided only limited visibility. The lot was crowded with two fire engines, their lights whirling and flashing, and three cars from the city station. From a fire hydrant a hundred yards down the street, hoses stretched along the street and across the grounds into the front door that had been caved in. A window on the street side had been knocked out. Fire crews were huddled in or near the trucks as though waiting for the order to reassemble their equipment, leave the scene and find some warmth at the station house.

Jason saw a fire chief standing just outside the structure and introduced himself. The fireman said, "I'm glad you came. We weren't sure what we were dealing with inside and didn't want to put our crew in danger."

"How much damage?" Jason moved to see into the fireman's ruddy face, bits of grime along one cheek. With a rough hand he brushed across his forehead as though erasing a headache. No doubt he'd been jerked awake in the middle of the night.

"It seems to be confined to the offices and the conference room, although some smoke drifted through the entire building. There's no sign of embers anywhere else. You were lucky."

"Who reported the fire?"

"The *Herald* distributor who drops bundles of papers to the carriers between three and five every morning. He saw the flames when he passed around three-fifteen this morning. He called 911. We had equipment and men here within ten minutes. But we didn't know who was responsible for the building. We called the police dispatcher who contacted Chief Hayden."

"Yeah, he called me," Jason said. "Is it safe to enter?"

He nodded and began walking toward the entrance. "In fact, we'd like you to walk through with a couple of the crew to confirm we've not missed something that might flare up later. With all those danger signs around, we were reluctant to move anything we didn't have to."

Jason led two of the crew through the labs. Nothing seemed amiss except for the smoke wafting along the ceiling and the odors of smoke and retardants used by the firemen. Water from the sprinkler system had doused everything. Fortunately, the equipment had been covered as part of the routine closing at the end of each day, but each piece would require checking out before any actual tests were run. None had visible damage, a positive sign, but not a fool proof one. Most of the water had drained through the floor drains, but the cement floor and the bench tops were soaked with puddles in low spots. The soles of Jason's running shoes were wet almost immediately.

The safety lab had escaped damage except for the sprinkler outpouring. The animal room was intact. The rats were stalking their cages amid all the noise and strange smells. However, the offices and conference room were a total loss. The desks and chairs had burned beyond repair. The water-soaked carpet reeked of smoke and burned fabric. A door to the hall had been charred and would have soon burned through had the firemen arrived much later.

Returning to the outside, Jason said to the Chief, "You're correct. Only the office areas were damaged. I don't see any problems beyond those rooms."

"I'm pleased you can confirm our thinking." He pushed his helmet back on his head, showing more of his ruddy facial features and allowing gray hair to appear. "Best we could tell, the culprits piled a group of papers in the middle of the office area, placed the chairs on top, and torched it. There seems to have been no fire enhancer involved or if there was, it didn't function very well. I assume they intended for the blaze to spread throughout the building and it might have except for the fortunate sighting by the paper guy. And the fact you had all the lab doors closed and locked helped. That kept fire out of those areas. And you know, had the flames reached the labs with all those volatile chemicals, we would have a total disaster."

"Perhaps the hazardous warning signs kept them away from some spaces," Jason commented, remembering how ominous those biological danger warnings could be, especially to the uninitiated.

"That may have been a factor in their actions or they believed the fire would spread from the office more quickly than it did."

"Could you tell how they got inside?"

"A window in the office area had been broken, the sash ripped away, likely pried loose by a crowbar, and the frame smashed by an axe or hatchet. You can see the slash marks. We believe that was both their entrance and exit since the outside doors were intact when we arrived."

The Chief turned away. “We’re going to return to the station, but if something crops up, give us a call. You may know that sometimes an ember we’ve missed catches and gets going. If no one notices, pretty soon the entire structure is blazing.”

“Thanks for your quick reactions and we’ll pay attention,” Jason said. He shook the Chief’s hand.

Jason paced around the outside of the structure as he thought about damage control and regaining lab functions. He’d get the contractor as soon as reasonable on a Sunday morning with the hopes he could get a crew to replace the gate, front door and window. Restoring the offices could wait. Then he’d call O’Hare who would have ideas about improving the security to prevent this again.

By the time he’d circled the building, the fire trucks had departed. He returned to the inside and checked all the locks. With the gate and front door missing, vandals would feel free to enter and wreak havoc just for the hell of it. And passing gawkers would be enticed to wander in and inadvertently break some vital piece of equipment. But he couldn’t remain here and make any progress.

He arrived home shortly after seven to find Kathryn preparing breakfast for the kids who were still in their pajamas and slouched on the den couch with the TV going. Without asking, Kathryn added eggs to the omelets she had going in an iron skillet, one Jason had inherited from his grandparents.

He caressed her shoulder and she leaned against him. “Are you okay? You smell smoky.”

He told her about the fire and the break in as he got the coffee pot going. "I need to do several things this morning since the lab is exposed to whoever is tempted to enter. The timing doesn't help since no one will be in their offices on Sunday morning."

She forked the omelets and slices of crisp bacon onto plates and called for the children to come. Toast popped out of the apparatus. Jason poured a mug of black coffee from the pot and brought it to his place at the table.

At eight-thirty he called the home number for the contractor and explained the situation and the need to get the gate and door repaired or install temporary barriers in place as soon as possible. He was relieved when the gruff-voiced owner promised to have a crew on the job within a couple of hours. He concluded, "We'll put up a temporary structure until I can get the right materials. Or we may be lucky and have those in our stock. I'll check before we come."

Relieved the man hadn't balked because of the weekend or lack of crew, Jason said, "I appreciate your help."

Then he called Tom O'Hare at his home to learn from his wife that Tom had gone to the office for some emergency on campus. Replacing the phone, he wondered if cops and firemen ever had a night without some call out.

Anxious about the entire situation, Jason left home again, drove by the lab facility to check. No one seemed to be around. He then drove to the campus police station and found O'Hare in his office, pulling his heavy coat on.

Jason rapped on Tom's door and said, "I know this is a bad time but within the next few hours I need some advice. I can come back later if you'd prefer."

O'Hare ran a hand through his hair and across his face as though trying to eradicate weariness. "Let's do it now." He pointed to a chair around a small table in one corner of the office. "Then maybe I can find a couple of hours of free time."

Jason said, "Thanks. I'll be as quick as possible." He explained the problem at the 29th Street lab and said, "I need some reliable security on site by tonight if possible. I understand this goes beyond anything you or Chief Hayden can provide. And the military and Homeland Security seem to have more pressing priorities."

O'Hare asked, "You're asking for a guard during the non-working hours, I take it?"

"I believe that would solve the problem short-term or until the feds can get their act together."

O'Hare stared at the table top for a moment. "There are a couple of private security firms around, but I don't know how reliable they are. You take a chance with either of them. They typically employ part-time people, often retired police or military, whose dependability varies all over the map. But off the top of my head, I don't know of another approach."

O'Hare pulled a Spencerville telephone directory from the credenza behind his desk, thumbed through the yellow pages, then showed a page to Jason. "Here's the listing. Three possibilities. I have some experience with this one, Spencerville Security. They helped us out with a elementary school problem three or four years ago and that worked out okay. I can't vouch for the others although they may be as good or better."

"I'll give this one a call," Jason said, standing. "And thanks for the advice."

"Let me know how this works out." O'Hare pulled his coat on again and followed Jason to the outside. They drove away in different directions.

From his office in Quincy Hall Jason called the security company. A sleepy voiced male responded, "Spencerville Security. What's the problem?"

Jason figured the supervisor was expecting a call from one of the operatives who'd been experiencing difficulties on a job. He ignored the question and explained his own situation and the need for assistance by nightfall.

Becoming more alert, the man said, "Let me send someone to look over the property before we commit. How about an hour from now?"

"I'll be there," Jason said, then repeated the address of the lab.

Rather than go home again, he called Kathryn to let her know the status of his quest. He got the coffee pot going in the office work room and paced the floor until a couple of mugs had brewed. He filled his cup and returned to his desk. Rather than waste the time, he spent the next forty-five minutes scanning memos from the dean and other administrative offices, another task he had to do on a regular basis to be certain he didn't miss something important to the department, but for the most part, the correspondence represented nothing more than information, the majority of which had no application to Biology.

At ten-thirty he met Jim Peters, the representative from the security firm at the lab. He walked through the building with Peters, showing him the various aspects of the operation and informing him about the biological hazard signs and the need to avoid certain spaces. Peters poked his head through every door, checked every window, and watched the animals for a moment as though fascinated by the caged rats. They traversed the fence, stopping at the place the vandals had cut through.

While they were at the rear of the property, the contractor showed with two panel trucks. With few or no instructions, two workers set about repairing the window and door. They prepared to knock out the damaged areas and replace them with new materials. The foreman nodded to Jason as he and Peters returned to the inside.

Standing in the office, Peters said, “Dr. Spradlin, we’ll have someone here starting at seven tonight. If you can provide a set of keys, we’ll be able to monitor everything pretty closely. And we’ll keep a guard here until seven in the morning. If there are problems at other times, we’ll rethink our approach.”

“That sounds good,” Jason said. “All the break ins and sightings of vandals have occurred during the night when none of our staff is around.”

“That’s typical,“ Peters said. “Tomorrow I’ll bring a written contract for your agreement and signature. We can leave the date open until you feel secure without our presence or until we apprehend the people doing this.”

“A federal agency will pay you directly,” Jason said, although he would need to confirm that with Johnson tomorrow morning when the D. C. offices were operating again. If for some reason Johnson denied his request, he'd have another issue to deal with, but the local security agency would be less expensive then sending a cadre of troops or federal agents to patrol the place.

As Peters departed, Jason turned to the foreman, Edgar Jennings, according to his name tag pinned to his coveralls, as he was removing plastic wrappings and wooden slats from a factory produced window. "I appreciate your coming so quickly," Jason said.

Jennings stopped his work. "We'll replace the windows and the door using supplies we luckily had in our warehouse. We'll repair the fence in the back. The gate will have to wait until we can obtain a replacement, probably a couple of days if the supplier has them in stock. If not, it'll take a week to ten days to order from the manufacturer."

"What about locks?"

"We'll key the new door so the ones you have will work."

"Anything else we should do to improve security?"

The older man eased his hard hat back on his head, revealing wisps of gray combed over a bald top. "Couple of things you might consider. One is putting up a couple or three light poles with strong beams focused on all the vulnerable areas around the property." He pointed to the warehouse in the adjacent area. "Those are what I mean. They're set to come on when there's decreased light, even on a dark day, and always at night. You'd be surprised how vandals fear the light."

"Another thing you might do is install an alarm system. It can be set to go off when doors and windows are tampered with. You're able to cut it off when you or other workers come in because there's a short delay. Plus, if Chief Hayden is willing, it could be rigged to ring the phone at the dispatcher's desk within a brief span of time. Cops could be here before the vandals realized they'd triggered the system."

He turned the window to a different position. "I can put those poles up if you say so. Probably get it done next week as things are slow during the cold season."

Jason responded. "Go ahead with both of those. Put up poles in back and a third near the loading dock. Do the alarm and I'll check with the Chief about connecting to the station."

He thought he should clear all of these expenses with Johnson before the administrator started screaming but his priority at the moment was protecting the laboratory.

Jason arrived home mid-afternoon. Without announcing his presence, he went directly to the kitchen and put together a sandwich from the ham they'd had the day before and pulled a beer from the refrigerator. With food in hand, he found Kathryn at her computer in the office. The kids were in their room, both engrossed with some toy they'd received at Christmas while they watched television. Faint sounds of a television or radio from the basement indicated Mrs. Carter had returned from her holiday.

He bent over Kathryn and kissed her forehead. "Lot of progress but I'm ready for a siesta. This four o'clock rising got to me."

She stood and looked into his face. "You never do that. Anyway, before you drop off somewhere, I'd like to tell the children about the baby. I told Mrs. Carter the day she left and I'd rather they hear the news from us than have her surprise them. And with her back, that could happen anytime."

When she stood, he realized she'd put on the dress sent by her father for Christmas. He said, "You look beautiful. The purplish color or whatever goes great."

"I wanted to try it before the pregnancy takes its toll on my figure." She took his hand. "Come on. Let's make the big announcement to the children."

Jason found the kids in the den where they were watching a rerun of a program they'd seen a dozen times. He turned the television off and said, "Kathryn and I need to tell you something, then you can go back to your TV. So come closer and give her your attention for a few minutes."

Grumbling because they'd been interrupted, Jennifer said, "Can't it wait?"

"It could but now is as good as any time," Jason said, taking her by the a hand and leading her to a chair. He pulled her onto his lap.

Kathryn sat on the couch. Tony dropped to the floor in front of her feet. Then she said, "We wanted to tell you I'm going to have a baby next summer."

Jennifer jumped to sit next to Kathryn on the den couch, grabbed her around the neck. "Make sure it's a girl. I need a sister."

As anyone could predict, Tony, now attentive and sitting up, chimed in. "Not fair. It has to be a boy."

Jason laughed at their excitement. "We can't control what it will be, but we'll all be happy with either a new brother or sister."

Jennifer asked. "Will your tummy get big like Mrs. Culpepper's did when she had her baby?"

Kathryn rubbed Jennifer's head and rearranged her hair. "It will. Within a couple of months you'll see a change."

"And you won't be able to walk very well. One of my teachers had a baby last summer and she couldn't get around when school was out. Looked like a whale out of water."

Jennifer and Tony lost interest in a few minutes and wandered away to their rooms, having forgotten the program on TV.

Jason said, "You interested in having a nap with me?"

Kathryn moved to take his hand. "I thought you were exhausted but if you are suggesting we do it in the middle of the day, I could be persuaded, but lock the door." She reached to kiss him, her lips open, her touch warm. He circled her waist as they headed for the bedroom.

Chapter 13

Jason left early on Monday morning to arrive to the lab before Helga or Ingrid discovered the chaos. By seven forty-five he was in the office, the desks seeming more charred than he remembered, the floor still damp in spots, and odors of smoke that would likely linger for days or weeks. Grimy footprints of the fire crew revealed where they had gone in quest of potential hot spots that could erupt into a full blown blaze before anyone realized what was happening. He shoved two partially burned chairs and small pieces of debris toward a corner.

Helga rushed in just before eight, stomping the snow off her boots, unbuttoning her heavy coat. "What happened?" Her mouth gaped open, her eyes taking in the chaos that had been a functioning office when she'd last seen it. "Have we been bombed?" She paced around the office, touching the desks and chairs piled into a blackened heap and now almost unrecognizable as the clean furniture she'd left.

Jason told her about the break in and the fire and led her into the lab. "I'd like for you to examine everything, including the test organism, to be certain nothing was damaged. I looked, but you'll know better than I. As for this mess in the offices, we can leave that for our cleaning service who is scheduled for this afternoon." When they'd occupied the facility, General Services Administration had contracted with a local service to come in weekly and clean the floors, wash dirty windows, get rid of trash, whatever was needed to maintain a clean environment. Usually Ingrid supervised the two-person crew to be sure they didn't disturb experiments or inadvertently wander into dangerous areas.

Helga walked through the labs, opened doors and drawers, examined carefully the large freezer where the precious organism was stored. She looked at Jason. "I think we're okay. We can mop up the remainder of the water and get back to our task."

Striving to divert her attention from the mess, he asked, "How was your holiday?"

Her face clouded and her lips came into a firm line as though confronting an unpleasant experience. "Jim's folks are great to me and go to extremes to make me feel welcome and part of the family, but it always contains a sad element without him there. We shared too many remembrances and everyone left somewhat depressed he was no longer with us." She shrugged her shoulders and pulled on her lab coat. "It's a mixed bag, so to speak. I don't know if I'll go again, especially during the holidays when the memories seem more acute."

Jason recalled the depression he'd experienced when his own parents had been killed in an automobile crash his senior year at Iowa State, then his utter devastation when Lucy had been killed. He wanted to express his condolences to Helga and tell her Christmas often brought back memories of lost loved ones, but thought it might be better to let the memory fade as rapidly as possible. And her work would be a reasonable antidote.

He touched her shoulder and said, "I'm going to my office, call Johnson about a couple of issues, place an order for new desks, chairs, and a conference table. If you need me, call."

She stopped him by saying, "Jason, this lab is in many respects a copy of those I worked in before. That is, everyone was isolated and seldom communicated. But this is different. You've made me feel like a colleague and being able to share and discuss problems makes this a much more rewarding experience. I thought about this a lot over the holidays and just wanted to tell you I appreciate your approach."

Taken aback by this revelation, he searched for a response before saying, "It's the manner in which academic types work all the time. It's nothing new to me, but I'm pleased you're happy here."

Remembering his agenda for the day, he zipped his coat, pulled on his gloves and headed for the door.

After getting a secretary on the line, Jason waited two minutes before Johnson came on. "Dr. Spradlin, How're things going?"

He told Johnson about the break in and his actions to improve the security, including the hiring of a private security firm, the additional expense involved with erection of the light poles, and the installation of an alarm system. Johnson didn't raise questions but agreed to support those efforts by telling Jason to submit the bills to the accountants as they came due.

Then Johnson asked. "What about the actual research?" Jason detected a change in his tone. A suggestion of encouragement, or more like a pressing desire to bring the work to completion as quickly as possible.

"We've made progress with the toxin and have eliminated several possible structures, but I remain concerned about the events that have occurred since we occupied the space." He outlined the unusual interest in the lab from the very outset, calls to the local paper, followed by break ins and the fire. He concluded, "It's becoming reasonably obvious someone or some group is determined to sabotage our work and this fire is their first serious shot."

Johnson seemed to take seconds before responding. "Maybe it's nothing more than curious idlers who have nothing to do. They somehow got into the building, and as a prank, decided to set things ablaze. You know it happens every day in our crazy society."

"I admit that's a possibility, but something bothers me about their approach. We haven't observed anyone around during the daylight hours. Every incident has occurred at night. Frankly, I'm concerned about the laboratory as well as the vandals who are likely to push their agenda and end up killing themselves or worse, a group of innocent bystanders." He thought to himself that if they were unable to produce a lethal toxin, the worry about bystanders was an empty one.

"Any threatening letters or telephone calls to you or the lab?"

"Nothing like that. Nor have there been demonstrations with people parading in front with placards."

Johnson said, "Let's let it ride for another month. See how things play out and if the vandalism continues, I'll try to do something from this end to beef up your security even more, but maybe with the alarm and lights around the facility that will be sufficient. But keep in your thinking, money is tight and most requests for things that seem non-essential are denied."

"I hope you're right about the new measures," Jason said. "I'll keep you up to date with our activities."

Then Johnson closed off by saying, "Keep pushing the real agenda. I'd like to have something tangible to show the Secretary by the end of this fiscal year." Jason interpreted Johnson's push as a sign the Deputy could be reassigned in the near future.

Thinking more about Johnson's response, he thought about the potential that the development of biological toxins as weapons could be shut down. Almost every day some group raised the issue about the damage being done to the country's image by stances taken by the present administration, including the treatment of prisoners, the unsigned Kyoto treaty, and the speculation that Homeland Security was not all it appeared to be to the ordinary citizen. If there was a change in administration in the coming months as appeared likely, appointees like Johnson could be on the outside looking in with nothing concrete to their credit in the war on terrorists. And that wouldn't bode well for those bureaucrats who floated from one position to another, never seeming to leave the D. C. area.

The Tuesday morning edition of the *Herald* reported on the fire at the federal lab on 29th Street. Under Susan Randolph's byline, she revealed some parts of her interview with Jason and hinted at the secrecy surrounding the laboratory and the work going on there.

Jason read the article carefully and knew Susan had been pushed by her editors to reveal more, but true to her promise she'd not gone overboard with speculation about dangers to the community evolving from the strange laboratory. She'd not mentioned Jason's name nor hinted at his affiliation. He shoved the paper to one side and trusted the issue would die from lack of interest. But his mind kept returning to the concern about the unusual interest in the remote lab from the first day.

The issue with Riley resurfaced when Kathryn was called by the City Prosecutor to provide a sworn deposition describing the incident in the Quincy laboratory. Concerned Riley was preparing a suit against her for assault, she began to prepare for the session with the prosecutor by writing out the statement she would make and get ready for any questions of clarification. She tried to resurrect the scene and described in detail the sequence of the confrontation. Then she rounded up statements from three graduate assistants who had seen Riley lurking around the halls near the lab in Quincy. One of them had seen Riley coming out of the janitor's closet one evening when he was leaving King's lab. While on coffee break and talking about her frustration of spending time on the statement with her colleagues in the Medical building, an intern volunteered to provide a statement about his seeing Riley near their lab. And to her surprise, a technical assistant in the Medical building gave her a statement indicating he'd bumped into Riley in the doorway of the laboratory in which Kathryn was working.

At Jason's suggestion she assembled the written documentation from all the witnesses, and took the packet to the university attorney's office for a review of the material before she met with the prosecutor. Stella Krause, who had worked closely with Jason on two other significant occasion, met with Kathryn after she'd read the material.

Kathryn felt comfortable with Krause whom she recalled from the hearings in Washington. Stella had shepherded them through the ordeal before the House Committee for Science and Technology, making certain they stayed on message and avoided opening cracks in their testimonies that could lead eager Congressmen into tangential areas if they thought it would generate publicity.

In Stella's office on the top floor of the administration building, Krause shook Kathryn's hand as she entered. "I haven't seen you since you and Dr. Spradlin married. How is he by the way?" They took chairs around the conference table.

"He's doing well, but always busy. I worry at times he'll explode because he seldom stops working." She continued, "About the only time he seems not to be thinking about work is when he's involved with his children."

Krause smiled. "That's how I remember him from the first time we worked together. Anyway, give him my regards."

Stella opened the folder with the statements Kathryn had brought over three days before. "You seem to have covered all the bases. These leave no doubt that Riley stalked you for quite some time, apparently waiting for the right moment to make his approach. Having others aware of his presence near your work places is a plus. The thing you can't document is his motive. Only he knows that, but the circumstantial evidence is sufficient in my thinking to demonstrate he had motives less than pure. Kathryn, a good attorney will rip him apart if he tries to prove you were the aggressor."

Kathryn asked. "Are you in a position to defend me if he files suit?"

"Since you are a university employee and all the altercations occurred on university property while you were working on university affairs, I should be available for you. To be certain I'll clear with the State Attorney General, who is my ultimate supervisor, but let's assume I will defend you if it comes to that. Feel free to tell the City Prosecutor if he asks about your attorney. And if for some strange reason my boss tells me I can't represent you, I'll give you a call and assist in finding an alternate."

Kathryn asked. "Should I do anything else at this point?"

"I don't think so. Stick with your story when you do the deposition and remind the others who provided statements to do the same. If you like, I'll go with you for the hearings after all the depositions are in. Sometimes these attorney's are out to make a name for themselves and get carried away in trying to poke holes in your story."

"I'd appreciate your being with me and I'll let you know the time," Kathryn said, as she stood. "It's nice to see you again."

Harris, Townsend and Pierson resumed their Friday meetings as the new term began. They draped their winter coats, scarves, and gloves on an extra chair at the table and reached for their first sip of the session. To their surprise Riley appeared, dragged up a chair, and waved to a passing waitress for a draft beer before he uttered a greeting of any form.

Townsend looked to his buddies as Riley eased into the chair, then said, "Hugh, it's a surprise to see you. How're you doing?"

Riley ran his hand along his jaw, still slightly black with hints of bruising. "I'm getting better. You no doubt heard that bitch Helweg fractured my jaw after she'd kicked me in the balls."

Townsend said, "I heard through our wives and remember, I saw you in the hospital."

Riley sipped his beer, sighed with contentment. "I don't recall much from that period. Too sedated with drugs."

"Are you teaching at the community college this term?" Harris asked.

"Two sections of beginning biology. Plus, I'm spending time with a lawyer and considering bringing suit against Helweg for assault with intent to do bodily harm. My attorney thinks I should ask for medical expenses and damages."

Harris and Townsend exchanged glances. Harris said, "Hugh, if I were you, I'd let the matter drop and count your good fortune she hasn't gone to court about your stalking and harassing antics. Remember you haven't been out from under thc limitations of the earlier restraining order very long. "

"My attorney disagrees. He'll argue I had the right as a citizen to be in those public buildings. And he'll make the point she didn't let me explain my intentions before attacking me."

"Maybe he's looking for a payoff himself," Harris persisted. "The more time these lawyers spend on the case, the more they charge you, whether it makes any sense or not."

Riley eyed his former colleagues. "We'll see. We're meeting with the City Prosecutor on Monday afternoon."

Townsend asked. “Will Helweg be present and will she be represented by an attorney?”

“I expect her to be there. She’s completed a deposition. My lawyer wasn’t there for that, but I suspect he’s seen the document.”

Harris grinned and drained his stein. “You know, Hugh, you’re lucky Spradlin wasn’t with her the night you tailed her into King’s lab. You might have more than a fractured jaw and bruised balls.”

Riley looked surprised at this reaction. “I thought you guys were on my side.”

Harris shook his head. “Hugh, it’s not about sides. We just don’t understand your animosity toward Spradlin. You’ve been trying to damage Jason Spradlin since the day he arrived on this campus and when that didn’t pan out, you took off after his wife. And we warned you on more than one occasion to cease your stalking of Helweg.”

“You’re wrong. This time I’ll come out the winner.” Riley swiped his fingers around the base of his mug and added, “Now there’s something you don’t know about Spradlin. He’s working on some secret deal with the feds in that laboratory out on 29th. You know, the place that pharmaceutical company built, then went bankrupt.”

Pierson, the newcomer to the group who seemed content to hear his friends pass tidbits of gossip each week, asked, “What do you think he’s working on?”

His voice dropping to just above a whisper, Riley said, “From what I’ve heard through some friends I met recently, they’re trying to create some biological weapon for Homeland Security. I’d guess it’s some kind of organism that can be released into a population and kill off thousands."

"You mean like anthrax?"

Townsend knocked his pipe against the table leg. "Hugh, how can you possibly know this for a fact. Are you certain it's not some rumor started by some pacifists group?"

Riley shrugged, a smug expression emerging across his face. "This guy I've met seems to have an inside source of information. He knows Spradlin has a contract with an Agency that's part of Homeland Security and has brought in this other scientist to help him with this stuff."

"That seems unbelievable," Harris said. "Not the part about the contract, but that someone is leaking information to locals. For what purpose?"

Riley stood, eased on his coat. "Time will tell." He turned away and disappeared toward the door.

Chapter 14

The City Prosecutor assembled the parties in his conference room in the administration building that housed most of the Spencerville offices and services. The attorneys and related officials occupied one floor of the huge building that had been renovated and added to several times during its seventy-five year existence. Portraits of the present and past Governors adorned the wall along one side of the rectangular room. Photographs of the Mayor and members of city council were arrayed along the other side, a couple hanging at a sloped angle as though they were about to fall from their position.

Reed Creswell, who had served as the City Attorney for twelve years, called the session to order promptly at the announced time of two p.m. He nodded to a clerk prepared to take notes and who switched on a recording device. "For the record the following are present: Dr. Kathryn Helweg, her attorney, Stella Krause, Dr. Hugh Riley and his attorney, Blaine Lamar. We are here for the purpose of attaining an agreement on the charges by Dr. Helweg against Dr. Riley for stalking and threatening her personal safety. It is noted that Dr. Riley has filed charges of assault against Dr. Helweg. Both have provided sworn statements as to the incidents on December 19th of last year. In addition, witnesses have filed statements on behalf of Dr. Helweg. I believe both parties and the attorneys have had an opportunity to review these documents. My purpose today is to seek an agreement between the two rather than take the issue to a court trial."

Creswell paused to allow the clerk to complete a section of notes. "I have read the depositions and have concluded that Dr. Riley did indeed stalk and threaten Dr. Helweg. He persisted in his trailing of her over a two month period of time during which witnesses were aware of his presence in or near the offices and laboratories used by Dr. Helweg. I cannot determine any reason for Riley to be around those areas of the campus other than following Dr. Helweg and apparently waiting for the appropriate opportunity to accost her and with the probable intent of doing her bodily harm and/or sexually assaulting her. His illegal possession of keys to rooms in Quincy Hall serve only to support his intent and his rather clandestine methods."

Creswell paused again giving Riley's attorney, Blaine Lamar, an opening to disagree with the statement. "I object to the prosecutor's opinion. There is no basis for the notion that my client intended to attack Helweg. You cannot know his motive based on the evidence and statements of witnesses biased against my client."

When Creswell didn't respond immediately, Krauss broke in. "The record is clear and persuasive. Riley was arrested two years ago for stalking Dr. Helweg and reached a plea agreement warning him against continued action to that end. Although he obeyed the terms of that court order by staying away from her and away from the campus for two years, he seems to have resumed his previous actions. While I cannot know his motive, it seems reasonable that Riley is obsessed with Dr. Helweg and cannot keep away from her. When a male persists in his efforts to reach a place and time that he is alone with his female prey in an isolated building and then confronts her in a manner in which she has no means of escape, in my opinion his motive becomes quite evident. Riley intended to attack Dr. Helweg and likely use his advantage in size to overwhelm her and then sexually assault her. He was surprised when she used her skills to resist and in the outcome, Riley was injured. For him to now consider charges against her is ridiculous. For him to not serve a prison sentence is ludicrous."

Lamar started to speak, but Creswell held up his hand. "I must agree with Ms. Krauss whose opinion is supported by the statements of those involved. Even Dr. Riley testified that he approached Dr. Helweg when she was alone in an isolated laboratory. He failed, in my judgment, to provide a motive different than his actions suggest."

The prosecutor looked at each of those present as waiting for comments. Riley jumped at the opportunity. He blurted, "I only meant to touch her and talk with her. I intended nothing more than that."

Stella said, "That's difficult to believe. You could have done both of those things in a public arena with other people around. And you know even touching her constitutes assault. Mr. Creswell, I find no credence in this lame rationale for what he meant to do."

In the ensuing silence, no one spoke. Riley muttered under his breath but then shrugged his shoulders.

Creswell said, "I will consider the depositions and your comments today for a time then render an opinion. Unless persuaded differently after my review, I will file charges against Riley for stalking with the intent to do bodily harm and recommend a jail term of up to three years followed by a period of probation. The fact that this is the second occasion for criminal acts by Riley does not speak well for his future. Of course, the court will have to agree with any recommendation from my office.

"If Dr. Riley wishes to pursue his suit further in the courts, I cannot stop him, but I'd suggest it would be a waste of his time and a cost of court time, which if the judgment of the court goes against him, he will be responsible for those costs. And I should remind him that the criminal case will receive first attention. After that is settled, Mr. Riley and his attorney can decide their next action."

Creswell stood, nodded to the clerk who turned off the recorder. "I will communicate my decision within the next week." He collected his papers and turned toward the door.

The others filed out, no one saying a word until they reached the hall. Riley was muttering to his lawyer about the unfairness of the system that always came down on the side of the female.

Kathryn and Stella let the others proceed out the front door onto the street then Stella said, "Creswell won't alter his opinion. As best I can tell, he's already reached a judgment. Riley may object, but he won't persuade Creswell to respond differently."

"What about this suit against me?"

"It's difficult to know what Riley and Lamar will do, but if they think about the consequences, they'll drop the idea and hope he can plead for a light sentence in the court. The fact is Creswell is giving him an easy alternative. Should this go to a trial, a jury and judge will likely put Riley away for several years. And if the court holds Riley responsible in the criminal case, his civil suit falls apart."

As they moved toward the outside, each getting into heavy coats, Stella said, "I don't mean to pry into your personal life, but are you coming down with something?"

Kathryn shook her head. A slight smile broke across her face. "Not many know yet, but I'm pregnant. That's the reason for my changed coloration." Several of her co-workers had raised the same question with her during the past three days.

Stella touched her arm. "That's wonderful and I should have guessed. Pregnancy seems to bring about a glow to the woman that is often suspected as some infection. In your case, it only heightens your natural beauty."

"Thanks Stella. And I appreciate your being here today." She reached to shake Stella's hand.

"I'll let you know if we need to do anything further after Creswell renders his opinion. We may have to appear before the judge if Riley contests the opinion or seeks to plea bargain and avoid any penalty."

Greg Harris had stewed about Riley's comment as he left the coffee group on last Friday, wondering if Riley really knew something or was guessing with the hope they would confirm his suspicion or be awed by his knowledge. After the weekend and a couple of busy days in his lab, Harris could not shake his concern.

He decided to talk with Townsend who usually had a good feeling for Riley's rampages. He found Peter in his office, rapped on the door jamb, walked in and closed the door behind him.

Townsend looked up from a set of quizzes he was marking for his class. "What's up? You doing okay?"

Harris dropped into the chair by Peter's desk. "I've been thinking about Riley's comment regarding Spradlin at coffee last Friday. I don't doubt Spradlin may be involved in some contract for the feds with the sudden development of that lab on 29th Street. And there's been no publicity about the grant, other than that short piece about infectious diseases, or however he's being supported. That in itself is unusual around the university."

Townsend said, "I've thought about it some, especially after seeing that article in the paper about a fire at the place. The reporter seemed to be speculating that the fire had been set deliberately along with a break in. You thinking Riley was involved with that little escapade?"

"That doesn't sound like Riley. He wouldn't have the guts to break into a place. But the thing I can't get out of my mind is his hint about inside knowledge and that there was a leak in the system providing him the information."

Townsend shoved back from his desk and pulled one of his array of pipes from a rack on the table near the window. "I drove by the lab on Saturday after Riley's suggestion. There's a heavy fence around the place and a group of signs warning people of biological hazardous materials. You know, that international symbol for biological dangers."

"So it's likely Jason and his cohort there are trying to develop something for the government. And with the secrecy involved, that likely means a weapon system built around a lethal organism. That's Spradlin's background—genetic manipulation of animals and intervention in humans to solve diseases. Those skills could be easily transferred to microbes of all sorts."

"Are you worried Riley is with some group planning to sabotage the effort?"

"It's a possibility. You know he'll do almost anything to damage Spradlin." Harris stood and walked to the window behind Peter's desk. "I need your advice though about my nagging notion. Should I tell Spradlin about my suspicions, especially this business about a leak?"

Townsend fumbled with the lighting of his pipe for several, seconds, puffed away to get the tobacco going. "I don't know what to advise. Frankly, I didn't take Riley's comment with any degree of credibility. He likes to drop little tidbits that leave you thinking he knows more than he really does."

Harris said, "It's one of those deals that whatever you do seems wrong. I don't wish to upset Jason but I'd feel guilty if something goes wrong and he or his colleague is harmed by some idiot like Riley."

"I understand the dilemma," Peter said. "But I'd tend to lean toward the side of believing Riley is searching for information rather than truly knowing something. He wouldn't know anyone in the federal system as a source of information."

"Suppose he's become involved with one of these splinter groups that rant and rave about everything the government does. Maybe the group has an insider in Washington."

"That doesn't seem like something Riley would become involved with. And where would he ever have made a contact with such a group. They'd be highly suspicious of some guy who's worked in higher education all his life."

Harris turned toward the door. "You're probably right. It's probably nothing more than Riley shooting off his mouth and my suspicious nature. I'll hold off on alerting Jason."

The comment made by Walcott about a contractor being the culprit in another federal project wouldn't leave Jason's thinking as he continued to be concerned about the safety of the lab. He'd hoped Johnson would have agreed to beef up the security or provide federal help to ferret out the individuals or group so interested in the lab. Attempts to shove the worry away hadn't succeeded. He'd talked briefly with Kathryn about it, trying not to reveal the nature of the research, but phrasing his concern in the context of protecting Helga and Ingrid from an outside force. Kathryn believed the fire and break ins were only vagrants with nothing more to do than try to disrupt anything associated with the government.

Finally Jason decided to act on his suspicions and established a meeting with the contractor who'd done the renovation work. He met Edgar Jennings at his office located in a warehouse type building with a fading sign **Jennings Construction** on a side road on the west outskirts of Spencerville. Jason wended his way through piles of construction materials, lumber, roofing tiles, sacks of concrete, barrels of nails, and tools arranged by size and function. An older man stacking two by fours in a truck pointed the way to the office, a partially walled-off room, in a rear corner of the building. Fluorescent lighting cast shadows in the corners.

Dressed in khakis and work boots, Jennings came around a scarred wooden desk with a computer on one corner to shake Jason's hand and ask, "You want coffee? We keep a pot going all the time."

Jason accepted the offer and followed Jennings to the opposite corner of the barn-like structure where a rustic kitchen had been established for the workers. A large refrigerator and gas range occupied the back wall. A table covered with crumbs, wadded napkins and two lunch boxes sat in the middle of the space.

As they walked Jason said, "Thanks for getting those light poles up so quickly. I went by last night and it really makes a difference. And the alarm system is going in soon."

Jennings handed him a mug and led him back to the office. Settled around a small table with blueprints shoved aside, Jennings asked, "What can I help you with related to security? You said you had questions about workers."

As Jennings sipped his coffee, Jason iterated his concern about the unusual interest in the lab and the safety of Helga and Ingrid. "I have no idea who would want to break into a sterile lab with nothing to take that they could market anywhere without being quickly identified. I've thought about possible groups who may wish to destroy anything they suspect is being associated with the federal government if there's a hint of the facility being used to develop biological agents. And those signs about biological hazards seemed to have exacerbated the vandalism rather than serve as a deterrent."

Jennings shook his head, raked a weathered hand across his face. "I can't help you. I have no idea who or why but I agree with your logic."

Realizing he was treading a fine line across which he might irritate

Jennings to the point he'd just not respond at all, but he wanted to discover anything Jennings might know about the community of workers who likely moved from one job to another. Jason said, "I expect you know the area pretty well and would know if there are groups who might be prone to vandalism, even violence, if they believed the government was into biological agents of any kind."

Jennings looked blank. "No notion at all. Haven't heard of any such group around these parts. They're mostly middle to low income citizens who mind their own business and don't stir up trouble."

He paused to sip from his mug. "But I don't know my workers beyond the job. If they do satisfactory work, I don't worry about what they do on their own time. It's none of my business."

"Have there ever been demonstrations around federal facilities in the past?"

Jennings shook his head. "Can't remember any. None that ever got the attention of newspapers or TV reporters."

Jason told Jennings the story passed to him by Walcott without identifying the federal official, then said, "I don't know where to look but thought if anyone knew about local groups or unhappy workers, you would likely have heard about them."

The telephone interrupted the conversation. While Jennings responded to a series of questions and promised he'd check out the work by tomorrow night, Jason gazed around the room, always intrigued by the papers, plans and drafts of sites piled without any apparent order on the desk, table and on two wooden chairs shoved against the wall. Another eight inch pile rested against the wall.

Jennings made a note on a pad after the phone exchange. “No, Dr. Spradlin, I don’t have a clue about disgruntled types. I’m sure there are some, but I’ve never heard of anyone trying to damage property.”

Jason pushed his agenda a bit further. “What about groups that broke away from a main line religion? Or groups that seem to hang together with some leader who wows them about his own agenda?”

Jennings scratched his chin, broken and uneven fingernails testifying to his type of work. “I’ve heard of one group who meet when this guy gets them together. Rumors are he preaches to them about the ways of Satan and his followers on the earth. I have no idea where or when they meet and don’t know anyone who participates in the group.”

Jason finished his coffee and stood. “Mr. Jennings, thanks for talking with me. Maybe the police or sheriff knows about this group.”

Jennings stood. “Could be. Those types, I call them sects myself, strain against the rules of normal society and often go too far.”

“I have a feeling we’ve run up against one here. And I’m concerned about the damage they might do to the local population and to themselves.”

Jason left the warehouse having learned nothing new that might in some way provide clues about the vandals and their motives. And wondering if his last comment to Jennings had tipped him off to the actual work going on in the lab.

Chapter 15

With the beginning of the spring term, Jason's responsibilities forced him to give attention to the administration of the department. Budget requests were due in another week and he'd prepared three different versions in line with the dean's charge for one showing a five percent growth, another with no growth, and a third with a five percent reduction. He detailed a plan for the utilization of the growth possibility knowing the department had grown in number of both graduate students and undergraduates. Classes were overrun. At times they were unable to accommodate the requests and scheduled the student in another term; something they tried to avoid as it could cause the student to spend another semester at the university thus costing the parents another tuition charge. And he made the point the department research expenditures had grown by twenty-two percent in the last year resulting in an increase of graduate research assistants. He tried to make a strong case that faculty were working diligently and were productive, bringing in grants and contracts which meant overhead dollars for the university. He feared, but did not include this in the presentation, that any reduction would be regarded as a slap in the face by those faculty who worked diligently to teach students and produce research findings to move the entire field of understanding forward.

But the discussion with Jennings lingered in his thinking, breaking forth when he made his routine daily visit to the lab to check with Helga.

She had rearranged the base pairs of the genome another time and wanted Jason to be present when she conducted the test with rats. Jason continued to think about the possibilities for another model for the genome and at intervals considered the real chance nothing would alter the organism into a toxin. No doubt Walcott and perhaps another colleague in the D.C. labs had randomly chosen a benign organism that had no potential for toxicity in its typical scenario, but hoped he and Helga could devise some lethal bug from the nucleotides present naturally. It continued to be a trial and retrial approach. And failure was a realistic outcome. The organism might not be lethal in any configuration and they were beating their heads against a stone wall.

In the second week of the new semester, he ran late because of a long and dull meeting with the dean and department heads during which a debate broke out about the proposed revised guidelines for tenure and promotion. Several wanted to push central administration to abolish the three year possibility for tenure and make everyone jump through the hoops at the six-year point, the traditional approach at most sister universities. Jason argued to maintain the present system because it rewarded promising faculty as soon as they had demonstrated their long term worth but still left open the six-year option for those who weren't ready at the earlier point. Others pushed for change. They left the session without a clear resolution as often happened with thorny problems. Jason knew the topic would appear on an agenda in the near future and they'd likely reach the same resolution. He continued to be amazed at the time spent hashing and rehashing the same issues.

Jason dropped his papers from the meeting in his office, checked a couple of messages left by the secretary and headed for the 29th Street lab, hoping to catch Helga before she left for the day. Traffic leaving the university at the end of the day slowed his progress to a crawl as the lines backed up at traffic signals. He reached the lab a bit past five-thirty with darkness descending rapidly. Seeing no lights in the building, he drove past, noticed a car parked across the street, turned around two blocks down the street and returned. The parked car remained in position and sparked his attention. There was no other destination near the vehicle and it posed a question about its presence in a vacant block unless they were experiencing car trouble on a cold night. He pulled in behind it and stopped within six feet of the rear bumper. He peered at the license plate and then at the two people in the front seat of the older Buick. He expected one of them to come and ask for help, but after a few seconds the Buick roared to life and the people drove away, spinning the tires and leaving burn marks on the pavement in their haste to disappear. Jason scribbled the plate number on a pad he kept in the door pocket.

He pulled across the street just outside the gate to the lab and walked in to find a note from Helga, reminding him to cut off the alarm before the cops showed up. And she had summarized their progress for the day; another configuration of the genome was coming into being and should be ready for a test run soon. He walked through the lab, everything covered and secure for the night.

On the way out, he remembered to set the alarm, the device mounted on the wall near the front door.

At eight the next morning he called O'Hare. He told him about the strange car near the lab and then asked, "Are you able to trace a license plate for me? I'd like to know who idles away their time apparently watching our lab?"

"I'll run the number from our computer, but are you certain it will lead anywhere?"

"That I can't know, but it's more than strange for the these guys to wait on a cold night for no apparent reason, then speed away when I stopped behind them. Had they been in trouble, you'd think they'd ask for help, not dash away like kids caught with their hands in the cookie jar."

O'Hare laughed at the analogy and said, "Give me the number and I'll work on it. Then I'll get back to you as soon as I have it." He paused, then added, "But don't go chasing these guys on your own. If it seems suspicious, we'll trace it to the owner."

Kathryn and Stella Krause were called to meet with Reed Creswell regarding the Riley decision. They settled around the table in the same room they'd met previously with Creswell across from them. The ever-present tape recorder hummed away.

Creswell shuffled through a folder, pulled a paper out, scanned it for a moment, then looked up at them. "I appreciate your coming on this brisk morning and I apologize for the delay in reaching a decision.

"I worried about the circumstances and read through all the depositions and witness statements to be certain I understood all the elements related to the confrontation between Dr. Helweg and Dr. Riley. I reached the conclusion that Riley should serve two years in jail with no condition of forgiving time. I took my recommendation to the presiding judge. He asked me to summarize the case, then asked several questions. He wanted to read the documentation himself and took all the statements.

"Yesterday morning he called to indicate he'd go along with my recommendation about jail time, but he would suspend one year of incarceration. After serving one year of state detention, Riley is ordered to stay at least five hundred yards away from Dr. Helweg at all times. He must give up the campus keys he'd accumulated, and not enter any of the campus buildings where she normally works. That would exclude those public spaces such as the library and sporting arenas. Failure to abide by the court order will result in additional time in jail."

Creswell continued, scanning his notes, "Dr. Riley, through his attorney, has indicated they will appeal the ruling, thus the jail sentence won't begin until that has been settled. During the appeal process, Riley must abide by the court order distancing himself from Dr. Helweg."

Stella broke in, her tone tense, showing frustration. "That's almost the same stipulations as before except for the actual one year sentence. I'd hoped for a five year sentence. I'm concerned Riley will serve out the time of his probation, then resume his stalking. You know he'll do the same thing again."

"I know," Creswell said, nodding his head, "and I argued that very point with the judge, but he wouldn't budge from his position."

Kathryn asked. "What other options do I have other than to accept this ruling?"

"You could appeal to the next level or ask for a court trial with either a judge or a jury making the decision, but I'd guess both of those will be rejected as a waste of court time and resources."

"You know, Reed," Stella said, "there is overwhelming evidence and hordes of precedents demonstrating these stalkers never give up. In the final outcome their victim is either killed or maimed. Then everyone wrings their hands as though they were unknowing bystanders and promises to review their thinking about such cases, but nothing ever changes."

"I pointed that out to the judge, but he believed the circumstances didn't merit severe punishment for Riley. He reasoned that Riley was attracted beyond his capacity to stay away and had no devious intent to do harm. Plus, the fact that Riley didn't actively attack Dr. Helweg may have been an issue in his determination."

Kathryn stood. "He didn't see Riley's face as he approached me in that lab. He had ideas of attacking me both physically and sexually. And I was lucky my resistance surprised him before he could manhandle me."

In the hall as they got into heavy coats, Stella said, "I'm truly disappointed at this. I thought surely the judge would send Riley away for a lengthy time."

Kathryn shrugged her shoulders into the coat, pulled a scarf around her throat, and said, "Since all of this happened I've been reading about stalkers and their habits. Scumbags like Riley always get off easy until they do permanent damage to someone. You were correct in what you said to Creswell."

"So be alert, will you?" Stella straightened Kathryn's collar where it had caught the scarf.

"I try to be, always."

Over lunch at the Faculty Club, Kathryn blurted out her frustration with the court's decision as soon as they'd placed orders and the waitress had left their table. "The more I've thought about this, the more irate I become. You have to be killed or severely injured to get the attention of these judges. Now Riley is on the street for at least six months or as long as he and his attorney can drag out an appeal."

Taking her hand, Jason said, "I wish there was something I could do, but there isn't. Let's hope the process of appeal goes quickly and Riley disappears for some time."

He'd never seen her so distraught and wanted to console her, but he didn't know what to say. He was as irritated as she and wanted to find Riley and give him a solid thrashing.

O'Hare phoned Jason the day after he been given the plate number. "I was able to get a name for that license number you gave me. It belongs to a person named Phillip Westlake who lives with a wife and two children in an rather isolated house on an unmarked lane off Route 23. He picks up his mail in a box in the central post office so there's not a rural delivery number."

"Thanks for doing this," Jason replied. "Any record of past problems?"

"We ran a background check. Westlake has been arrested once for disorderly conduct during a demonstration around a dam site the U. S. Engineers were building on the Beaver River to prevent flooding of nearby farms. Westlake and his group opposed the construction on the grounds it interfered with the natural habitat of the area. I talked with Chief Hayden who believes Westlake is the leader of a group of radical types who resist anything associated with the government."

"So seeing those signs about biological hazards could set him off?"

"Probably. And if he was involved with the break in, the presence of signs inside the facility may have warned him it could be dangerous in those labs. Or the fire proved difficult to start and the fire people arrived before they could complete their plan. But this is all speculation."

"But his parking in front of the building suggests he has an interest and maybe is trying to decide what he could do next. Or he was trying to decide how to work around those new lights that reveal any one prowling around the building."

"Maybe. Let's keep alert to any other activity around the lab. We can't bring Westlake in on the basis he was parked on a public street without some evidence he intended to damage the property."

"Does Westlake have a job?"

"He's a mechanic at the community college. He does maintenance chores and minor repairs on the vehicles and machines the college has. I haven't checked out his record of performance, but it must be okay. He's been there several years."

"Okay," Jason said. "We'll be more vigilant for anyone lurking around and thanks for your help." But as he dropped the receiver into the cradle, he knew they'd done all they could do except alert the security person or remain in the building every night.

Holding to a long tradition at the university, President Snyder invited groups of department heads and deans to his campus home for dinner at intervals throughout the academic year. Snyder routinely expressed a desire to know the lower echelon administrators better and to meet them in a social setting and used these dinners to accomplish his goal. Jason and Kathryn had been invited to the mid-January event and felt they couldn't turn down the invitation for the reception at six-thirty followed by a formal dinner.

As Jason dressed in a navy blue suit sent to him by Kathryn's father, he became aware of her pulling out several dresses and holding them in front of her before the full-length mirror attached to the back of the bedroom door.

He moved to stand near and said, "You can't decide or you're concerned about the fit now?"

She smiled and turned toward him, holding a black sheath in front of her. "I think this one. I'm not showing much yet and it has a bit more play around the middle than most of these." She nodded toward the five or six piled on the bed. "But it's a bit short and I don't like to be too noticeable at these university affairs."

Jason remembered the dress. It touched the top of her knees and revealed her knees and a stretch of thigh when she sat and crossed her legs. "It'll be fine. I like for you to grab their attention and have my colleagues admit you're the most beautiful woman of the bunch."

A minute later she said, "Could you help with this zipper?" She turned her back to him and waited for his struggle to raise the resistant clasp to the top of her shoulders.

Jason said, "It'll be more exciting when I help you take this off."

She turned to face him, her face uplifted to stare into his eyes. "Maybe. We'll see."

At the reception they stood around for thirty minutes, mixing with the others, engaging in small talk about university events, drinking wine or non-alcoholic punch, nibbling on tiny bits of cheese and crisp bread, before Snyder invited them to the dining room where they found place cards around the table for twenty. Husbands and wives were separated and Jason found himself between two women he'd met briefly during the reception period. Kathryn was situated at one end next to Snyder and the department head of Physics.

The heavy four-course meal was served by a cadre of professional staff and students who worked in the President's house or assisted with social events that went on continuously during the year. Jason had often wondered how the Snyders tolerated the schedule, but he seemed to thrive on it, always smiling and conversing easily with everyone.

Conversation lagged during the various courses of soup, salad, entrée, and dessert as the waiters performed proficiently. They kept the lag times between courses at a minimum and refilled the wine glasses on a steady basis. At one point Jason's eyes met Kathryn's and they smiled. He responded to questions from the women on either side of him and they discovered commonalities in their children and school activities which seemed to dominate the lives of both women.

As the dinner ended and movement away from the table began, Snyder approached Jason and said softly, "If you have a couple of minutes, I need to tell you a couple of things in private. My wife will see that Kathryn is comfortable and, by the way, I enjoyed talking with her tonight. She's doing well in her position in the Medical School."

Snyder led Jason down a short hall to an den-office set-up and pointed to chairs in front of a darkened fireplace. "I won't take much of your time, but if you need to discuss these issues further, set up an appointment at the office."

"First thing is about your contract with Homeland Security. Somehow the Governor has heard rumors about this and has called to ask several questions. I have no idea of his interest other than he likes to know anything related to the federal government that goes on within the state institutions, nor do I have any idea of how he learned about the work. But I thought you should know in case some state official comes around."

Jason said, "I suspect there's an information leak in the agency but I'm guessing. There's been unusual interest in the lab since the day we began renovation, such as strangers coming around the place, a break in and fire in a part of the building. I've contacted the local police who have increased patrols in the area. And we've hired a private security firm who provides a guard during the night and over weekends. And this week we installed an alarm system that alerts the police to any break ins."

"I read the item in the paper about the incursion and wondered about how secure the place really is, but you seem on top of that issue."

Snyder leaned forward in his padded chair and his voice seemed to drop as though to avoid being overheard. "The second thing on my mind is Dean Hawthorne. He is in the running for two or three presidential positions at other institutions and I expect he'll be offered by one that contacted me earlier this week. And they'll want him to move as rapidly as possible, likely before the end of our spring term. Whenever his departure occurs, I'd like you to function as Interim Dean while a search goes on. And I hope you will be interested in the position on a permanent basis."

Jason knew his features revealed surprise and dismay, but Snyder pushed on. "I've watched you over the years and have always been impressed with your sensible, low-key approach to events that most others react to as though the fate of the world is in the balance."

"I don't know how to respond, Dr. Snyder. I've never had ambitions for upper administrative posts." He recalled telling Snyder the same thing before he became department head.

Snyder stood. "Those who harbor those feelings typically fail in the job because they're so caught up with their unrealistic visions of power and prestige, they are unable to handle the nitty-gritty chores, not to mention the difficult conflicts that require our best efforts and sensible judgments. I don't know how this thing with Hawthorne will go, but I wanted you to know my thoughts and not be surprised when I make a formal request."

He touched Jason's arm. "Now let's find our wives and let you be on your way."

Kathryn and Snyder's wife were seated on each end of a couch in the living area when Jason and the President found them. Both stood and Mrs. Snyder said, "We've had a good conversation while you guys tended to pressing affairs. Kathryn was telling me she's expecting in the summer. I'm excited for both of you."

Jason and Kathryn looked at each other, but neither ventured a comment sure to lengthen the discussion..

At the door, Snyder said, "I'm pleased you came and, Jason, think about the possibility of the interim position."

In their car Kathryn asked, "Can you tell me what the President was hinting about?"

Jason pulled away from the curb along the private drive to the mansion. "He thinks Hawthorne might be leaving State and, if that happens, Snyder wants me to serve as the interim administrator of the college."

"And then he'd want you to become the dean," she responded, her hand on his arm.

Jason nodded as they turned into their driveway and waited for the automatic garage door to open. "That's what he wants me to consider, but I'm not ready for that job."

"He must think so or he wouldn't broach the subject. I recall your saying you weren't ready to be a department head and now, look at how the department has progressed." They entered the downstairs foyer and trying to remain quiet and not rouse the children, eased up the stairs to their bedroom.

Kathryn untied his tie and looked into his face. "Now you can help with the zipper." She pulled his head down to kiss him on the lips, her lips parted, her body warm against his.

He turned her to move the zipper down, then he eased the garment from her shoulders. He kissed her neck, his hands caressing her shoulders and breasts as he pulled her against him. "You shouldn't wear such provocative clothes."

"I know, but otherwise, you might not pay attention to the important things in life."

Chapter 16

At intervals throughout the year Roy Blount, his former post-doc and now an Assistant Professor in his second year on the faculty, came by the office to update Jason on the progress of the Redlake Industries effort in which Jason had played a key role. Redlake's goal was to market pork products started from embryos grown in cell cultures and then implanted in host sows for the gestation period. Normal pigs would be born and raised to market size by a group of farmers. Redlake believed the product would be more uniform, thus attractive to consumers who could know the quality before they bought. Plus their market analysis predicted the product would be less expensive than pork products from the traditional methods. The tall red-head came in at seven-forty-five knowing he would catch Jason before the daily meetings and other tasks filled his calendar and took him away from the office.

Roy dropped into the chair by the desk as Jason signed the last form in the stack left by Audrey the day before. "Dr. Spradlin, I wanted to let you know the Redlake project is moving forward. You remember we've cleared the hurdles of FDA although they insisted the product be identified as the outcome of embryo transplantation."

"I remember. Any repercussions because of that labeling?" At the time Jason could envision demonstrations about alien products in the food supply and editorials from critics of anything that smacked of the unnatural. And the worst he could imagine was the refusal by consumers to purchase the product.

"Thus far, the marketing has been limited in part because of the short supply of product, but it's sold well and there've been no complaints from consumers. Redlake is gearing up for full scale production. They're enlisting more growers and the supply will jump soon. Then increased sales should follow."

Thinking about the initial agreement with Redlake, Jason said, "At this stage, we've fulfilled our portion of the contract and should bow out of the picture. Redlake can take it from here. Your friend Cynthia has the skills to continue the cell culturing process."

"That's right and is another issue I wanted to pass by you. By the third quarter of this fiscal year, Redlake plans to begin paying the dividend as outlined in the contract. Brenda Fallon wanted me to confirm how you wished your stipend to come—through the university or directly to your private account."

"I should check with the Research Office about the correct protocol but off the top of my head, I'd think my portion could go directly into my bank account. The institution is also due some payoff. Let me confirm that today and I'll leave a note in your box or send an E-mail." The agreement between Redlake and the university was typical. When a commercial process that had utilized faculty consultants generated profits, the university received a small portion of the proceeds in return for the original use of state facilities. The primary investigator usually received some payment for services and expertise. Most often the returns were small but there was always the potential for huge payouts.

Roy stood. “On another matter, I’m submitting a request to continue funding for the cystic fibrosis project. I think I’m in good shape. We’ve made good progress and have several publications. Plus, I’ve been invited to participate on a symposium panel at Federation of American Societies of Experimental Biology in April.”

Jason stood, always looking up toward Roy’s face. “Great. I thought the work had good potential and am pleased it’s paying off.” The cystic fibrosis work had been initiated by Jason during his first year at State and had continued without interruption. As Jason had taken on more administrative duties, Roy had assumed leadership for the research and now had become the principal investigator.

Roy stopped moving. “Do you wish to continue as a co-investigator? Having your name on the proposal might enhance our chances of renewal.”

“I’m not able to contribute much and it seems to be more difficult to get into the lab. But I’ll leave the decision about including me up to you. And understand, I won’t be offended if you don’t.”

Roy grinned. “I’d like to list you. That’ll give me an opening to get your advice if I need to.”

Watching Roy leave, Jason felt good about the transition, but accepted his days in the research lab were approaching the end. While he missed the aura of the laboratory with its attendant odors and working through snags with graduate students, he’d found new challenges in the leadership role for the department.

While the issue of Redlake payout was on his mind, Jason called an accountant with whom he'd dealt in the Research Office. On the line with her, he said, "Jill, I need advice." He explained the situation with Redlake and the question of how to deal with funds coming from the company.

"Dr. Spradlin, I'd suggest they pay directly into your private account. That keeps it clear of any complications with the university's share." She laughed and added, "And it's one more transaction I won't have to deal with and explain to some administrator."

He thanked her and put a note in Roy's mail box.

Responding to a summons from Johnson's office, Jason and Helga flew into Reagan National. Sparks was waiting for them at the terminal as they came through the gangway into the terminal.

Sparks took Helga's briefcase from her hand. "Dr. Grimes, I haven't seen you in a long time. And Dr. Spradlin, good to see you again."

They followed the usual procedure, trailing Sparks through the crowded terminal to a government sedan, a forty minute drive into the Virginia suburbs, and into the lot behind the nondescript building that housed some of the most dangerous experiments in all of the federal system. Conversation was almost non-existent during the drive. Helga seemed content to review familiar surroundings. Jason thought about the impending session with Johnson, then another with Walcott, to update the officials on progress and problems associated with the development of the biological toxin. His mind drifted to the upcoming changes in his household with the addition of a new child and the departure of Mrs. Carter.

Sparks led them to Johnson's below-ground suite after they'd stopped briefly in rest rooms along the hallway. The secretary rang Johnson and said, "He's ready for you and Sparks will come back for you."

Johnson was standing in front of his desk when they entered. Smiling, he shook their hands and ushered them to a conference table. "I know this is a rush meeting and I appreciate your bending your schedules to come today. Let me arrange for coffee and we'll get started." He picked up the phone and spoke to a secretary. There'd been no recognition of Helga beyond the usual greetings as though nothing had ever occurred to drive her away from the Agency.

While the secretary brought in beverages and shuffled papers out of the way on the table top, Helga and Jason removed the relevant documents from their briefcases. Before they took first sips, Johnson said, "Now tell me about your progress."

Helga took the lead as she and Jason had decided on the plane. "We've gone through a dozen different configurations of the genome without satisfactory results. We're close though because we had one set-up that put the test animals out immediately, although they recovered. The genome acted as an anesthetic rather than a lethal substance. We believe continued efforts near to that specific set-up will provide the desired outcome."

Johnson held up his hand. "But you need more time?"

"We hope Dr. Walcott can be able to give us ideas of improving our chances of success," Helga said. "And it may be nothing more than trying to incorporate a more concentrated level of the organism into the aerosol before release. Basically, we would overdose with the configuration that knocked them out for several minutes and trust it would result in death of the test animals. We've discussed that possibility, but haven't tried it yet."

Johnson said, "You must know I'm getting pressure from the Secretary. No doubt he's being pushed by the White House to bring this to a successful conclusion within the next year."

Jason realized the few months would bring an effective end to the present administration and there was no guarantee the work would continue. If speeches from the leading candidates for both major parties were an indicator, development of all biological weapons would cease and the U. S. would once again abide by international treaties they'd agreed to previously but had quietly ignored. He said, "I understand the situation. We're moving as rapidly as possible to find a solution. As Dr. Grimes has said, we believe we're close, but we can't predict a time frame to attain our goal."

Johnson shifted focus. "How about the administrative arrangements? Payments coming okay? Bills processed on a timely basis?"

"It's worked well." Jason said. "No complaints from contractors or vendors thus I assume they've been reimbursed as expected." He made a note to check with a couple of the contractors when he returned to be certain payments were being made as promised.

"Walcott will review the scientific aspects with you, but are there any difficulties I can perhaps smooth over?"

Jason said, "I'm certain you're aware because of our conversations, but we've had unusual interest in our facility, including a break in and a fire in the office part of the building."

"I remember your asking for increased security and I'm disappointed we could not deliver that. But who seems to be the culprit in this vandalism?"

"I'm reasonably certain a group opposed to federal activities has been watching the facility and likely were the ones involved in the break in. I suspect they have somehow learned about the work we're doing and will attempt at some point to stop us by damaging the building and the equipment."

"How could they know?" Johnson asked, his mouth agape, his face showing disbelief . "It's been hush-hush from the very outset. No one other than Walcott and I know about your activity in enough depth to be concerned."

Jason said, "I have no idea, except I was told a couple of days ago that the Governor of the state has learned somehow. And you now from your experience, if politicians learn about it it's only a matter of time before the press knows. I understand you may not believe me, but I'm reasonably certain someone from this end is leaking information."

"That's preposterous, Dr. Spradlin," Johnson almost bellowed in indignation and leaned forward in his chair, knocking a coffee mug askew. Fortunately the mug was empty except for the final dregs and the table was spared a dousing. "Who would do that. None of the scientists here know. The technical staff are beyond reproach. Plus they are not privy to any work except that in their private labs." Johnson's face had gone from its usual pasty white to a deep red as he ranted his frustration.

"What about administrative support staff?" Jason persisted in getting Johnson to focus on the problem. "What about accountants, lawyers, others who have been involved with contracts, payment of vouchers, and the like. They're intelligent people who can easily make the necessary connections between the type of equipment we purchased and the research itself. They've seen the contract and the numerous purchasing agreements and arrangements with local contractors. They know the mission of the Agency. It's not a big leap to think about a weapon system."

Johnson raked a pudgy hand across his face. "It's hard to believe anyone of that group would leak information to a Governor, much less to some group of crazies intent on doing the project harm."

"I understand, but I'm confident that is what's occurring," Jason stuck with his feeling about the basic problem.

Then he added, "I've checked out the potential leaks at our end and there seems to be nothing reasonable. The only people who've been near the facility were the contractor who did the renovation. Neither he nor his workers have any notion of what we're about. All the scientific equipment is foreign to them."

Johnson stared at Jason for several seconds as though preparing to have some guard come and toss him out. Then he muttered, "I'll have someone check on this, but I must admit I don't see much credence to your accusation."

"It's worth checking out," Jason said, "and I'd appreciate your looking into the situation."

Then to ease Johnson's frustration, Jason added, "And I'll continue to examine potential problems at our end."

Johnson came around the table to shake their hands, "I'll try to get the Agency security types to investigate and determine if there truly is a renegade in our midst. And now Sparks will get you to Walcott's office."

Walcott was ready for them when Sparks ushered them into his office. "Dr. Grimes and Dr. Spradlin, good to see both of you." He motioned toward a small table in one end of his square office, an underground space with the whirring air system providing ventilation.

"So how's the project going?" Walcott asked as they found chairs and settled around the table.

Helga pulled out a folder and passed it to Walcott. "Here's a summary of our experiments for your files, but to update you in person, we've attempted a dozen different arrangements of the genome without success."

She summarized their efforts by showing him the various alterations within the genome and the results of the tests with animals. "The fact is we've about run out of options in altering the genome itself, except we've not attempted to concentrate the one option that showed the most promise and determine if the level of the toxin being released is key."

Walcott said, "That might be worth doing and if that doesn't work, let's try adding genes from a known toxin, such as ricin or tularemia. I'll have someone work on that and determine which is most likely to be effective. The bottom line is still to come out with an agent that is lethal within minutes and then dissipates so no one can detect its presence."

Jason asked. "Did you select this particular organism for some reason or was it a random shot?"

"I, along with a couple of colleagues, thought this specific one might lend itself to easy modification but we know nothing about the potential for toxicity, except most in its class demonstrate some level of toxicity to humans and to most animals species. And at approximately two hundred thousand base pairs, it's one of the smallest discovered so far. We thought that size would be more easily manipulated. However, there's a lot we don't know about it's actions in the native form."

Walcott spent five minutes in silence scanning the results of their experiments, turning pages in their notes. Then he said, "You know, it might be worth trying a random regeneration of the genome. Break it into the ten or twelve segments, reassemble those, then conduct a test on animals. We've done that on other occasions with mixed results, but you could try it. It seems you've tried every iteration reasonable without success. Or, maybe just eliminate the very end of the genome, say the one you found worked as an anesthetic, and add components from known toxic agents. That's a promising step if we can figure out how to make it a permanent effect."

Walcott continued. "There are scientists around the world who know a lot about these microbes, but I'm concerned about contacting them because of security issues, but if your next few trials don't pan out, I might bring one of them in to confer. There's no need to keep shooting in the dark and failing to make progress. But let's try the things we've discussed today before we resort to that."

Jason asked. "In your thinking, is there a huge rush to get this done?"

Walcott shook his head. "Of course I'd like to complete the project as soon as possible, but I'm not concerned about a due date in the near future. If you're thinking about the coming change in administration, I wouldn't worry about that. We've been working on these weapons for a long time and changes at the top seem not to matter. There's a lot of press about a new administration ending the development of biological weapons but the fact is, no one wants to close out our efforts. As long as there are terrorists in this world, we'll be searching for measures to counteract their plots."

He looked at his watch and said, "Let's go to the cafeteria and have lunch. Then Sparks should get you started to the airport. No need to get caught in the rush hour and miss your flight."

Standing and collecting their papers, Helga said, "You should know I'm enjoying the work although it's frustrating with the lack of results."

Walcott held the door for them. "So you aren't bored in the small town atmosphere of Spencerville?"

"It's been wonderful. Much less traffic compared to the city and the people have been kind and helpful to me. Plus, I've found the give and take of ideas between Jason and me to be stimulating."

They found their way to the small cafeteria on the ground level floor and engaged in small talk while consuming sandwiches and coffee. Walcott seemed interested in Helga's experiences in Spencerville and continued to pose questions. Jason had begun to think there was a personal relationship between the two that had never surfaced before.

As they finished the meal, Sparks came in, glanced at Walcott, and grabbed Helga's briefcase. "Better get going. There's been an accident on our usual route and we'll need to take another which is a bit longer."

Jason arrived home after eleven to find Kathryn pacing the floor. As soon as he entered, she came toward him, her features showing concern. "An explosion at the lab on 29th occurred around seven tonight. The police dispatcher called around eight-thirty. He didn't know the extent of the damage but they've cordoned off the building in case there's a secondary blast and to keep gawkers off the premises. Then O'Hare phoned and recommended you wait until morning to check on things. By then the bomb squads and fire people will have completed their preliminary investigation. There's nothing you can accomplish tonight."

"What about the security guy?"

"He was taken to the hospital with minor burns, but O'Hare thought he'll be okay."

"Good Lord, I'm glad no one else was there when it happened. I guess they have no clues about who did this?"

"Neither the dispatcher nor O'Hare had any idea." She took him by the arm. "Come on, let me make you a drink and a sandwich. I know you won't be able to sleep until you know the details, but try to get some rest."

"I'll settle for a Scotch and a bit of soda. And I'll call Helga to let her know."

With the drink in hand he tried to relax on the couch with Kathryn, but he kept thinking about the car he'd encountered near the lab and the likelihood those guys had been involved. But this episode may get Johnson's attention enough to mount an inquiry among those who knew about the work.

Chapter 17

Unable to sleep, Jason tossed and turned most of the night as images of the potential damage to the facility, the expensive equipment, and the loss of the organism captured his mind. Thoughts about failing to adequately secure the property interrupted his drowsiness. Finally when he heard the newspaper hit the front walk, he eased out of bed, tucked the covers more securely around Kathryn, pulled on his sweat suit and running shoes, grabbed a heavy coat from the downstairs closet and left the house.

Inside the fence police tape circled the entire building. A police cruiser with two uniformed officers sat near the gate. When Jason parked near them, one emerged from the warmth of the car and came to meet Jason who'd left his car and started toward them.

Jason identified himself and asked permission to walk into the building. The cop nodded but insisted he come with Jason. "I don't want to get in trouble with the Chief and need to be certain you don't touch anything that might be important to the investigation."

"I understand," Jason said, as they eased through the front door.

"The primary blast was near the loading dock at that end," the cop pointed to the hall leading to the animal room, a storage area, and onto the dock which had not been used since they'd moved the larger pieces of equipment into the lab. The heavy wooden double-doors onto the concrete slab had been shredded by the explosion. Debris littered the hall and animal room. The six test rats had been killed by the rush of air and the flying objects, their bodies mute on the concrete. The metal racks holding the cages had been upturned. Cages had been ripped from the rack and were scattered across the floor. The glass water bottles were broken. Ceramic feed dishes were strewn across the floor.

Jason rubbed his eyes in disbelief and turned to enter the lab areas. "There seemed to be little damage to this end," the cop explained as they opened the door to the lab. "I suspect those thick doors acted as a shield and the blast didn't penetrate this far." Now Jason felt vindicated for insisting they install those solid doors between the lab area and the other parts of the building, although at the time he'd thought more about isolation of the actual research from the other parts of the structure. He'd never dreamed they might protect the expensive equipment from idiots and their explosive devices.

The cop was correct. The equipment seemed intact with some dirt and debris scattered around the floor and on top of the vinyl coverings. Neither the safety lab nor the testing hoods had been damaged.

Jason asked. "How's the security guard?"

"Don't really know. He was shook up pretty badly with minor burns and several bruises from flying objects, but he could walk. The paramedics took him to the emergency unit at City General Hospital and I haven't heard since. My guess is he'll be okay. Maybe a bit of shock."

"Could you tell how the culprits got past the fence?"

"The place they came in is around back. I can show you if you'd like, but the best we can figure, they used two ladders. One guy climbed to the top, pulled a second ladder and secured it on the inside, then climbed down. His buddy followed and then they left by the same route, pulling the ladders away. We can tell from footprints there were two guys. They apparently parked a vehicle in the lot next to that warehouse where the lights fail to cover. And they'd obviously scoped out the place and knew when and where to get close enough to plant the device. It's pretty clear they jammed it as close to those double doors on the platform as possible. Apparently it was detonated by a timing mechanism. But the crime scene boys will take a look and do some measurements when it's daylight. And we'll look more closely in the daylight at the places they scaled the fence and left their vehicle."

The cop grinned and shoved his cap back on his head. "They'll confirm what we know, but they might find some clue that's not obvious to us."

Jason took another turn around the lab and asked. "When will we be able to function again?"

"Soon as the crime tech guys release the scene we'll give it back to you. You'll need to make certain your utilities are working."

"There's a lot of damage," Jason said, "but we can work in the labs okay and bring in a contractor to restore the offices and the animal area. I'm not concerned about the dock area for the present time."

Jason headed for the front door. "Thanks for letting me in here. I'll try to go by the hospital this morning to check on the condition of the guard and maybe get his version of what happened."

The cop returned to the relative warmth of the cruiser as Jason backed away from the gate and turned toward home. The clock in the car indicated it was seven a.m. He'd be home in time to help get the kids ready for school and grab a bite of breakfast.

An hour later as he reached his desk in the office, the telephone rang. O'Hare was on the line. "I heard you'd been by the scene. I wanted to check but you likely know as much as I at this point."

"Have you talked with the guard? I don't know why he didn't see these guys before they set off their explosive."

"I talked with him a few minutes ago. He's in the process of being released from the hospital. They treated him for minor burns and scrapes where he'd been hit by flying objects, but he'll be back at work tonight. His story about the incident is he made his rounds and had been back in the office where he hangs out for about twenty minutes when it happened. My guess is the perpetrators watched him make the circuit and as soon as he disappeared back inside, they went into action —scaled the fence, ran to the area of the dock, jammed the device close to the structure, then left. They removed their ladders and very shortly the timer kicked in. They were likely in their vehicle by then and sped away as soon as they knew they'd been successful."

"So they had this planned to the last detail. They had the timer set before they went in thus they knew how much time they'd need."

"I'd guess that's right. They couldn't risk having the guard come around again. I bet they were within the fence less than three minutes."

"We can work around the mess and I'll get the contractor to repair the damaged areas."

"I'll let you know if the crime techs discover anything significant in the light of another day."

"Thanks for calling, Tom." He replaced the receiver and scanned through his file until he found Johnson's number in D.C.

He called Johnson, who always seemed to be in his office early, and told him about the explosion and the manner in which the deed had been conducted. Johnson listened without raising questions then concluded, "I have a promise from the security people to initiate an investigation into possible moles in our support group, although I don't have much faith it will lead to anything."

Jason asked. "Would you be amenable to doubling the security guards around the facility? Having only one is obviously not sufficient to protect the place."

Johnson hesitated for the first time an expense had been broached. "I'd better check with accounting about our budget for the project. We're under the gun to rein in expenses. And I raised the possibility of a cadre of troops with the a Deputy Assistant close to the Secretary of Defense. He didn't turn me down on the spot, but I'd be surprised if they help because of the demands for troops in hot spots around the world that they view as more strategically important."

"Do they understand the importance and potential dangers if these toxins are released in a public place? They'd have a public relations nightmare on their hands that would equal the one with the hurricane that hit the Gulf Coast and New Orleans."

Johnson responded after thinking for a few seconds. "I doubt they'd think in those terms, but you're correct."

Jason concluded. "Maybe these guys around here have made their statement and will go away." But he didn't believe for one moment this was the end of the problems. Whoever was doing this intended to close the facility and stop the research.

Then he called Jennings, the contractor who committed to putting the pieces together again as quickly as the officials released the building and he could assemble a crew. Jennings laughed as they ended the conversation. "Maybe you should hire me outright."

Pleased someone could find a tad of levity in the chaos, Jason responded, "Could save a lot of phone calls."

Kathryn approached the formal three-year review hearing with some concern as did everyone whose career could be derailed by a negative outcome. She knew she had the backing of her immediate section chief, but it was unpredictable how a panel of faculty might evaluate her accomplishments and how they might predict her future worth to the institution. She accepted she could be dealing with some big egos.

And she hoped the pregnancy didn't become a factor although it was possible for some of these older males, and perhaps females, to view it as an obstacle to sustained productivity. Jason encouraged her, telling her she had an outstanding record with solid promise for the future, but she sometimes thought he was shielding her from the real facts.

She'd submitted her credentials by the deadline, had met with her section chief, and now she faced an interview with the Dean of the Medical School, an older physician-researcher whom she seldom saw in the halls, one of his Associate Deans and a group of faculty representing the various components of the school. The interview phase was unique to the Medical School as no other unit of the university put faculty through that hoop.

Knowing the passage by this group of senior officials and elected faculty would be tantamount to gaining tenure at the three-year review, she fretted about every detail. With Jason's concurrence, she'd decided to appear in her typical professional garb; that is, a modest dress that covered her knees, nylons and medium heels. She thought males wouldn't worry about dress as much as she but didn't voice that opinion to Jason who seemed to wear the same sets of slacks and sport coats day after day.

She waited in the outer office of the Dean's conference room with three others confronting the same ordeal as she, but conversation was limited as each thought about their own plight and promise. Kathryn smiled inwardly as she recalled the same feelings on the day of her preliminary exam in graduate school. All the others were male and she realized she'd attracted the attention of her peers when they kept glancing at her. Now she was pleased she'd chosen the blue dress that showed promises of her figure without an overt flaunting of her physical attributes.

The door to the conference room opened and a male, probably in his mid thirties, emerged, a deep frown on his face. He rubbed his ruddy face and balding head as though trying to erase an unpleasant experience, not a good omen for those waiting their turn. He marched straight to the exit without looking to anyone, seeking a quick escape.

A secretary responsible for maintaining the order of candidate's appearance before the panel, called out, "Dr. Kathryn Helweg."

Kathryn steadied herself and walked quickly into the room to face a long table of seven males, all watching her. She smiled as she was shown to her chair at the end of the table. Papers and Styrofoam coffee cups littered the table. A coffee urn, a stack of paper napkins and remnants of food were on a side table.

Dean Rupert Gordon wasted no time on formalities. From the other end of the table, he said, "Dr. Helweg, we've reviewed your record and have been impressed you've accomplished so many things in the three years you've been on our faculty. Before I permit questions, do you have a statement indicating your future plans and goals?"

Kathryn had been alerted to this by her section chief and had prepared a brief comment. Without notes and looking around the table, meeting the eyes of her judges, she smiled and said, "I've enjoyed working in the School, teaching the sections of biochemistry, and conducting a research program. I believe I've been successful in those endeavors. I look forward to continuing to improve my teaching approach and perhaps taking on different classes to enlarge my knowledge of the various subjects we deal with. I anticipate I will be able to generate additional outside grant support for my research and I have a grant proposal pending at NIH. In addition, I will strive to be a good citizen by serving on committees and panels when asked." Her voice had been steady and she had not gone overboard in promising things she couldn't deliver.

She stopped and looked toward Gordon who'd given attention to her short speech. He nodded and said, "Now I'll give anyone an opportunity to ask questions about Dr. Helweg's record or her future goals."

A tall male, his long arms resting on the table top, seated along the right side of the table asked, "Will you continue your virus work with Preston King in Biology?"

Focusing on his face, she said, "I expect to do that. Dr. King and I are preparing a continuation proposal due to NIH in six weeks. We have the draft essentially finalized and are prepared to meet the deadline of the agency."

The same person asked. "Have you enjoyed the teaching phase of your appointment?"

Kathryn smiled and replied. "For the most part. I struggled some early on but I seem to gain good responses from students and I believe they are learning the essential material. Several have come by to tell me they've been able to utilize the concepts in their advanced courses." As part of her documentation submitted for the review were student evaluations of her courses, and a few comments from students who praised her as an instructor.

A burly man at the far end of the table and sitting adjacent to the Dean asked. "Has being a female in a predominantly male school been either an advantage or a disadvantage?"

Kathryn nodded her head. "I've perceived neither. I've been treated cordially and professionally by colleagues who have been supportive and open to my requests for advice and assistance. I have been accepted as a member of the faculty and have not felt I was a hire to meet any equal opportunity needs of the school." She smiled and added. "This is not to say I'd not like to see other qualified women brought onto the faculty."

"Is there a reason for your saying that?"

"Yes. I believe additional women would demonstrate a better model for our female students who represent approximately half of each class. Those young people need to see that women can succeed in what has long been a male dominated profession."

"Do you harbor any ambitions of becoming an administrator?" Also coming from the same source who seemed to dominate the question phase. She wondered if the query was indeed to be a trap. She had learned that many females, especially those who had entered the profession after having a family, pushed for leadership positions citing their age and experience as sufficient reasons to be promoted.

Kathryn shook her head. "I have no aspirations to do that. I am quite happy to continue doing teaching and research. But if asked to fill a need of the school, I would do my very best in an administrative role."

"Do you have a role model in mind?" The guy wouldn't stop and she wondered if ever the Dean brought closure to one individual's interrogation.

"As my credentials show, I am married to Jason Spradlin who is department head of Biology. He seems to thrive in the position, although he stays on the go all the time. He is a model I would try to emulate to accomplish the numerous tasks that come to your desk."

Finally Dean Gordon broke in. "Yes, most of us know him and he's a model for almost everyone who attempts to be an effective administrator and maintain a research program. We could all learn from him."

Gordon looked at his colleagues as though indicating this interview had run its course. When no one raised a query, he said, "Dr. Helweg, thank you for coming in and we'll inform you of our decision by the end of tomorrow."

Kathryn was hanging her coat on the rack when her office telephone rang. She'd just returned from lunch at the Faculty Club where she and Jason had enjoyed the daily special and time for a private conversation in the middle of busy days. It had become a ritual both looked forward to and when they could not meet, they felt something missing in their day.

"This is Dean Gordon's secretary. Can you come to his office?"

"I can come immediately," she said, hoping to get this behind her before walking across campus to do some work in King's lab.

Gordon was seated behind a huge desk, almost bare of papers or bric-a-brac. She was reminded of Jason's desk in Quincy except for the size difference. Both seemed to move the endless flow of paper as efficiently as anyone she'd known. Most desks of other administrators and faculty were always piled high with stacks of papers, some of which had been there for weeks or longer.

Gordon stood and led her to a group of soft chairs arranged in a half-circle at one end of the large office. She realized she'd never been in here before. She dropped into a chair, crossed her legs and smoothed her skirt, wishing to wipe the moisture off her hands but not wanting to soil either the skirt or the chair..

Without preliminary small talk, Gordon said, “Dr. Helweg, I am pleased to tell you we have agreed you are most deserving of tenure and promotion to Associate Professor. We were impressed with your record and your interview.”

Gordon smiled and continued, “I was impressed too by your somewhat understatement of future goals and hopes for the future.”

“Thank you for the vote of confidence. I am pleased and, of course, relieved to have this hurdle behind me.”

“I met your husband when he was working with John Hadley on the Wilson’s disease project. Hadley is a long time friend and colleague of mine and he had a fine relationship with Jason. But spouses aside for the moment, I will have an Associate Dean retiring within the next two years and hope to bring a female into that slot. In fact, what you said yesterday about role models for young women cemented my notion that it was the right thing to do.”

Kathryn said, “That would be a step forward for all women in the medical and allied health fields.”

Gordon leaned forward. “This is much too early to make any commitments regarding that appointment, but if things work out and if you are interested when the time arrives, I hope you might consider submitting your credentials for that position.”

“I’m flattered you consider me a fit for the office. I will certainly think about it, but in the meantime, I realize I must continue to perform as a teacher and researcher.”

Gordon stood. “Dr. Helweg, thanks for your contributions to this faculty and best wishes for the future.”

As she stood, Gordon shook her hand and led her to the door.

Back in her office, her first inclination was to call Jason. Then she remembered she intended to work some in King's lab. She'd drop by his office and give him the news in person. When she arrived at Quincy Jason was in a meeting, this time with the department accountant, Miriam. Audrey, the secretary, invited her to have a coffee in the work room, telling her Jason would not be long.

Five minutes later and sipping coffee, sitting alone on a high stool as the copy machine whirred out multiple copies of some document, Audrey came to tell her Jason was free. She went immediately to find him focused on a paper. As she entered, she closed the door behind her, the click of the bolt causing him to look up.

He smiled and came toward her. "This is a good surprise." He squeezed her hand.

"Dean Gordon just told me I've made the cut and I wanted to tell you as soon as possible."

He pulled her closer. "Great, I'm proud of you. We'll have to celebrate, maybe dinner at a good place."

"I'd like that, but this time we should include Jennifer and Tony. It's time they participated in adult activities."

When his phone rang, she dropped his hand and said, "See you tonight and we'll figure out how to celebrate getting past one more threat in our lives."

She watched for a moment as Jason talked on the phone, his focus on the conversation, then he made a couple of notes on a pad. When he looked up, she waved and left through the door.

Chapter 18

Jennifer and Tony were excited having dinner with Kathryn and Jason on one of their 'date' night affairs. They always wondered what went on and had talked about the things that might happen. Their parents seemed secretive about it, only saying it was their one night each month when they celebrated alone. Their spirits soared when Kathryn had told them they were invited to go with them this coming Saturday evening.

Now the big event was at hand. Jennifer was thrilled to try out her new brown/beige dress, one sent by her 'Grandfather Helweg', and she had new brown shoes to match. Tony had doubts about getting dressed in a suit and tie, something he wore only when forced by his father. And the fancy restaurant rather than a fast food place didn't match his idea of anything special.

At Alberto's, an upscale Italian restaurant in the downtown area, they were led by a hostess in a black dress to a table for four in one corner of this posh place, candles on each table, linen napkins, silver forks, knives and spoons arranged by each place, crystal goblets which were filled with water after the woman had given them menus. Several tables around them were occupied even at the early hour of six-thirty.

Jason said, "Look at the menus on page four, see what you might like. And drinks are listed on the very back page." When Tony had trouble managing the heavy menu, Jason reached to help him, flipped to the right page and pointed out several possibilities.

Jennifer frowned and said, “There are too many choices. It’s hard to decide.”

Kathryn said, “Maybe something like the pork chop with potatoes would be nice, You both like that at home. Or you could get slices of pizza, or a calzone, to try something different.”

“Pizza is okay by me,” Tony responded. “And maybe a root beer or coke.”

More venturesome than her younger sibling, Jennifer said, “I’m going to order the calzone. The picture looks nice.”

Jason grinned at their confusion, remembering the first times he’d gone out with his parents when he was Jennifer’s age. Then Kathryn helped them with drinks. ”Your father always orders a wine. But I’m going to have the sparkling grape juice. You would enjoy that and it’s different than the typical soft drink.”

They nodded, glad to have the decision made for them.

The meal progressed without incident, no spilled drink, no food dropped on the floor, but the kids were sedate, remembering Jason’s admonition they had to behave like adults or the hostess would have them thrown out.

As they neared completion of the meal, a pianist started playing soft music. Jason said, “Jennifer, would you like to dance with me?”

She looked at Kathryn who nodded approval. Jason led her to the small dance floor and made sure she knew where to place her hands, although she’d taken a few lessons in an after school program. Within a few steps she caught on to the beat and followed her father through the tune. Jason led her back to the table and held the chair for her. She looked up at him, smiled and said, "Thank you."

When Kathryn suggested to Tony they could try the dance, he rebelled. "I don't know how and would be embarrassed."

Kathryn didn't push him. "That's okay. Maybe next time."

In the car on the way home, Jennifer piped up from the back seat. "That was different, but not very much fun. I was worried about making a mistake."

Jason said, "You both did fine. I'm proud of the way you handled everything. Next time we'll go to a different place. Keep practicing what you've learned at those dance classes."

"That'd be good," Jennifer responded from the back seat.

Tony punched her in the arm. "I'll stay home with Mrs. Carter. None of this dance stuff for me."

Helga and Ingrid were able to focus on the reconfiguration of the genome again as the contractor banged away at the other end of the building, putting the offices and animal rooms back in shape and installing steel doors on the loading dock. Jason had ordered a new animal cage to replace the scarred and bent one that had been flipped around by the blast.

They'd decided to take Walcott's suggestion and chop the genome into pieces of forty base pairs, then randomly mix them and check the results. Possibly the mixture wouldn't even rearrange itself into an intact strand, but it was worth the effort. If it failed, they could eliminate one more possibility. And Helga had called Walcott to ask that he send to them an active gene of a known toxin.

Two days later Walcott phoned Jason just before lunch. "Dr. Spradlin, I'm sending a mycotoxin to you. We recovered it from an insect a few months ago. Another investigator has worked on it and he's identified the active gene fragment that is extremely toxic. I believe if you can incorporate this into the genome you're working with, we might achieve success."

Walcott seemed more talkative than usual and went on. "We know this mycotoxin is lethal within minutes by impacting the airways and leading to death for the lack of oxygen. In its present form we've not been able to effectively put it into an aerosol because of its size. But by incorporating the gene fragment of approximately forty base pairs into the genome you have, I think the size problem will be overcome. We'll know after you and Helga give it a try."

Jason asked, "How are you sending this?"

"There's a military plane transporting a half-dozen troops to Spencerville for deployment to Crews. We'll put the gene piece, probably in a freeze-dried state, on that plane. It's to arrive at your place at seven-thirty tonight. I trust either you or Helga can meet the plane and take the package to the lab."

"One of us will do that," Jason said.

Walcott continued, "I heard about your latest problem with the vandals through Johnson. He asked me to let you know he can't afford a second security guard. The budget is too tight."

"I'm disappointed but understand. We'll need to rethink our approach to security. I'll talk with the organization providing the guard.

They will no doubt have encountered such situations before."

"Good luck. This interference into the lab is beyond my scope of thinking. We've never had those problems before. But this is one of the few times we've contracted work out to a university."

Jason said, "The primary thing is to get the toxin to work effectively. And hope these disruptions don't set us back."

Jason and Helga met the plane to receive the small package from Walcott. As the troops debarked and struggled with backpacks and other gear toward a transport truck parked inside the loading area, the co-pilot brought the canister to them and asked for a signature indicating receipt.

Prepared to turn away, the officer said, "This must be precious stuff. The person who gave it to us warned about not dropping it or removing any portion of the covering."

Jason signed the receipt form, shook the airman's hand and said, "Thanks for getting it here in good shape." They turned toward the entrance and to the parking area.

Twenty minutes later at the lab, they prepared to store the canister in the large freezer. Seeing no sign of the guard, Helga asked, "Have we given up on security or is the guy goofing off somewhere?"

"He's around," Jason said. "I saw his car across the street when we came. They've decided to patrol the fence line rather than do random checks inside the facility and a quick walk outside. He's trying to position his car to observe the entire property from one vantage point. And I believe he'll move around so vandals are never quite sure where he'll be." Jason had talked with the Security company after the bomb blast and the person in charge suggested they use this approach indicating it had worked at other facilities that had been frequently vandalized. He thought it would keep the vandals from learning the guard's position or his schedule they could work around.

"Let's hope that works better than before."

"It almost has to be an improvement," Jason commented, as they set the alarm and closed the front door.

Riley had become a regular attendee at the Friday beer sessions with his former Biology colleagues. The four settled around a corner table which Harris had grabbed when a group of undergraduates left leaving their mugs on the table with spillage across the top. Soggy napkins added to the mess, but a waitress came soon to wipe away the chaos and take their orders. The cold day led to a haze in the air of the crowded tavern as snow melted from shoes. Coats and mitts were shaken to rid them of flakes and added to the mixture of cold moisture mixing with the warm air.

As the waitress left, Riley opened the conversation. "I guess you saw in the papers and on the TV news about the explosion at Spradlin's lab on 29th Street." He glanced at each of the others to determine if they heard his news, his smug expression indicating he knew something they weren't privy to.

Townsend sipped his draft Budweiser. "It was hard to miss. I heard it on the TV news then read about it in the morning paper. Lucky someone wasn't killed."

"They knew no one was there. They all leave at five or five-thirty."

"What about the security guard that ended up in the emergency unit?" Harris watched for Riley's reaction.

"I guess he took his chances when he signed on with those feds and Spradlin who are out to make biological weapons that will kill millions of innocent people."

Harris pressed. "How do you know that?"

Riley smiled, a sly grin that spread across his face. "Someone I know has inside information. His source hasn't been wrong yet."

Townsend said, "So this is another of your approaches to damage Jason?" He continued, "And I saw in the paper you are appealing the court decision regarding your encounter with Helweg."

"My lawyer thinks we have a good chance of having the verdict overturned, but it's going to take a while, maybe even six months."

"I wish you well, but let's face it," Peter said, "you were stalking Helweg again or you wouldn't have been in King's lab that night."

Riley's face clouded, his mouth twisted into a scowl. "You guys have become Spradlin disciples. I shouldn't tell you anything more."

Harris said, his voice somewhat like a parent disciplining a wayward child. "We just don't understand your obsession. Some day it will get you in deep trouble, more than you're already in because of your stalking his wife. You need to move on and forget any past grievances. Let it alone, Hugh."

His face turning dark, Riley stood. "I'm right. Spradlin disciples is the only way to describe you guys." He grabbed his coat from the back of a vacant chair and stomped out of the place, leaving his beer mug three-quarters filled.

The newcomer to the group, Pierson said, "Spradlin must have done something pretty drastic to get Riley stirred up like he is."

Townsend puffed on his pipe. "No, he just called Riley's hand on his antics within the department. Riley never forgave him for being called on the carpet by the former head because of some crap he'd pulled with Jason's graduate students."

Harris added, "You have to understand Riley was always a trouble maker in the department. He gave the former head fits by passing rumors and false information around until Rogers figured him out. Riley became even more devious after Rogers died and during the search for his successor he did everything possible to undermine Jason's candidacy for the headship. Then Jason and Dean Hawthorne worked out some strategy to buy Riley out and get him out of the department."

"It's been a much more peaceful place since Riley left. We all get along and no one is out to do a colleague harm." Townsend continued, "But I give Jason much of the credit for the improvement."

Harris stood. "Peter, you're absolutely right about the environment in the department." He pulled his coat from the pile and zipped the front to the top. "Sorry to leave early, but I'm meeting a friend for dinner. See you next time."

As Harris weaved his way through the crowd near the door, Pierson said, "He's meeting that woman from Sociology. I suspect they are living together at her place but I don't know for sure."

"What about his wife? Does she know about this affair?"

"Harris told me they were divorcing. All their kids are grown and gone from home. He and his wife agreed it was time to stop fighting and go their separate ways. Greg is living in a small condo near the downtown area."

Harris continued to be nagged by the rumors Riley was passing around about inside information. He had no idea how Riley managed to find out about the culprits who'd damaged the lab and it could well be Riley was guessing and trying to impress them. His conscience haunted him until he felt he had to get the concern off his shoulders and set up an appointment to see Spradlin.

Jason came around his desk to shake Harris' hand and lead him to the conference table. Jason said, "Greg, I don't see much of you these days. I assume things are going well. I saw where you received a new grant from NIH and intended to get by your office to congratulate you, but things became too hectic."

Harris settled into the chair, crossed his legs, picked at the seam of his gray trousers before looking at Jason. "Yeah, things are going well. No problems I know about."

Jason waited several seconds, knowing Harris had something important to communicate as he didn't come into the head's office unless summoned.

Harris looked up and met Jason's eyes. "I need to tell you something I'm bothered about. I've stewed about this for several days and concluded yesterday I should let you know my suspicions."

Having broken through his inner resistance, Harris rushed on. "I believe Hugh Riley knows who is behind those incidents at the lab on

29th Street."

He stopped, apparently thinking there needed to be some background, then started again. "You probably know some of us meet every Friday after hours to have a beer. Riley started the group but dropped out for about two years because of his teaching schedule at the community college. But he started coming back last fall and has on two recent occasions hinted he knew who was involved with those incidents. He's mentioned he had inside information about the work going on in the lab and the people who've tried to sabotage the efforts. But you know Riley and he could be just blowing smoke. Anyway, I thought you should know."

Jason sat mute for several seconds, digesting the information from Harris. "There has been a lot of interest in the lab since the day we began renovation which seemed unusual to me. I've thought for some time there is a leak in the system and somehow people know our mission that is classified secret. I have no idea where the problem is located, but I've asked contacts in the federal system to begin checking."

"So that much coincides with Riley's boast."

"It does, but how does Riley fit in? Has he become a member of some anti-government group?"

"He hasn't divulged that, just hints he knows more than I think he should."

"Has Riley made new friends or become acquainted with people who might desire to stop any research involving the federal system?"

Harris shrugged, but feeling more comfortable in talking with

Jason than he had in a long time. "He intimates the research is related to the development of biological weapons."

Jason didn't know how much to trust Harris who'd been Riley's buddy since he'd been around the department. Henry Rogers had warned Jason about the liaison between Riley and Harris and their tendencies to create problems, but the only issue he'd ever had with Harris was his urge to hit on females under his charge. And he recalled Kathryn telling him about Harris trying to get close to her during her post-doc days with King. The fact that Harris was forthcoming with this suspicion about Riley changed the nature of their relationship, at least for the present time. But it was too early to reveal confidential information.

"I appreciate your sharing your concerns, Greg, but where do I go from here?"

Harris seemed reluctant to respond, perhaps not knowing what Jason might ask of him. "I don't know what to suggest other than have the cops bring Riley in for a session. Scare the hell out of him. He might give a name to the police."

Jason decided to push Harris a bit. "Would you be willing to query Riley the next time he brings up his suspicions? See if he'll divulge his contacts."

"I don't know if I can do that. It smacks of ratting out a friend."

"I understand how you might feel, but if the opportunity is there, push him a bit about local connections. We know one of the males who has been interested in the lab works at the community college. That could put Riley and him together."

Harris shrugged. “I didn’t know that.” He stood, his face revealing his uncertainty. “I’ll see how the next session with Riley goes. If I can lead him into some revelation about the source of his rumors, I’ll let you know.”

Jason stood and walked to the door with Harris. “Thanks, Greg. You never know what little bit of information can be important. And keep up the good work with your research program.”

Chapter 19

Helga and Ingrid prepared for the next testing of the modified genome, this one a random rearrangement of the original as Walcott had suggested. Jason brought another group of adult test rats and allowed them to adjust to new surroundings for three days, not wanting the stress of new quarters to be a factor in their response.

Jason came to assist with the trial. Without noise and being as gentle as possible, he transferred the animals in their cages from the animal room to the test facility, a reverse air hood which would contain any toxic substance within the system and not allow it to spread throughout the laboratory. They waited thirty minutes for the rats to settle down after being shifted from one space to another. When all was ready and the system checked, the genome within the aerosol was released into the environment of the rats. The animals sniffed the strange mist invading their cages, but then returned to their positions of nibbling at their food, or lying quietly in their security. No evidence of toxicity appeared. After ten minutes of watching, Jason and Helga knew the trial had failed.

Jason asked, "Did the genome pieces truly form a new structure?"

"Yes, the parts came together with apparent ease and connections were made between them so we had a genome of two hundred thousand base pairs again but in a different configuration."

"So our next attempt should be to insert the gene material sent by

Walcott, but the question is where and in what arrangement of the genome?"

Helga pondered the question for a bit, walking around the office and looking at Jason. "I suggest we go back to our initial trial, put the pieces into that arrangement and place the mycotoxin in the middle of that. We know that brought the reaction we wanted, but it was not toxic enough to be lethal. We could then deliver two potential toxic shots in one blast. If that doesn't work, I'm at a loss as to what's next."

"I don't have a better idea," Jason said, as he nodded agreement. Then he turned to leave to meet an appointment with a search committee for a prospective faculty member in for an interview. The young woman, a doctoral graduate from Berkeley with a year of post doc work at Wisconsin, had caught the attention of the search committee. If she impressed the faculty during her seminar, Jason was prepared to make her an offer. The committee was scheduled to provide Jason the results of the faculty poll just before Ann Mitchell's appointment later in the morning.

At the office door, newly installed but not yet painted, Jason said, "I'll give you a couple of hours tomorrow but if you need me before then, give me a call." He wanted to achieve success with this project and move on to other things. The continued failure to meet the goal had begun to frustrate him and he wondered if Walcott had given them the best advice. But it could well be that Walcott was searching for the answer himself.

"We'll be okay," Helga said. "Ingrid has become quite proficient with the methodology and we work well as a team."

Intertwined with the meetings about the faculty vacancy, the speculation of Harris about Riley festered in Jason's thinking until he decided to act. He'd met with Mitchell and offered her the position to begin the next fall semester. He called O'Hare and asked if he would be willing to set up a meeting with Chief Hayden of the Spencerville police.

He and O'Hare met Hayden in the Chief's office. Jason outlined his issue and then asked, "I wonder if you could assign a detective to investigate this. I know it may be a dead end, but the rumors persist."

Hayden seemed reluctant and O'Hare chipped in. "Maybe I can put a man on this for a few days. After all, it does involve the university, although not located on the campus proper. To do this, I'll need a copy of Westlake's file."

Hayden dialed a number on his phone and requested a clerk bring in the folder. He scanned through it and said, "Tell you what. I'll give you the entire file. You can return it if it doesn't pan out, but for now, we have no use for it. He hasn't committed a crime in our jurisdiction in the last five years. It's archived in our data base."

With Jason leaning over his shoulder, O'Hare flipped through the slim folder containing scant information about the suspected sect leader. Jason stared at the grainy photo of Westlake for several seconds, believing he'd seen him around campus, but he couldn't be certain. He was now convinced Westlake was the man he'd seen in the car parked on that cold night across the street from the lab.

"Maybe we should focus on Riley," O'Hare said. "He seems to be the individual with the important information. Or at least the one spouting off about what he knows."

Jason seconded the idea. "Tying the two together may be the key. Understand, I don't know for sure if Riley knows something or is trying to impress his buddies."

"How would he know about the biological weapon development?" Hayden asked.

"He could be guessing. But he knows enough biology to put the weapon development concept together with a classified federal contract, plus he knows my background in genetic manipulation. He could put those facts together and come up with a reasonable assumption about what we're doing."

O'Hare closed the file and stood. "I'll continue thinking about the best approach, but at the moment I'm inclined to investigate Riley. And if he and Westlake are meeting somewhere, we'll discover that."

The connection between Riley and Westlake came more quickly than anyone hoped and in a setting no one would have considered a likely possibility. On the spur of the moment as they walked away from Quincy, Jason and Kathryn decided to try a new diner near the campus for lunch. They arrived just before the noon crowd eager to test the new restaurant now in their second full week of operation after months of renovation of the space previously occupied by a clothing store. They were seated quickly in a back booth and menus delivered. Both ordered soft drinks, scanned the two-page listing of lunch specials and settled on the soup and salad.

Kathryn said, “King and I finished the grant application for continuation of the virus work. He’ll run it by the Research Office for their checks and sign-offs and then we wait for the verdict of the agency.”

“Are you confident about it?”

She smiled, her dark eyes shining, and said, “I’m always confident. We’ve done some good work and there’s no reason not to be continued. My only reservation is the time I’ll need to commit to the research during next year when I’m supposed to be on leave.”

“The positive aspect is you can manage your time and work in the lab when you can be most productive.”

“I’ve been thinking about the time when Lillian Carter leaves us. I’d like to look for a nanny type who can serve as a reliable backup for those times when I need to be two places at the same time.”

Jason mumbled his agreement, but his attention was focused on the head waiter as he led four men to a table in the middle of the rectangular room. The loud conversation caused Jason to glance up to see Hugh Riley, Phillip Westlake and two companions being seated. All except Riley were dressed in heavy coveralls, baseball caps, and work boots covered with mud and grime. They apparently hadn’t shaved in days as scraggly beards masked most of their facial features. Jason looked closely again as they settled into the chairs to be certain of his identification of Westlake.

Realizing he’d become distracted from their conversation, Kathryn asked, “What is it?” She began twisting in the booth to look across the restaurant.

"Don't look around but Riley and Philip Westlake, this suspected leader of a dissident group, are at a table with two other seedy looking characters. Riley can't see us and I'd just as soon he didn't."

"Westlake's the one you saw in the car in front of the lab?"

"Yes, O'Hare ran his license plate number for me. Now O'Hare has a detective trying to connect Riley and Westlake. I'll call him when I'm in the office."

The conversation at Riley's table became heated within minutes. Westlake and another man, his cap in place, seemed to be arguing, pointing their fingers at each other. Their faces becoming red, the confrontation gaining the attention of nearby diners, as their voices elevated in volume. Riley remained silent as he watched the exchange. Jason wished he could overhear, but the noise and the distance prevented any chance of that. At one point the man arguing with Westlake pushed back his chair, bumping a waitress as she maneuvered through the tight space. Realizing they'd become the center of attraction when others stopped talking and gave their attention to the fracas, Riley said something that seemed to calm the two. The debate simmered down and Jason focused on his lunch.

Their food eaten and the bill paid, Jason and Kathryn lingered over coffee. Jason looked at his watch again and said, "Let's walk out and hope Riley doesn't notice. I'd hoped he'd leave before we had to, but I can't delay any longer and make this appointment I have at the office."

As they gathered their coats and gloves, a waiter came by. Jason stopped him and on a sudden whim asked, "Is there a back entrance we could use?"

The young man looked perplexed, glanced around for some problem, then nodded. "There's a side door past the rest rooms. It'll push open from the inside but you can't enter that way." He took a couple of steps and pointed down a short hallway.

Jason grabbed Kathryn's hand and led her to the secondary exit. They came out into an alley that led to the main street. The gravel drive was covered with remnants of snow. Papers and cardboard containers had been blown against the wall of the building. One of the garbage cans had been overturned by an animal or a careless worker to scatter more debris.

Outside in the cold air, she said, "Nothing like being a spy to get into a messy place."

Still holding her hand, they eased their way through the chaos. Kathryn skirted away from a pile of gravel to avoid wrecking her low-heeled shoes.

As they passed the front of the restaurant, Jason glanced in. Riley and his cohorts were still there. Their heads were bent over their plates.

Back in his office, he called O'Hare and told him about the sighting of Riley and Westlake. "Now we know they communicate with each other but beyond that, their relationship remains a mystery. But their being together is important to learn."

"I'm going to have my detective follow Westlake for a couple of days. See if there's some sort of meeting with others who are plotting to do more damage."

"I'd appreciate it," Jason said. "We've made the initial connection. For some reason, I suspect Westlake is the one receiving information from a contact in the D.C. offices. He seems to be around the scene more than others and remember he's been at odds with the feds before. Now maybe we can determine their scheme and perhaps their source of information within the federal system."

"We'll run a background check on Westlake. Search any service records, prison sentences, places he's lived and who knows what else we might find. And if the Agency security people suspect anyone as the mole, we could try tying them together."

"I'll try to get the name of a contact for you," Jason volunteered, but he suspected that might be difficult within the secret organization.

"Let's keep in touch."

Jason had forgotten about President Snyder's warning regarding the Governor's potential interest in the project until he received a telephone call from the Governor's deputy asking that Jason come to the capitol and update the Governor. Thinking he had no choice, Jason agreed to come two days later for a two o'clock session with the State's Chief Executive. He called the President's office to discover Snyder was out of town. Jason left a message and indicated he'd check in when he returned from the capitol.

Jason decided to drive the one hundred and twenty-five miles to the capitol rather than brave the small commuter line that made two round trips daily from Spencerville. During the drive along the interstate his mind wandered, initially on the upcoming meeting with Governor Charles Brewster who had the reputation of being antagonistic to everyone except those close to him or to supporters who could keep him in office. Then he thought about Kathryn's pregnancy that had progressed without a hitch thus far. She was in good physical condition and still ran with him each morning. But her mid-section had begun to swell as expected and he knew she would have to forego hard exercise soon. He thought about Riley and what he might do next or what role he played in the group led by Westlake. He grinned to himself as he neared the exit to the Governor's mansion and the capitol, thinking he'd not had so much time alone in months to ponder the events swirling around him.

He parked on the top floor of the garage adjoining the capitol building, stopped in a rest room, and found his way to the Governor's office ten minutes ahead of the appointed time.

Fifteen minutes after the scheduled session, Jason was escorted into the office of the Governor by a middle-age secretary who smiled as she showed him the door. A male associate appeared from a side office and followed him into the inner sanctum.

The Governor, at five-ten, was essentially Jason's height, but his tailored suit failed to cover his bulging mid-section. His dark hair was turning to gray and neatly combed to cover emerging bald areas. Brewster came around his massive desk littered with stacks of papers amid several memorabilia representing associations with groups of supporters or special occasions. "Dr. Spradlin, I appreciate your coming. And please meet my assistant, Gene Throckmorton, who will sit in with us." He pointed to a group of chairs around a large coffee table.

Without delay Brewster said, "I've heard about your contract with

Homeland Security and am curious about the work going on in your lab. I understand from my source that the work is related to biological weapons and has a top security clearance. But I need to know what goes on in state facilities." His eyes bored into Jason's face as though daring him to evade the issue.

"You're correct about the focus of the research and it is classified secret by Homeland Security. I can tell you that very few people know about the research and its purpose." Jason returned the Governor's stare.

Throckmorton spoke up. "I learned about your contract through a source close to the Secretary of Defense."

Turning to face the aide, Jason said, "I'm surprised he or she revealed anything about the work. I've been told from the outset to maintain close secrecy about what we're doing and I've tried to do that. Only a couple of university administrators have been told because I thought they should know how I'm spending my time."

Brewster said, his voice authoritarian and demanding, "And you never thought to advise this office about this top secret mission?" His blue eyes stared into Jason's face.

"No, Governor, I didn't. I've tried to follow the guidelines established by the Agency regarding who should know. Obviously the fewer people involved, the less chance there is for the press to discover and spread rumors about the work."

Brewster turned to his assistant. "Are any of our Congressional delegation in the loop about this?"

"Not to my knowledge, but perhaps Dr. Spradlin has an idea."

Jason shook his head. "I'm not privy to what our representatives or senators have access to. Members of the House Committee for Science and Technology probably have been briefed, although I can't be certain of that. I've discussed the matter with Congressman Wilke who chairs the committee that has oversight for science and technology activities within the Agency."

Brewster stared at Jason for several seconds, then said, "And what would you do if I ordered you to close down your secret operation and get out of that research altogether?" His features remained impassive. Jason couldn't detect anything but a person intending to use the authority of his office to have his way.

Jason wanted to tell Brewster he couldn't do that, but decided to pass the buck. "That would be a matter between your office, Governor, the Secretary of Defense and perhaps responsible Congressional committees. If there is an agreement between those parties and you, then I'd have no choice but to stop."

Brewster changed course. "Dr. Spradlin, what are the possibilities this weapon you're developing will kill millions of innocent people? We've all heard about the anthrax problem that got the Congress in a dither, but what you're doing might be worse."

Jason shook his head in disagreement. "We're working on a unique weapon intended to thwart terrorist groups rather than one that is to be used against a population."

"But it could happen, couldn't it, placed in the wrong hands?"

"It's possible, but highly unlikely." Jason thought about going into details but decided the press would soon know about the approach they were using. Then his entire effort could be wasted as the Agency would quietly close up the lab and move the research to another site.

A knock on the door took Throckmorton to meet the secretary who whispered something. Throckmorton returned to stand next to his chair. "Governor, that was a reminder you have a session with a delegation from the Farm Bureau. They're waiting in the conference room."

Brewster stood. "Dr. Spradlin, I'll consider my possible actions regarding this developing weapon system, then I'll communicate my decision to your President. But I'm more than a bit concerned state personnel are involved with these type ventures."

Driving away from the capitol Jason decided he should alert Congressman Wilke of potential interference with the work by the governor and to tell him about leaks to Throckmorton and likely to others. And he must warn President Snyder about the call forthcoming from the Governor's office.

Chapter 20

Jason's alert to Wilke resulted in a trip to D.C. to visit with the Congressman and a couple of his aides. They assembled in Wilke's conference room, an adjunct to his office adorned with numerous photos of the Representative, smiling constituent groups, and big donors. Jason suspected the staff worked diligently to ensure those visitors saw evidence of their session with Wilke through photographs, maybe even tapes of their meetings. Wilke shook Jason's hand as they gathered and introduced him to two assistants.

Settled around the table with a silver coffee service in the center, Wilke began. "So, Dr. Spradlin, you're concerned about information leakage around the biological weapons project. And so am I. But I'm not surprised. It's almost impossible to maintain any secrecy around this place. Politicians and those who work for politicians have this innate characteristic I call diarrhea of the mouth. If they know something, they must pass the information to others regardless of the potential consequences."

The aides and Jason laughed at the characterization. Jason said, "In this situation, the leak has gone not only to government officials, but to a group of dissidents who seem intent on continuously disrupting the research or closing us down. In fact, they've already caused some damage and resulting delays." He described the series of events around the lab and the measures they'd taken to secure the place. "And all of this started as soon as the renovation began."

"Have you alerted Deputy Director Johnson?"

Jason nodded. "He's promised to have the security people look into the problem, but I don't know if they've discovered the source yet or even if they've initiated an investigation."

Wilke shook his head, a frown across his broad face. "Eventually they'll locate the problem but it may take months or years. Remember how long it took the FBI to ferret out those rebels within their own agency."

Jason recalled vaguely the publicity about moles within the Bureau, but he asked, "Then what should I do? Keep plugging along and hope we can complete the task before serious damage is done?" He didn't say but thought "or until someone is killed."

Wilke nodded and picked up his coffee cup, sipped from the fine china, gently replaced it on a saucer. "That's the best approach, but I'm more concerned about your Governor's threats to shut down the operation. I really don't understand his motive other than seeking revenge for not being included in the loop from the outset. And that's my fault. I should have called him before we sealed the contract."

"That may be the issue," Jason acknowledged, thinking it rather juvenile but nothing else jumped out to describe Brewster's pique.

"Let's keep going until he does something. Then I'll have the Secretary of Defense give him a call. If we can't obtain his cooperation in any other way, we could threaten to cut off all defense contracts in the state. That could mean millions of revenue and hundreds of jobs down the drain. And if that got into the press, Brewster could be finished in public life." Wilke smiled as he thought of the potential consequences for an executive aligned with the opposition party.

Jason said, "We'll keep at it. I believe we're close to success but we won't know that until it's there. We've been close before only to have the effort fizzle."

"Do you need more resources, personnel, equipment, operations?"

"I would like to beef up the security by having funds to hire a second guard. I believe that would deter the vandals. Director Johnson was unable to support that request because of funds."

Wilke nodded to an assistant. "See what can be done about that. It shouldn't require much for the next few months. But it seems you've done about as much as possible short of a 24-hour military presence." He stood, suggesting it was time to move on to the next agenda item on his busy schedule.

Wilke shook Jason's hand. "Thanks for coming and keeping me in the loop. We'll let you know within a couple of days about this increased security support."

Jason left the House building feeling he had accomplished his goal of heading off the Governor if he should interfere. The potential for funds to bring on a second guard had been a plus he hadn't counted on. Of course, that hadn't come to fruition yet.

With time to spend before his flight, he dropped into a large department store and purchased small gifts for his kids who always expected something when he traveled. Two doors down the street he walked into a jewelry store and after viewing items for several minutes and discussing his desire with a female clerk, he purchased a gold necklace for Kathryn. She had another, but this one was different with a tiny heart-shaped pendant at the end and it would surprise her since he seldom bought gifts except on special occasions and Christmas. Maybe he would save it until their upcoming date night.

He wandered to the metro stop and made his way to the airport with time to spare.

In his office the next morning he found a message to call President Snyder or make an appointment to visit today. He called Snyder's office and established a three o'clock time that afternoon. Replacing the receiver, he realized he'd come to prefer face to face meetings rather than phone dialogues, maybe a sign he was rebelling against high-tech gadgets, or he preferred seeing expressions on faces rather than trying to guess how the other person appeared as they talked.

For once Snyder was on schedule and Jason was ushered in at the appointed time. Snyder came to the point of the meeting immediately. "So, Dr. Spradlin, our Governor has given you his famous chiding. And he called me this morning to let me know we should have included him in the group who were privy to your secret research. It was not a pleasant conversation to say the least."

Jason leaned forward in his chair. "Is he still threatening to close us down? That was his parting shot to me."

Snyder grinned. "No, but he was more than a bit miffed that Congressman Wilke phoned him late yesterday to let him know any interference in the project could have serious consequences. He seems not to know how Wilke found out about his interest, but he suspects you tipped him off."

Jason said, "I probably shouldn't tell you. If the Governor forces the issue, you can plead innocent."

"And if he calls you directly?"

"I'll tell him the truth."

Snyder smiled. "At any rate, Brewster isn't likely to raise the question again. I suspect Wilke got his full attention when he suggested federal resources within the state could be impacted. And by the way, Wilke let him know he has considerable admiration for you and the way you tackle issues."

Jason shook his head in mild disbelief that Wilke would tell the Governor about him. "Wilke is the reason I'm involved with this research. He recommended me to the Agency."

Snyder changed the subject without a preface. "Dean Hawthorne has accepted a president's position at another university and they're discussing starting dates. My guess is it'll be the first of next month and I'm still hoping you will agree to serve as acting dean while a search goes on. I'm alerting you now because there won't be much time between his announcement and his leaving."

"Since our earlier conversation, I've thought about this. I'm open to serving, but I'd like to inform my department faculty before any announcement about the interim appointment is made public."

Snyder stood and Jason followed as they moved toward the door. "Yes, that would be appropriate and you should think about an interim head for Biology. You can't do both jobs. There are inherent conflicts of interests not to mention the demands of the positions."

Jason walked quickly through a cold April wind toward Quincy. His mind overflowed with the issues soon to confront him, administrative problems he'd never faced before and trying to complete this biological weapons project as soon as possible. Notions that the Governor hadn't fired his last shot persisted. Wilke's acknowledgement that he knew Jason should be enough to tip off Brewster that Jason was the rat who squealed. But now he had to turn his attention to the biological weapon and meet with Helga.

When Jason arrived at the 29th Street lab near four, he found Helga at the desk in the office, now fully restored after the latest vandalism. She looked up from a journal paper she was reading, smiled, and said, "We're ready for the next test run."

Detecting her enthusiasm, Jason grinned and asked. "Then I assume the mycotoxin meshed with the genome okay?"

"It did just as we thought it would and today we've been able to prepare the aerosol. We don't have much of the genome but I believe there's enough to run a test with the rats."

"And you have some reserve of the genome?"

"Yes, there's sufficient to do other trials if needed. Walcott will want some of the new configuration if we're successful with our test, but we can reproduce it easily."

Jason said, "Let's do the run tomorrow. Maybe around ten in the morning."

Helga stood from behind the desk. "Good. That'll give us time to get set in the morning. Both Ingrid and I are too tired to do that now."

"I'll come soon after nine," Jason said, turning to go into the animal room and check the rats. He wanted the animals to be in good condition when they ran the trial.

The next morning they were ready at nine-forty-five, the animals in place and acclimated, the test hood firmly sealed and the air flow checked. Helga released the aerosol, the fine mist floating into all parts of the hood. The animals jerked up at the sound and the strange spray around them. Then they began to gasp, their small jaws opening and closing, pawing at their noses, their movements unsteady, then almost in unison, the five rats collapsed. After several spasms their bodies stilled and their eyes closed.

Helga, Ingrid and Jason waited and watched, remembering the false alarm in the early trial. After fifteen minutes none of the animals had moved after dropping to the floor of their cages.

Ingrid peered through the glass, her face pressing against the barrier. "I believe we've succeeded. They're not moving at all. You can tell they're no longer breathing."

Jason and Helga shook hands. "Yes, it's worked."

Jason said, "After the aerosol has completely dissipated, I'll take the rats to a pathologist in the Vet School. He can confirm for us they've died of pulmonary failure or if something else occurred."

"And I," Helga said, "will call Walcott. He'll want enough of the genome to test on primates to be certain it'll work on species other than rodents. Ingrid and I will get busy preparing sufficient sample to satisfy his needs and retain some should we need to run confirming tests."

Jason nodded agreement, but added, “Let’s store some in another place. I can fit a canister into the walk-in freezer in Biology.” Faculty in the department were assigned shelf space on a needs basis and, if required, small lockers in the huge freezer. Jason retained both types of storage for his various research projects and recalled he had sufficient room for another canister.

Then he asked, “Will Walcott send a plane to pick it up?”

Helga looked blank for a moment then said, “My guess is a military plane comes to Spencerville on a regular basis to change the troops at Crews, but Walcott will know.”

O’Hare phoned Jason just before eight the next morning. “I wanted to update you on our surveillance of Westlake and Riley. Last night they met with several other males in an old house on rural route 1629. There’s no house number or even a mail box. The detective has followed Westlake there on two other occasions and he believes Westlake may live there alone in spite of our thinking he had a wife and kids. Yesterday he followed Riley to the place and waited in nearby woods until others arrived. He intends to check it out today to ascertain if it’s a livable place, but the important thing is we know Riley and Westlake are in cahoots. And others are involved.”

“I suppose he couldn’t get close enough to overhear conversation?”

“No, it was too risky. The meeting went on for almost two hours with guys coming and going all the time. I’m guessing they’re planning their next venture.”

Jason asked. “Where did Riley and Westlake meet?”

“No doubt at the community college where both work.’”

“What’s next?”

“I don’t have the manpower to maintain a tail on either of them. And we can’t do anything about arresting them until they’re caught in a criminal act or we have more evidence they’re planning an act. Now they could tell us they were meeting for beers and poker. But one thing I’m considering is planting a recording device in the house. We could accomplish that during the day when no one is around. Maybe we can overhear the next session and figure out what they’re planning, if anything.”

“That sounds good to me,” Jason said. “Let me know how it goes.”

Jason walked to the window in the office, still thinking about the connection between Riley and Westlake. He fully expected another episode at the lab and made a mental note to alert the security person.

Chapter 21

President Snyder called Jason on the following Monday, the middle of April. “Dr. Spradlin, Dean Hawthorne will reveal in a news conference at four today his resignation to be effective at the end of Tuesday. I plan to immediately announce your appointment as Acting Dean effective Wednesday morning. Hawthorne will begin the process of vacating his office immediately after his pronouncement. You should be prepared to occupy the Dean’s office as soon as possible.”

Snyder continued. “I’ve talked over the situation with Vice-President Hayes and he’s in agreement with my decision about your interim appointment.”

Thinking about wounded feelings within Hawthorne’s immediate circle, Jason asked, “What about the Associate Deans? They’re going to be surprised and maybe irritated they were passed over.” He could envision working with a group of disgruntled associates determined to make his task as difficult as possible. And they would know more than he about the issues confronting the dean’s office.

“Vice-President Hayes will meet with them immediately after Hawthorne’s declaration. In fact, one of them may follow Hawthorne to Oregon and the second one who deals with undergraduate affairs likely would not anticipate moving up at this point in her career. Hayes tells me she’s only been in the slot for a few months.”

After the conversation Jason knew he had to do some things

immediately. He asked Audrey to send an e-mail calling a meeting of department faculty at four this afternoon. When she looked questionably at him, no doubt wondering about the short notice, he decided he had to tell her what was going to happen. They'd been through too many trials together to leave her wondering and then find out after all the faculty. And he knew she'd keep the information to herself.

Jason motioned for her to sit in the side chair, then said, "So you know what's going on, Dean Hawthorne is leaving the university and the President has asked me to serve as the Interim Dean starting Wednesday morning."

Her face blanched. "Oh, my. That means you'll no longer be here." She brushed mist from her eyes. After a moment, she stood, "Now I understand why the rush for a faculty meeting."

"As soon as that meeting starts, you may tell the other staff in the office."

"I will." She touched Jason's shoulder as she stood near him at the desk. He wanted to pull her close but shoved aside the inclination.

Then he called Kathryn at her office. He started. "Well, it's going to happen. Snyder called me a few minutes ago to confirm Hawthorne's leaving and my interim move to the dean's office."

"I'm not surprised except at the swiftness of the change."

"There's a lot to get done within the next few hours, but let's get together at lunch as usual."

"Faculty Club at noon."

Since Snyder's initial hint about the interim appointment, Jason had thought about the department head slot. Two or three faculty could do it well and keep Biology moving forward. He'd seriously considered Ben Ramsey, a reliable professor who took on numerous tasks for the department and everyone trusted his judgment. But he'd finally settled on first approaching Pamela Sturgis, a person with whom he'd worked on joint projects since his first year at State. He appreciated her intelligence and the level-headed approach she brought to problems. She been promoted to the rank of Professor two years ago, thus removing any notion she had not been productive in her position. And it was time for a qualified female to assume leadership roles. He called her and they settled on a one-thirty appointment. Then, thinking about his authority to act without clearing with an official above him, he mulled over the ramifications and grinned to himself. This appointment would constitute his first act as a dean.

Sturgis appeared at the appointed time, dressed in her usual creased slacks and matching blouse. She sat in the chair next to the desk and looked at Jason. She was taken aback when Jason revealed Hawthorne's pending announcement and his shift to the Dean's slot. But she was surprised more when he said, "I would like you to serve as the interim head of the department. I've thought about the various possibilities and I believe you're ready to take on this role. I realize it comes fast and the future is uncertain but I have confidence you can provide the essential leadership during this time of changes within the college and the department."

"And you'd like me to start immediately?"

Jason told her the timetable established by the President. "I'm to be in the Dean's office by Wednesday morning and you should plan to assume these duties at the same time. Of course, I'll be available to help wrap up any pending issues."

Sturgis examined her shoes for several seconds, then looked at Jason. "I appreciate your confidence. We've known each other for all the time I've been in Biology and you know me as well as anyone. And knowing how you operate, you've thought about this for some time."

"I've considered several faculty members, but I hope you'll agree to do this."

Sturgis smiled at her trusted colleague. "Will you be a candidate for the dean's position?"

"The President expects me to be but I'm on the fence about becoming a full-time administrator."

"And if you were a candidate and didn't get the job, would you like to return to the head's position?"

Jason ran a hand through his unruly hair. "That might depend on you and whether the faculty insists on a national search. If they did, I might come back to avoid that. But I'd not wish to replace you just as you settle into the responsibilities. I could return to a faculty position and be happy there."

Sturgis reached across the corner of the desk to take his hand and looked into his face. "Let's agree on this. I'll take on the interim position but you must promise to come back to the head's slot if the dean thing doesn't work out. I've been so pleased with the way Biology has gone since you became our leader and I'd not stand in your way if that's what it comes to. And I doubt I'll become so enamored with this administrative stuff, I'd desire to stay. "

"I'll agree with that approach, "Jason said, "but I'll give you the option of changing your mind if all the parts fall in place."

"When will you tell the faculty?"

"At the meeting scheduled for four today. The President plans to announce my interim appointment tomorrow morning. I wanted the faculty to know before it goes public."

Sturgis stood. "Jason, I guess I should thank you for this opportunity to try my hand at administration, but I may call on you for advice more than you wish."

"Any time, just call me." He stepped toward her to shake her hand but she moved even closer, hugged him, then turned away. Watching her leave the office he felt good and knew his judgment about her was correct. In his experience with her, she remained calm under all circumstances and would seek advice from trusted faculty colleagues as she felt the need. He remembered Snyder's comment about those who aspired to administrative roles but couldn't handle the nitty-gritty of the daily details, not to mention the big problems. Sturgis was not among those.

As Sturgis left the office the telephone rang. Helga was on the line to tell him Walcott wanted the genome sample put on the plane arriving on Friday morning.

"Can you have the amount he needs by then?" Making copies of the genome was a laborious task that required time and attention to detail.

"Yes, we can but it helps he doesn't want it in an aerosol form. He'll do that in the D.C. labs and then conduct tests on two or three primates at Fort Detrick."

Helga said, "I'm going to prepare sufficient as a backup and I intend to place some in an aerosol to learn how stable the mixture is. Once the Agency takes it for use in the field, no telling how long it will be retained before the actual use. If it's not stable, we have another problem."

Jason wanted Helga to learn about his next assignment from him rather than hear it through the grapevine or read it in the morning paper. He told her about the upcoming announcement from the President.

Helga gasped, "That's wonderful, but it's going to take you away from any research, isn't it?"

"Very likely, but I plan on completing the projects I have going, including this contract with the Agency."

Helga said, "You know, I've been so intent on doing this contract, I've not thought about my future. The Agency will not maintain this facility after we've completed the present assignment and I doubt I'd be welcome back in D.C. But if you know of something around the university that might fit with my background and experience, I'd like to apply. I've loved Spencerville and the local people have been wonderful to me." She paused then added, "And if that shouldn't work out, I'll begin applying to other universities. I'm sure I don't wish to return to a federal job."

Jason hadn't thought about Helga's future either, as it seemed not to be his concern, but there were always openings in the large university. It was a matter of locating the right one at the right time. "I'll make some calls in the next few days, Helga. I suspect there are possibilities." Helga could possibly fit Biology but he wanted to involve Pamela Sturgis in any decision affecting the department and he didn't want to make a commitment until they'd conferred. He dug out Helga's credentials and stuck the file in his briefcase intending to review those before raising the possibility with Pamela.

Jason had not looked forward to the meeting with the department faculty. Telling his colleagues he was moving to a new assignment could be difficult. They gathered in a large classroom assigned to Biology, their usual meeting site, on the first floor of Quincy. As they entered they were quietly conversing and debating the reason for the unusual session. No agenda had been circulated, a break from the usual.

Behind a table at the front of the room, Jason called the meeting to order immediately after the electronic bell signaling the start and close of class periods sounded the four o'clock time. All but three of the forty faculty were present and Jason knew two of those were away at scientific meetings.

He started by saying, "I've called you together to inform you that as we're meeting, Dean Hawthorne is holding a press conference to announce his resignation from State University to assume a presidential position in Oregon. His resignation is effective at the close of tomorrow." A few murmurs arose, but most of the faculty had little or no contact with the dean and were typically not affected by changes in administrators beyond the department level.

Jason continued, “President Snyder and Vice-President Hayes have asked me to serve as the interim dean while a search for a permanent replacement moves forward. I have agreed to do that with serious reservations as I have enjoyed my time as department head and as a faculty member in Biology.”

He waited until the murmurs had subsided. “To provide leadership in the department I have asked Dr. Pamela Sturgis to act as head until all these administrative upheavals are settled. She has agreed and her appointment is effective Wednesday morning, the same time I assume the dean’s duties. All of you know her and respect her. I trust you will support her as she assumes the leadership role.

“I realize this all comes as a surprise to you and I ask that you continue your usual responsibilities in the way you have performed them in the past. Remember your teaching and research are the most important facets of the department. Those should not be forgotten in the midst of these changes.”

A hand went up as Jason seemed to wind down. Ben Ramsey said, “Will you become a candidate for the dean job?”

Jason shrugged and responded. “I have no idea at this time. I haven’t even found the office yet, so to speak.” A few quiet laughs followed his attempt to insert some levity into the situation.

Ramsey continued, “I for one hope you will and provide the same leadership for the college you have given Biology. And I intend to give Pamela my full support.” A chorus of voices seconded Ben’s promise. A sensation of pleasure rose up in Jason as he knew choosing Sturgis had been a correct decision.

Another voice from the back of the room. "I assume you will close out your research projects?"

"I will," Jason said. "It has become increasingly difficult to maintain currency with the technological and scientific changes from my present position and it will be impossible to do so with increased administrative responsibilities. I will discuss projects with some of you in the next few days to determine any interest in picking up those lines. And in certain cases there are natural inheritors because you are a co-investigator. Then I will get out of your way."

George Stuart, the senior member of the faculty and retiring at the end of the academic session stood in the middle of the room. "Jason, I think I speak for all of us when I tell you we have been most grateful for your efforts on behalf of this department as well as for each of us individually. You have made us all better. Our students are served better than before and we have all become engaged in worthwhile research or service projects. I thank you for all you have done and wish you well in whatever direction you take in the future." Applause started in the back rows and spread throughout the room. Then everyone stood.

Jason walked to the front of the table. "Thanks to each of you. I never realized how eager you were to see me get off your backs." Laughter broke out and people began to move about.

Jason said, "This meeting is adjourned and again, thanks to all."

Most of the faculty came forward to shake his hand and wish him well in a personal way. He and Pamela were the last ones to leave the room. She said, her hand on his arm, "That went well. Now if I can live up to the standards you've set the department will be okay."

"You will. I have great confidence in you."

"And I wish you the best in this new venture, especially since I'll be reporting to you."

From his office just before five he called Hawthorne who invited him over for a short chat. Hawthorne was removing the last vestiges of his lengthy presence in the office. Outlines of pictures and plaques showed on the walls where light had faded the surroundings. Boxes were stacked along one wall. On the desk top Hawthorne's briefcase seemed filled to overflowing.

They shook hands and Jason said, "I wish you good luck with your new position, but I don't look forward to following you."

"Hayes told me just before you called. You'll do well once you get past some hurt feelings of those department heads with longer tenure than you. But ignore that and move forward. Hayes will give you good advice if you need it."

Jason asked, "Any pressing matters I should be aware of before you leave?"

Hawthorne shook his head. "None I'm aware of. We're past the tenure battles and the budget issues for the year, both of which require inordinate amounts of time. No doubt there'll be new appointments to consider but for the most part department heads have made good decisions." He closed a box and placed it on the stack near the door.

"What about the Associate Deans? Will they accept this new person okay?"

"They both know you and there should not be problems. Hayes may have told you that Jensen is coming with me but will remain here through this academic year. Jane Pearson is relatively new at her job and is doing well. The support staff is stable and competent. Your secretary, Bridget Dawson, has been here for several years and knows the ropes. She will keep you on schedule and out of trouble."

Hawthorne looked around the space he'd occupied for years, then opened the desk drawer and pulled out keys on a metal ring. "Here are keys to the office, the outside door for the building, and file cabinets in case you need to get into things over weekends or evenings. Bridget can show you the system of filing which I never figured out myself.

"I'll be around tomorrow, but need to clear with personnel questions related to insurance, retirement, unused leave days, who knows what else. If you need me, Bridget will know how to find me. Movers will get these boxes out of your way in the morning." Hawthorne moved toward the door. Jason followed into the outer suite. They shook hands and Hawthorne left through the front door, leaving Jason alone in surroundings he visited numerous times. But the situation had shifted dramatically.

The next two days became a blur. On Tuesday evening with Kathryn's help, he moved his personal things from the Biology office to the dean's office. Knowing they had to cross a quadrangle, Jason borrowed a cart from his lab and loaded it to the brim, then gingerly rolled it through the backdoor of Quincy, down a handicap ramp, along bumpy sidewalks until they reached Gallagher Hall, up an elevator to the second floor and into the suite. Most of his journals and files could be moved by campus crews on Wednesday or Thursday.

With her help and advice he decided where to position pictures. He dropped into the desk chair then realized he needed to adjust it to accommodate his size. The desk drawers were bare until he began placing pens and other things in places he would locate easily.

On Wednesday morning he was the first in the office. Soon Bridget arrived bringing a stack of papers to be signed.

She said, “Dr. Spradlin, welcome. I look forward to working with you. Audrey has told me how the two of you functioned and how much she hates to see you leave Biology.”

Jason stood to shake her hand. “Don’t change anything until I figure out the way you operate. I can adjust as needed.

The day went quickly as well-wishers came by to congratulate him on his appointment and perhaps to size him up in this new role. He signed several papers following the guidance of Bridget and the accounting staff. No major problems arose the first morning.

After lunch with Kathryn at a campus diner, he went to the lab on 29th Street. Helga and Ingrid were engrossed in replicating the genome and preparing a portion in an aerosol. Helga stopped her work and came toward him. “We’re moving along pretty well, no snags thus far. And Walcott phoned to confirm a military plane would be here Friday afternoon to pick up samples. I’ll make sure they get to the airport on time.”

Helga pointed to a canister on the desk. “That’s the sample you wanted to stash in Biology. Just so you know, I think that’s a good idea with all these break ins and bombings. I’d hate to lose all our supply.”

“If you’re set and don’t need my help, I’ll take this container. It’ll be stored in a locker I still have in the Biology walk-in freezer. If you need to get to it when I'm not available, the technician in my research lab will help."

Chapter 22

Friday morning in the Dean's office, Jason confronted a continuing stream of visitors, some wishing him well, others bringing problems to the new guy with the hope he might be more understanding than his predecessor. The department head of Psychology came in with a complaint from a faculty accusing the administration of short changing him for travel funds.

Patterson, the head, said, "I promised to bring this to your attention although Hawthorne had denied his request for support to attend a meeting in an exotic location during the summer session."

Jason listened, then asked, "Did you support him and do you have funds in your budget?"

"I turned him down but he wasn't satisfied and raised the issue with the Dean who sent it back to me. I don't have funds to send him off on a trip that seems to be more pleasure than business, but he insisted you review the situation."

"Is he presenting a paper or chairing a panel?"

"Nothing. He just thinks we should support him to do whatever he pleases."

Jason shook his head. "I see no reason to go against your judgment. My policy is going to be if the head can't approve the request, neither will I." He acknowledged to himself there might be unusual situations he could break from that guideline, if he thought the faculty was being held back by a head who for some reason didn't approve of the actions.

Jason watched Patterson leave, suspecting the head couldn't be strong enough in his argument with a disgruntled faculty member looking for a travel perk at the expense of the university. Or maybe Patterson was playing some game with the new administrator. He remembered Henry Rogers telling him about such antics.

During an hour period in which there were no scheduled appointments, Jason left the office and walked Helga's file over to Biology. While walking he accepted he could have saved time by mailing the dossier with a note, but he wanted to give it personally to Pamela. He found Sturgis in the department head office and rapped softly on the door frame after he'd spoken to Audrey.

Pamela looked up from a stack of papers, smiled and said, "So you're back already." She started to rise, but he waved her back. He sat in the chair next to the desk, another acknowledgement of his changing role..

"That might be a good idea. The college office is very different than this one and the problems seem strange, although I've had only a couple thus far. But the reason I dropped in was to pass this credential file to you." He told her about Helga, her background and experience with the Agency labs near D.C. and her desire to locate a position at State.

Sturgis flipped through the first pages of Helga's file. "Why did she leave the Agency? That would seem like a secure position."

"Under strange circumstances from my perspective. She violated a rule about not seeking advice from colleagues under an administrator who demanded everything be secret, even among co-workers. Another scientist verified her story and after working with the Agency people and dealing with the Deputy Director who fired her, I can easily believe her."

Pamela asked, "Have you found her easy to work with and can she function independently?"

"She's actually been the leader of this work at the 29th Street lab, although the Agency holds me responsible. I'd have no problem recommending Helga Grimes to anyone. My feeling is she can tackle most problems related to genetics. And I believe she would be a competent instructor. She's bright, organized and articulate."

Turning another page in the dossier, Pamela said, "I see she taught beginning biology while a grad assistant at Hopkins. So she has some experience in the classroom."

Seeming to wait for the downside, Pamela continued to look at him for several seconds. Then she said, "What would you think of putting her in my position for the coming months. I have several research projects and will need assistance. Then when all these administrative issues are resolved, we could likely locate another slot for her. In fact, I could try her in a section of beginning biology next fall term." She grinned and added. "That's where we all begin."

"I'm sure she'd agree to that. And probably by the end of fall semester, we'll know the outcome of the search process."

"Let's do it," Pamela decided. "And you probably recall, Biology will have two vacancies after next year because of a retirement and a tenure denial. She could apply for those. And by then we'll have a solid perspective of her capabilities in the classroom and the genetics research lab."

Jason stood from the chair next to the desk he'd occupied for four years, still feeling a bit disoriented in the side chair. "I'll have her come in next week to talk with you. I won't promise her anything, but will let you decide after you've met with her."

Pamela stood. "I appreciate that. You know, most former heads would just make the decision and let the new person live with it."

The Friday beer club met as usual with Riley the first one present on a sunny spring- like day. By the time the other three walked in, he'd consumed one-third of his stein. As they pulled out chairs, he said, "What's up? I thought for a minute you weren't coming today." No evidence of his snit at the last session manifested itself in his friendly demeanor.

Townsend dropped into a seat and pulled his pipe from his pocket. He glanced at his watch. "We're here at the usual time. You're early. Must be thirsty."

After beers were ordered, Harris said, "I guess you saw in the paper about Hawthorne leaving and Spradlin taking the interim job."

Riley wiped his mouth with a paper napkin. "I did. So you guys have him out of your hair or at least one level removed."

"We're not so sure it's a good thing for us," Townsend said, 'but he will do the dean thing okay."

Pierson, who seldom spoke in the group, said, "I saw his wife last week in King's lab. She must be about five or six months pregnant, wearing maternity outfits. But she still looked beautiful."

Townsend changed the subject. "So Riley, how's the community college scene? You about through for the year?"

"Another week of classes, then exams. But it's a snap compared to the university. Just go to class, give your lectures, and you're free for the rest of the day. No hassle about research projects, getting grants, that kind of crap. And the students are good. Most of them are working part-time and taking classes to improve their job skills or qualify for admission to the university."

"So you must get bored," Harris said.

"There are always things to do. I've met a lot of people not associated with State since I left the faculty." He paused as though considering his next comment. "I'm meeting with this group who are planning a big operation soon. It'll shake up the old town. Get everybody's attention, especially Spradlin." He sipped from his beer and looked at his buddies, waiting for their reaction.

Pierson asked. "What do you mean?"

"I can't tell you more, but you'll know when it happens." Riley's smirk suggested the coming event would get media coverage and more.

Harris wanted to press Riley into revealing his big secret but then decided he didn't want to know. As far as he knew his telling Spradlin about Riley before hadn't gone anywhere. Why bother and only irritate Riley.

But he said, "You guys should know I'm getting married again in June to Janet Webster, the woman you've seen me with in here. She's tenured in Sociology and is doing well in her profession. I think this will work out good for both of us."

The others offered congratulations but wondered if a new marriage would truly cure Harris from trying to hit on other women. But none wished to raise the issue and the conversation moved on to rumors of events around the university and the city, the coming summer break, and the opening games of the major league baseball season.

Harris left the session before the others with his thought on Riley's statement. He accepted Riley would do almost anything to damage Spradlin and his inner being told him to warn Jason. But he didn't know enough to get his attention. He just hoped the big thing Riley was connected to didn't end up damaging Spradlin or his family. He could speculate the 'thing' was associated with the 29th Street lab but it seemed insufficient to chase Jason down and warn him. In addition, Jason no doubt had a full plate with the dean's position. As he walked along Main Street toward the parking lot, he thought more about his relationship to Jason over the years. His last meeting suggested it had taken a turn for the better. He'd been turned off by Jason's warning about his trying to seduce a graduate assistant, but Spradlin had been nothing but professional in their dealings since then. He'd actually come to admire the manner in which Jason operated.

At about the same time as the beer group was meeting, the military transport arrived at the Spencerville airport. While Helga waited for the co-pilot to meet her, six soldiers came off and four boarded, all young looking and loaded with packs, representing the continuous exchange of troops as they moved to new assignments, perhaps to some war zone where their lives would be in danger every day. Helga transferred the package containing a freeze-dried sample of the toxic genome to the young looking airman who was expecting it as he strode rapidly to meet her.

The aviator asked, “Any special precautions? We were alerted it could be dangerous material.”

“Just keep it in the sealed container and you’ll be okay. But if something drastic happens and the seal is broken, get away and stay away. It’s not lethal in the form you have unless you ingest it or somehow get it into your body.”

He turned toward the plane. “We’ll be careful.” He seemed to handle the package more carefully after Helga’s instructions and warnings.

She waited until the plane departed, a sense of relief washing over her, mixed with a feeling of accomplishment. Now she’d hoped the toxin would be effective with primates and she could move on with her life. During the afternoon she’d contemplated calling Jason to remind him of her need to find employment, but she restrained herself, thinking it would border on nagging. Nevertheless, she hoped he wouldn’t forget in the midst of all the turmoil in his life. She smiled to herself as she thought he seemed never to forget.

Kathryn and Jason had looked forward to their coming ‘date night’ and had planned to have dinner at a long-established restaurant in a nearby town, although it would require a thirty minute drive. Renaldo’s had a reputation for excellent food and an elegant atmosphere. And it would not be filled with university people wanting to offer congratulations to Jason and, in some cases, attempt to get his ear about some personal concern.

Jason had decided this might be the best time to give her the necklace he'd purchased in D. C. and had been hiding in his sock drawer, hoping she would not go roaming around in the pile. He watched her as she pulled on the black silk maternity dress sent by her father after he'd learned of her pregnancy. As she deliberated over the appropriate jewelry, he walked over to her, touched on the shoulder and said, "How about this one?"

She looked carefully at the necklace, laid it on the dresser to see how it looked when fully extended. She turned to him and pulled him close, not concerned about wrinkling the dress or messing her hair. They arranged the piece with Jason doing the hook at the back. They turned to look in the mirror. The gold necklace and pendant looked elegant, the perfect fit with the dress.

She fingered the piece on her throat. "You always surprise me at the most unusual times. I'd never dreamed you'd think of something during all the stuff you've been through." She leaned against him and put her arms around his neck. He held her close, caressing her back through the silk fabric, and nuzzled her neck, then said, "We'd better keep moving or we'll not make our dinner appointment."

She pulled away. 'That might be okay. We could get a burger later at McDonalds."

The restaurant lived up to all the promises. They enjoyed the food, danced a couple of times as the pianist shifted from jazz to some of the slower rhythms that suited Jason better than the fast tunes. Over coffee and dessert, Kathryn said, “This worked out wonderfully well. I’m glad you found this place.”

The maitre’d appeared at their table. “Dr. Spradlin, you’ve a telephone call. I can bring an extension to the table or you can come to the desk.”

Jason looked at Kathryn, shrugged his shoulders. “I have no idea unless there’s a problem with one of the kids. I left this number with Mrs. Carter just in case.” He followed the host to the desk.

To his surprise, it was O’Hare. “Dr. Spradlin, I’m sorry to bother you while you’re at dinner, but there’s been a major disruption at the lab on 29th. Chief Hayden called me forty-five minutes ago. It took me a bit to track you down as your housekeeper was reluctant to tell me where you were. She said these nights were almost sacred but she relented when I suggested it was urgent.”

Jason’s mind was racing at the probabilities. “How bad is it?”

“I’ve just come from there. I’d describe it as a disaster of the first order. I don’t know much about the equipment, but most pieces have been smashed.”

“What about the guard? Where was he?”

“At the moment he’s on the way to the hospital via ambulance. The best we could tell from his rather incoherent statements, he made his round just after seven-thirty, decided everything was quiet and under control, went for a burger at the restaurant down the street. When he returned just after eight, men were waiting for him inside the building. The hit him across the head, knocked him around pretty good until he passed out. When he came to, the vandals had gone but the place had been trashed."

"What about the alarm? Did they trigger it?"

"Apparently they knew how to cut it off. It never rang in the Spencerville station."

Jason said, "I'm out of town but can get back in an hour. I'll go by the place but it sounds like there's nothing I can do tonight."

"The city has stationed patrols around the lab but they will expect you. I believe the leader knows who you are and will allow you to enter. But as you'd know from experience, we'd like you not to move anything or even touch broken equipment until the forensics people have had a look."

"I understand. I'll talk to you later, Tom, probably tomorrow morning."

Back at the table, Kathryn's initial question was, "Trouble?" She had shoved her dessert aside and was sipping decaffeinated coffee.

He summarized O'Hare's message for her, his thoughts swirling about what to do next and who was responsible. He tried to focus on finishing his dessert and coffee, but the pressure to get going overwhelmed any desire for food.

"Thank goodness, it's not one of the kids," Jason said, "but the lab has been trashed again. And it sounds like this time, they really did a thorough job of it."

He drained his cool coffee in one large gulp and stood. "I'll need to go by there, but before I leave here, I'm going to call Helga. She will be better able to assess the damage than I."

Kathryn stood and took his hand. “She’s probably in bed.”

“I know and we should be.”

“You’re right. Remember your promise.”

He circled her waist as they moved toward the front door. “I’ll make it up to you.”

Helga was waiting at the entrance when Jason arrived just before midnight. She came toward him. “They wouldn’t let me in until you arrived.”

The patrol leader, a long-time city policeman whom Jason had met previously, permitted them to enter the front door, but warning them not to touch or move anything. They stepped gingerly over and around shattered glassware, pieces of small equipment, and broken parts of the lab benches. Each of the signs warning about biological hazardous materials had been ripped off or marred with a sharp instrument.

Helga said, “They didn’t miss anything. Everything has been damaged in some way, much of it beyond repair.”

“It’s obvious they came prepared with heavy malls, hammers, and cutting tools.”

In the animal room the metal cages had been battered and bent by a heavy force. The steel racks were overturned. Water bottles and feeding dishes were broken and scattered on the floor. Even the mops and brooms had been broken, handles snapped in two pieces.

In the controlled lab the reverse air hood had been attacked, the sash broken off the hinges, the glass shattered. They were unable to tell if the air system had been damaged, but chances were it had.

Helga peered into the large freezer that had been locked but now the doors hung loosely with the hinges broken. Suddenly her mouth gaped open, she shook her head in disbelief. Turning to Jason she said, almost a whisper, "The canisters containing the toxic samples have been taken."

Chapter 23

Jason knew immediately the missing toxins posed a serious problem. If some fool broke the seal on the aerosol canister, people would be killed. Even the freeze dried sample could become lethal if mishandled, the nitrogen released, a bit of water from the atmosphere could potentially result in a deadly toxin permeating the air for a brief period. The typical vandal wouldn't know enough to avoid tampering. He could envision them cracking open the containers out of sheer curiosity as though they'd discovered gold when in fact they were confronting death.

He turned to Helga. "What should we do? My first thought is to notify radio and television stations to broadcast warnings about the dangers of these containers, but that lets the public in on the secrecy of this work."

Still stunned over the development, Helga shook her head. "I'd like to call Walcott for his advice, but I hate doing that in the middle of the night."

"We shouldn't wait until morning to contact him. I'd like the media to issue warnings first thing in the morning before people are moving about, on their way to work, children headed for school, university students and faculty on their way to classes and labs. Even that could be too late but I think it's the best we can hope for."

They edged back toward the front door, avoiding the rubble on the floor. Jason said, "Let's go to my office and call Walcott. And I'm going to call O'Hare. He might have ideas."

He nodded to the patrol leader as they passed. "Thanks for letting us in. We'll have to think about what to do about the mess."

"You could burn the entire building."

Jason smiled at his attempted humor in the midst of chaos. "That may be the best thing to do."

In his recently occupied office in Gallagher Hall, Jason used the phone at his desk. Helga took an instrument at Bridget's desk in the college suite, careful not to disturb the files and stacks of papers on the desk top.

Jason called O'Hare at his home. After several rings, a groggy O'Hare muttered, "What's up?" No doubt his usual response to calls in the middle of the night from some patrol having problems with students on or near campus.

"Tom, Jason Spradlin. Sorry to wake you. This is the night to interrupt everyone's schedule, but I have a major problem." He told him quickly about the missing toxins and the potential danger, then asked, "You have advice?"

O'Hare didn't respond immediately as he considered the implications of an issue coming at him in the middle of the night as he struggled to come fully alert. "I'd get the media to alert the public of the danger. The radio stations probably have someone there all night and could arrange to air the message within minutes. But I think the TV people, except for some technical staff, close down around midnight. I'd call them around five-thirty or six in the morning. They'll all cooperate by doing public service announcements."

"My other concern is this will blow the secrecy of the entire operation, but we're contacting officials at the Agency also for their input and clearance on next moves. It's one of these deals that whatever you do is going to result in some kind of problem."

"I understand, but I'd err on the side of caution when lives are in danger. People need to be warned of the dangers and told how to respond in case they are near those guys and the packages."

"I'll talk to you in the morning. By then we'll know what the Agency wants us to do. Go back to sleep."

Jason replaced the receiver and walked around the office. He could hear Helga on the other line. Her elevated voice suggested she was not happy with the progress of the conversation.

Two minutes later, Helga came in. "As you heard I reached Walcott. His advice is do nothing. Take a chance nothing will happen. He's taking the view because of the warnings signs in the building the vandals will realize the possible danger and not tamper with the canisters. But as you might guess his primary concern is revealing the development of the weapon. That would damage or destroy all the efforts and expense expended in preparing a secret device."

"I'm not surprised by his stance," Jason said, "but I can envision innocent people being killed if these nuts tear open that aerosol sample in or near a public place. And they might well do that in trying to impress others or they have no idea as to the contents." He could envision Riley in his bluster ripping open the package to demonstrate what he knew.

"I pressed Walcott pretty hard about our concern. He stood by his initial advice but did promise to call Johnson and maybe the Director of the Agency. He'll try to get back to us by mid-morning at my home number or at this office."

"I hope he can find those guys on the weekend."

"He will. They all have mandates to always be available, but he may have some tracking to do."

Jason paced more, frustrated he could not move forward with the media. He could see small kids lying on the floor, dead as a result of some nut letting the aerosol loose in a household. But his hands were tied by the Agency. He dared not go against their orders or he'd be in deep trouble with the feds. He thought about calling Congressman Wilke early Monday morning although he didn't want to go around the Agency leaders. He decided he'd think more about that possibility in the light of another day.

Helga was experiencing the same turmoil. She looked at Jason, then finally said, "Jason, let's go home. Maybe we can get a couple hours of rest before we're forced to act by the Agency."

"You're right. No need to linger here." And he knew Kathryn would be concerned about him. He wanted her to maintain a sensible regimen as the pregnancy progressed and refrain from worrying about him and his hectic schedule. He wanted to get home and reassure her he was okay. Pacing the floor and worrying about him were not the things he wanted her to do.

The front page of the Monday morning edition of the *Herald* led with a huge headline: **FEDERAL LABORATORY DESTROYED**.

The article accompanied by graphic photographs of the lab, provided solid testimony as to what had occurred in the late hours of Saturday. The writer detailed the damages, speculated about the purpose of the facility, and wondered about the rationale of those who succeeded in destroying the recently renovated laboratory. In closing, Chief Hayden was quoted as promising a full investigation. He hinted there were plausible leads to be followed.

Jason, relieved names of investigators had not been released, scanned the article as he finished coffee at the breakfast table, then turned his attention to helping the kids organize their backpacks for school. He wondered if all the books and materials were necessary for elementary school children and how long before they'd experience back troubles. He hoped there'd be a communication from Walcott by the time he reached the office. He decided to have a second cup of coffee as he struggled to become fully awake.

But they didn't hear from the Agency until mid-morning Monday when Johnson called Jason.

Johnson started by reminding Jason of the need for utmost secrecy about the weapon development. "Walcott and I met this morning with Director Huffington to review the situation and have agreed we should not release any information to the public. Any tidbit will spur the press to dig deeper until they discover what's really going on. In addition, there was some fear that informing the vandals what they really possess might encourage them to use the weapon against a government facility and the people who work there."

Jason broke in. "We're concerned about innocent lives, Director Johnson. Doesn't that trump the secrecy issue?"

"Not from our perspective," Johnson said. "Those idiots should know better than to tear into a place with warning signs prominently placed where no one could miss them."

"It's not the vandals I'm worried about, but ordinary citizens who happen to be in the wrong place at the wrong time."

Johnson's tone calmed a bit. "I understand your feelings and we debated the potential for a major disaster but our need for secrecy prevailed. Let's take our chances, Dr. Spradlin."

Jason wanted to argue his position more, but knew he'd be wasting his efforts to persuade Johnson who could be doing nothing more than reflecting the views of those above him. He was concerned the bureaucrats failed to comprehend the dangers involved and that neither Johnson nor Walcott was able to convince them to take a different stance.

Jason called Helga at her home to pass along the message and suggested she remain at home until a decision about the future of the lab had been reached. She had already informed Ingrid of the situation.

Then he called O'Hare. "Tom, any breakthrough?"

"Nothing yet. Patrols have been trying to locate Riley and Westlake, the primary suspects, but to no avail. Soon after the incident was discovered Saturday night Chief Hayden sent detectives to the place they've sighted Westlake previously, but the place was dark and apparently deserted. No cars around. No one has been seen there. And it's so isolated, neighbors are too far away to notice anything short of a parade of vehicles."

"Did Riley or Westlake show for work today?"

"We checked around nine. Neither had come into the community college by that time. We found an address for Riley, an apartment in the basement of a residence on Sycamore but he isn't there. The owner of the house hasn't seen him since Saturday morning when Riley drove away in his Toyota truck."

"Is there a possibility they're delivering these containers to some terrorist group for a huge payoff?"

"I wouldn't think so, but it's the kind of thing you'd expect from a group out to undermine the government. They tend to forget the potential consequences in their quest for money or to satisfy their desire to damage this country."

Jason said, "But that doesn't sound like Riley. He just wants to hurt people in authority over him or make them look bad in the eyes of others. I've never suspected him of being anti-American or having the courage to deliberately kill anyone."

"But Westlake may have brain washed him or Riley can't control what Westlake and his group want to do."

"My own suspicion is they're holed up somewhere and will wait until the pressure subsides to make some move—maybe threaten to release the toxin to a rogue group or blackmail the U.S. into some goal they hope to achieve."

"Could be you're right. Anyway, we'll keep looking until we find some clue that will tell us what they're planning or until we locate them."

Jason had difficulty focusing on the tasks at hand in his new position. He met with a couple of younger faculty who had just received tenure and were seeking his permission to organize a new university-wide center for the purpose of investigating approaches to attack the global warming problem. They both seemed bright and had ideas about beginning steps, traits he admired in those around him. He encouraged them to develop a brief proposal and have it reviewed by department heads and perhaps the Research Office before creating a full blown proposal to be sent to some agency. They seemed to have no idea of who might be interested in supporting the idea but Jason promised he'd help them find either an agency or a foundation with potential interest. He knew from his own experience the university couldn't afford to put much money into the project. He didn't want to discourage them but he tried to insert some realism into their dreams.

The investigation became more complicated on Tuesday morning when the same two agents who'd initiated Jason's involvement with the contract appeared at his office. Feller and Sparks shook Jason's hand, asked how he was, putting on a friendly face for an acquaintance or co-conspirator. Jason invited them to chairs at a conference table and offered coffee which they declined.

With the greetings behind them, Feller said, "We've been sent by Deputy Director Johnson to investigate this disaster at the lab. We know the local authorities have been probing leads, but we've been assigned the task to broaden the search, arrest the perpetrators, and bring them to justice."

Jason nodded at their optimism and responded. "You should talk with Chief Hayden of Spencerville and Detective O'Hare from the university. They know the details of what they've done thus far and what leads have not gone anywhere. There's no need to cover the same ground."

Sparks asked, "What can you tell us?"

Jason figured they would compare his story to those of Hayden and O'Hare but he related everything he'd been privy to, including the disappearance of the deadly toxins and his concern for the safety of innocents who might inadvertently wander into the wrong place.

Sparks continued in the lead. "And they've put lookouts at this Westlake's house?"

"That's my understanding," Jason said. "Thus far, no one has appeared there since the break in."

"Have they obtained a warrant to search the place as well as the apartment of this Riley character? Sometimes these guys leave clues about their intent and even their plans after the deed has been done."

"Yes. O'Hare called me late yesterday. They had obtained search warrants and intended to enter both places this morning."

Feller stood suddenly. "We need to be in on that. Let's go, Sparks, and meet O'Hare." They charged out as though the last plane were leaving for the moon.

Just before noon, O'Hare phoned. "Jason, I wanted to update you on our investigation although we really know nothing more than we did yesterday."

"Did those security agents guys catch up with you?"

"They were waiting on the street when we got to Riley's apartment. Basically they want to take charge and argue this was a federal facility thus it's a federal matter. Of course, Hayden and I objected and after debating the issue a while, we agreed to cooperate. But the Feds will take any credit for an arrest if we get that far."

"You don't sound optimistic about an arrest?"

O'Hare's restrained laugh revealed his frustration and perhaps his weariness. "We struck out at Riley's place although we took his computer to have our tech guys check it out. There may be something on his hard drive worth following up on."

"What about Westlake's place? Have you gone in there?"

"We scoured it after we'd finished at Riley's. It's a ramshackle place and as best we can tell, he lives there alone. No evidence of another person. Only clothes and meager belongings for a single male. And again, nothing to suggest his involvement or intentions related to the lab."

"Did Westlake have a computer. He's been communicating with someone about this lab."

"None in his place, but he might have used one at the college. We'll need to check that out."

"What's next? Have you exhausted leads?"

"Nothing obvious jumps out, but the federal agents intend to talk with acquaintances and co-workers of both Riley and Westlake, starting with co-workers at the community college. It may provide another idea worth pursuing, but time is running out if we're to prevent a disaster with those toxins."

"Unless they didn't know what they had and just dumped the containers somewhere."

O'Hare closed out the conversation. "But not likely. Riley would know enough to make an intelligent guess just based on the Agency sponsorship and the secrecy around the lab."

Jason hung up the phone, acknowledging O'Hare had a valid point. Maybe he was trying to avoid the obvious and his friend, the detective who'd seen a lot of bizarre behavior during his career, wouldn't go along.

His afternoon schedule was crowded, but now he was headed for the quadrangle bordering Gallagher to meet Kathryn, always a bright spot in his day.

Chapter 24

Jason tried to focus on administrative responsibilities, the documents requiring his attention and signature and several visitors to the office during the afternoon, but his mind remained fixed on the potential fallout from the lab break in. As the office door closed behind the staff leaving for the day at five and the office became eerily quiet, O'Hare phoned.

The university detective sounded excited, his voice more animated than usual. "Jason, we have a promising lead. Sparks and Feller have been interviewing co-workers of Westlake. One of them, a mechanic at the community college, knows about a hunting cabin used by Westlake and his buddies during the open seasons. In addition, Westlake invites buddies there for weekends of drinking and card playing when the weather is warm. He guessed if Westlake wanted to disappear, that would be the place. This co-worker has been there for a deer hunt and it's very isolated with only a crude trail the last five hundred yards. There's a parking area among a group of trees where this trail begins."

"Is someone checking it out now?"

"Hayden and I are sending deputies up there now. Westlake's buddy from work volunteered to show them the way. We should know something later tonight. I'll give you a call if it goes anywhere. At the present I wanted to make you aware and to be alert for any call later."

"I've promised I'd go with Kathryn to a function at Jennifer's school, but that should conclude no later then eight. After that, I'll be at home all evening."

But as he cut the connection, he thought the lead would go nowhere. Why would the vandals scurry to an isolated destination with deadly toxins? Surely if they had a potential buyer or intended to use the weapon themselves, they would have planned that ahead of the break in. Or, maybe Riley alerted them to the potential of the toxins after the destruction of the lab and now they were trying to decide their next move. And, maybe they'd snatched the canisters with no idea of the danger and no plan for their disposal. Bottom line, nothing made logical sense.

He and Kathryn sat in the fourth row of parents, grandparents, aunts, uncles and neighbors, some nodding, their eyes closing, others smiling, as the third grade class displayed their budding talents on the stage, reenacting the well known fable, *Goldilocks and the Three Bears.* Jason watched his daughter in the lead role of the small girl invading the homes of the animals and her reactions to meeting the irate bears. It was one of those rare occasions now that he was reminded of Lucy as Jennifer increasingly had taken on the emerging adult appearance of her mother. Everyone clapped at the end as the would-be actors and actresses took their bows, no doubt pleased the ordeal had passed without major problems. But throughout the performance, Jason's mind veered to the search going on in some remote cabin and hoping this could bring closure to the festering issue of the missing vandals and the potential dangers of the lethal toxins. He could not erase images of those toxins being released into a crowded neighborhood or public gathering with the resulting death of scores of innocent people.

As they waited for Jennifer in the rear of the school auditorium, Kathryn grasped his hand. "Stop worrying. O'Hare will let you know as soon as he knows something worth reporting."

Jason squeezed her fingers. "So you could tell my brain was elsewhere?"

She leaned against him. "Of course, I know. But I have news you haven't dreamed about yet. I'll tell you after we're home and the children are in bed."

"Is it good? I need something upbeat for a change."

"You'll have to decide but I'm pleased."

"If you're pleased, I'll be happy."

An hour later, Jennifer and Tony had donned their pajamas and lasted through Kathryn's reading of a story before dropping off to sleep. Jason's watching of a rerun of one of the CSI series was interrupted when Kathryn sat on the couch next to him, her shoulders touching his, her hand taking his, then taking the remote from the coffee table and darkening the TV. He placed his arm around her shoulders and pulled her close.

Kathryn said, "Now, the big news I have."

The smile disappeared from her face. She focused on his face. "As you know, I had a routine appointment with the gynecologist this afternoon. After she'd done the usual checks, she said, "I think we'd better confirm with an MRI what I suspect. So we did that and she came back into the examining room to announce that I was going to deliver twins."

Jason twisted to look into her face, covered in a wide smile, her eyes bright. “Is she certain?” You don’t seem to have gained that much weight.”

“Dr. Ames was positive about the results of the test. And she’s reasonably sure both are healthy. She wants me to come back in two weeks for a confirming set of tests.”

“Wow, this will change our lives for sure.” He stood and paced around the room for a couple of minutes, his eyes coming back to Kathryn’s face.

Returning to the sofa, Jason said, “This means we should begin to search for a next Mrs. Carter. Twins will be too much if you continue to work.” He laughed. “Maybe we should both take a year off.”

Her smile disappeared. “I’ve thought about it more since we last talked. I’ve considered dropping out of the profession until they begin school. But five or six years out of circulation would mean starting over, not to mention I’d be so out of date I’d probably never catch up with the field.”

“Dropping out completely is not a good idea. But let’s talk with Mrs. Carter tomorrow or wait until the confirming tests come back. She might have ideas about a replacement.”

As she started to respond , the telephone rang. Jason grabbed it by the second ring, hoping it had not jarred the kids awake.

O’Hare was on the line. “Dr. Spradlin, I promised to get back to you tonight, although I don’t have much to share.”

“But you found the cabin?”

“Yes, as he said, this co-worker knew the way, but it was dark by the time we arrived. Using the flashlights we had, we weren't able to see much except it's a large rectangular room with a wood-burning stove at one end, several assorted wooden chairs, three cots folded against one wall, a table in the middle of the room— just what you'd expect in a lodge meant for roughing it for a couple of nights. But Sparks and Feller are going back in the morning. They've obtained a warrant to enter and look for any evidence of Westlake and his cronies having been there lately. If not, we've run out of clues as to where to look next."

"Any signs of a car having been around the place recently?"

"None. And remember it rained the day before the break in, so it would have been soft enough to leave tracks. I think they went somewhere else but we'll keep looking for possibilities."

"Or until they contact us about the toxins." He didn't say, but thought, or until they use it against some group hostile to their beliefs, including people around the university who'd worked on the weapon. And, knowing Riley's history of damaging Jason at every opportunity, he and his family could be the target.

"True. Let's see what the Homeland Security guys discover tomorrow."

"Thanks for keeping me in the loop." Jason replaced the phone and turned back to Kathryn's questioning expression. "Nothing definitive yet, but they'll keep at it."

He told her about the isolated cabin.

Vice-President Hayes had scheduled a meeting with Jason at nine the following morning. After contemplating canceling or putting the session on hold until he'd heard from O'Hare, Jason arrived five minutes early and paced in the outer suite until Hayes came to the door of his office and beckoned him in. They settled in soft chairs grouped around a glass-topped coffee table.

Hayes started immediately without preliminary small talk. "I've been thinking about the permanent leadership vacancy in Arts and Sciences. It's time to get started on the search process but I wanted your concurrence and ideas about the timing."

"Dr. Hayes, I haven't thought about the details, but if we could get a committee formed and agree on the job announcement before the spring semester is over, we could use the summer to solicit applications. Perhaps by the beginning of the fall term we could schedule interviews and bring the search to closure by the middle of the term or surely by the end the Christmas break. I realize that doesn't give much time to form a committee before faculty begin to disappear for the summer."

"We have about three weeks and some of those faculty will be on summer appointments for either teaching or working on research projects. I'm inclined to initiate solicitation of potential committee members in the next couple of days."

Jason nodded. "The faster, the better from my perspective."

Hayes laughed, a deep sound in his throat. "Sounds like you're an advocate for moving rapidly. And I hope you've thought about your own situation and will become a candidate for the position. I've not heard complaints from anyone about your style which is a plus."

"I expect the difficult decisions had been made before I got into the office. I've spent most of my time sorting through a couple of personnel problems and trying to wrap up projects in Biology." He paused and added, "I'd hoped to meet with each department head by now, but I've not been able to schedule those sessions yet." He wanted to learn more about the departments within the college, gauge the depth of commitment and leadership style of the heads, and learn about continuing problems or issues.

Jason added. "In all the turmoil of changing positions, closing out projects, and dealing with this federal research lab disaster I've not thought much about my aspirations for the permanent slot."

"There's plenty of time for that, but if you're in agreement, I'm going to set about forming a search committee. I'll keep you informed about the committee composition and send a draft of the job announcement before we release it."

Hayes leaned forward as ready to stand and added. "Remember that President Snyder expects you to become a candidate."

Jason stood to shake Hayes' hand. "I know."

Jason had been back in the office ten minutes when O'Hare phoned. "Jason, progress report. Feller and Sparks entered Westlake's cabin this morning. They found no evidence that anyone had been there for several days. But coming back along the trail, they noticed a place where a group of scrub trees and high grass had been smashed by a vehicle that had run off the road. They scrambled around and found Westlake's big Buick jammed against two large trees. Inside there are five bodies."

"Were they able to identify the individuals?"

"No, but they've never seen Riley or Westlake if indeed they're the ones in the vehicle. They want you and Dr. Grimes to come to the site because they're afraid to open the doors and perhaps contaminate the area with toxins."

Jason sat stunned for a moment with all the implications cascading through his mind, before responding. "I'll locate Helga and prepare to come, but we'll need a guide or directions."

"Meet at my office as soon as possible and I'll lead you there. And you may need protective clothing, but you know better than I about precautions to be taken."

"It may take us a while. We'll need to go by the lab to get protective gear and hope it's still intact.."

"I'll meet you there," O'Hare said, "and save you coming back to campus."

Jason called Helga and outlined the sequence of events and their need to go to the scene, then he called Bridget in to rearrange his schedule for the day. He said, "If the Vice-President calls, tell him I've been called to an emergency about the 29th Street lab disaster. He'll understand. But no one else needs to know where I am."

At the lab, still untouched after the vandalism, Jason and Helga pulled out from the overturned and dented metal lockers the protective masks, gloves, and coveralls to be worn in case they were needed. She folded several large plastic bags together in case they had to collect the toxins and any contaminated materials.

Jason followed O'Hare's official car as they headed west on 29th

Street, then onto a state road out of the city limits. After four plus miles they turned off the main highway onto an essentially ungraded road, rutted and pitted by traffic and weather with no hint of having ever been graveled or having received any maintenance. Within the first mile they passed a few house trailers with the usual stuff in the front, too overgrown to describe as yards. But after those, there was no evidence of people living near. Jason eased his car to a crawl and attempted to avoid the major dips and ruts, but still bounced around.

At one point, Jason growled, "This will be the death of my old car."

Helga responded, "Not to mention throwing our spines out of kilter."

Approximately two miles along the trail, they came upon Feller and Sparks standing by their government vehicle on a grassy spot just off the primary surface. O'Hare had pulled off the trail and parked on the grassy shoulder.

Sparks waved to them as they emerged from their cars. "This way. We were lucky to see where they went off the road."

The group peered down a sloping embankment to see the rear of Westlake's 1989 Buick. Bushes and grass had been mashed some, but the causal passerby would not notice the wreckage almost out of sight among a group of trees and undergrowth about fifty yards from the road.

Following the car tracks, Sparks led them down the slope, pointing out a couple of holes to avoid. At the vehicle, Sparks pointed to the inside. "Two guys in the front seats, three jammed into the rear seat. There is no suggestion they ever left the car. From best we can tell none of the doors had been opened. Just skidded down this bank and stopped. As I told you over the phone, Feller and I were afraid to open the doors for fear toxins would escape and we'd end up like these guys."

Jason said, "You did the right thing. Why don't you go back to the top and let Dr. Grimes and me sort this out. We'll do our best not to disrupt the scene."

While the others retreated up the embankment, Jason and Helga edged close enough to see through the dusty windows. None of the doors or windows had been opened. All seemed peaceful, no signs of struggle, expressions on their faces not revealing any pain before dying. Jason recognized Westlake as the driver and Riley in the front passenger seat. One of the canisters lay on the floor near Riley's feet. It appeared to be intact. Moving to look through a side window into the back seat, he saw three men in various forms of collapse. Jason recognized the burly men as those who been in the diner with Riley and Westlake. The ever-present baseball caps had been pulled tight. The third man, apparently much younger than the others, had the second canister jammed between his legs. It had been opened, the top lying in the middle passenger's lap.

Jason said, "Let's put on the protective gear and get inside."

She nodded agreement. They pulled the coveralls over their regular clothing, Jason removing his sport coat to have a more comfortable fit. He draped it across a nearby bush. With masks and gloves in place, Jason eased open the right rear door. They retreated several steps and waited five minutes. Then Jason pulled the canister from the front floor and handed it to Helga.

She looked it over for several seconds, ran her fingers around the top, and said, "This is the freeze dried specimen and has not been opened or even tampered with. All the seals are intact."

Jason edged inside the car and removed the container from the lap of the middle rider. The top was off. He said, "They knocked open the aerosol version. The way it's arranged it seems they did it purposefully rather than accidentally."

Helga said, "Now we know what happened. They tampered with the seals and released the aerosol. That would have killed them within seconds."

They inserted the canisters into a plastic bag, tied it securely, and brought the package up the slope to the others and explained their suspicions of what had gone wrong. Jason said, "This toxin is intended to kill within seconds after breathing it. And within the closed vehicle, they never had a chance. I expect they died of pulmonary failure within seconds. Westlake lost control of all his senses and the car skidded off the road. My guess is Westlake didn't even kill the engine, but it ran out of gas after a period of being jammed against those huge trees."

"That seems to fit," Sparks said. "We could see that the gear shift was still in drive position. We couldn't see the gauges and haven't tried checking the tank itself."

Standing three feet away from the others, Feller said, a tone of authority in his voice, "We can't let the public know what happened here. Let's take those canisters away, along with any other evidence they were killed by those toxins. Let the Medical Examiner determine the cause of death but we should not admit what we know as the actual cause. The Agency will insist we keep this undercover."

O'Hare asked, "What about any residual from the aerosol? Won't that tip off the forensics investigators?"

Helga spoke up, "The system is designed to dissipate within minutes. There should not be any remaining trace of the toxin."

O'Hare paced along the trail for a bit, then turned back to the others. "This is most unusual for me, but I will not reveal the toxins were the likely cause of death. I'm going to refer all questions of that nature to the Agency people." He stopped for a moment then added, "To bring this episode to closure, I must notify the city police and the county sheriff in whose jurisdiction this occurred. They will investigate, bring in the Medical Examiner, and the forensics types as in a typical crime scene." He moved toward his car.

Jason and Helga stowed the containers in the trunk of his car and reversed direction to head toward the lab.

After a half-mile of bumping and jarring along the trail, Jason said, "I'm not completely comfortable with this cover up, but I guess we have no choice."

"Releasing any information," Helga said, "would compromise the entire development of the weapon. I think we have no option other than to maintain secrecy."

"Well, we can inform Johnson and Walcott the toxin worked as planned. They may not need to run additional tests."

"I'll call Walcott from home," Helga volunteered, "as soon as I can clean up a bit."

Jason nodded and added. Let's hope that the press doesn't figure out what happened. If they do, there'll be hell to pay. Every official in state government, not to mention the federal agencies, will be hot after the facts."

Chapter 25

The morning edition of the Spencerville *Herald* featured on page one the headline **MYSTERIOUS DEATHS IN WOODS.** The story following revealed the strange deaths of the five men, suspects in the vandalism of the 29th Street laboratory being used for research by the federal government. Names of the deceased were listed along with a photograph of the Westlake's car almost buried in shrubs and jammed against trees. The reporter speculated that the deaths were the direct result of contact with a deadly substance although there was no evidence discovered by the forensics technicians that a toxic material was in or near the vehicle. The Medical Examiner had released a preliminary opinion that the cause of death was pulmonary malfunction, but suggested further examination might reveal more definitive causes.

The article became as much speculative as factual, as it continued on the third page. "The research laboratory has undergone a number of incidents in its short history since the federal government leased the property from a former pharmaceutical company and converted the facility into a secretive operation. International signs and symbols warning of biological dangers appeared only to attract vandals or groups who seemed intent on shutting down the work. Now their mission seems to have led to their deaths, although the local police crime scene investigators could not confirm the presence of toxic substances. On the scene agents of Homeland Security Agency would only say the research was classified secret thus preventing them from comments. They refused to speculate about the cause of death."

It continued with background information. "Phillip Westlake, the apparent leader of the group, has a criminal record and is known among his neighbors and co-workers at the local community college to foster disruptions of government facilities that go against his personal beliefs. He was apparently not a member of any organized sect or religion but he does have a small number of ardent followers. One of the victims, Dr. Hugh Riley, retired from State University two years ago and has been an instructor of biology at Webster Community College. He has a police record and recently was the object of a court order for stalking the wife of his former department head, Dr. Jason Spradlin, after being arrested and charged with stalking with the intent to sexually assault. The outcome of these charges is pending an appeal by the defendant.

"Both the Agency and the local police departments promise a continuing investigation."

Leaning over Jason's shoulder at the breakfast table, Kathryn scanned the article and commented. "Thus far they have not revealed either you or Helga as being connected to the lab but I don't like this reference to Riley's stalking. That will get my name in the news."

Jason drank the last of his coffee. "The media will be out in full force to discover as much as possible and connect the players."

Jason's prediction proved correct. A reporter from the *Herald* came into his office as soon as the doors opened for the morning. He introduced himself, Joel Ruffin, handed Jason a business card and reached to shake his hand.

Ruffin didn't waste time on preliminaries. "I'm following up on the morning's lead story about the deaths of those five guys and their connection to this research lab you're associated with."

"I saw the article," Jason said.

"Can you tell me more about the series of incidents and about the mission of this laboratory on 29th."

"Your paper has covered the various vandalism events in previous editions. As to the mission of the facility, I can tell you it operated under a federal contract, but I cannot reveal the nature of the research itself. As the article indicated, the work is classified secret."

Ruffin made a few notes in his pad. "What can you tell me about your relationship with Dr. Riley?"

"At one time we were both faculty members in Biology but did not work closely together."

"I understand from another source you were the department head when Dr. Riley was forced into early retirement."

"That's correct, but I'm not going to reveal the details of that separation because it's a private personnel issue."

Ruffin appeared to become frustrated with the lack of openness on Jason's part. "You know, Dr. Spradlin, we'll keep digging until we find out what really went on in that lab and what happened to those five guys."

Jason smiled and said, "I acknowledge that's your mission, but I'll not be the person who tells you about highly classified work. And if I discover who does reveal that, I'll do my very best to see them severely reprimanded."

Jason stood and moved toward the door. Ruffin followed, his face a cloud of frustration mixed with determination to discover the truth by any means. And Jason accepted that Ruffin or some colleague would eventually find out what had gone on. He was reminded of the likelihood of a source of information within the Agency who had apparently kept Westlake informed.

When Jason arrived home Kathryn was staring at the early evening broadcast of the news. He dropped his briefcase near the door and sat on the couch by her. The anchor reiterated much of what had been reported in the paper bolstered with graphic pictures of Westlake's car, the trampled brush near the car, his isolated cabin, and the damaged laboratory. Both Jason and Helga were mentioned as the primary investigators in a highly secret operation funded by the Federal government.

She said, "There's nothing new, but they'll stay with the incident until something breaks to show what really went on in the facility."

"Maybe, but if nothing crops up in the next day or so, I hope they'll move on. They tend to lose interest or something else takes center stage."

Helga's report to Walcott about the death of the vandals prompted their being summoned to Washington by Johnson. Jason and Helga arrived at Reagan National mid-morning to be met by two different agents. They'd expected this as Feller and Sparks were still in

Spencerville investigating the deaths of those five vandals. Conversation was almost non-existent as they drove the familiar route to the facility in Virginia. Again Helga seemed intent on looking at sights she'd lived with for several years.

They were led to Johnson's office, never out of sight of the guardian agents. Walcott appeared as though on a prearranged signal when Johnson greeted them and led them to a conference table in his office.

With no preliminary conversation, Johnson initiated the session. "Well, it's good to see both of you and to know you've been successful in the endeavor."

Jason nodded and said, "We're reasonably certain the aerosol delivery system worked as planned and the toxin reacted as predicted. But as you know, the test on human subjects was an accident and was not conducted under controlled conditions. You might argue we don't know for certain the toxin was the cause of death of the vandals, but it's as definitive as one could hope for under the circumstances."

Walcott leaned forward to put his arms on the table. "Based on the report from Feller and Sparks and your own description of what transpired, along with our tests with primates, I'm willing to call the mission a complete success. I haven't told you but we ran a test on four monkeys and another on four pigs using the sample you provided. All died within seconds of exposure. At some point in the future, we'll have an opportunity to use the weapon in the field. Then we'll know with absolute certainty, but we can't do more than we have to this point."

Johnson beamed, the first time Jason had seen the hint of a smile on the rotund face of the Deputy Director. "I agree and I have reported this to the Director and to the Secretary of Defense. We now have this capability in our arsenal we've never had before. Of course, we hope we never have to utilize it, but we'll be prepared if and when the circumstances demand our employment of the system."

Walcott added. "I believe we can stop any further investigations and close down the lab in Spencerville. There are a few bugs to be worked out, such as the stability of the aerosol under various field conditions and handling methodology by individuals not familiar with the toxin, but we can do that better from here."

Jason looked at Helga, then asked, "Do we need to do anything further at the lab?"

Johnson chipped in. "Based on the report from Feller and Sparks, all the equipment was destroyed beyond repair, but if you feel differently, we'd like to know."

"Helga and I have examined each of the pieces and agree with the agents. Restoring the major equipment back to a serviceable condition would be almost impossible, not to mention very expensive. My advice is scrap it all although we might be able to salvage some of the smaller pieces that escaped the attention of the culprits."

Helga chimed in. "The building itself was not damaged except where they crashed through the door. The infrastructure, including the safe lab and the test systems could be made functional with minor repairs."

Jason added. "If you plan to abandon the facility and return it to the original owner, State University would be interested in picking up the remaining time on the lease or perhaps purchasing the building. We seem to always be short of adequate research space and this lab could be quite useful." Jason had in fact discussed the possibility with the Director of the Research Office, the administrator responsible for research functions, including laboratory space at the university, and had taken the administrator on a tour of the facility.

Johnson said, "As you know, we leased the building for three years, but we could forfeit the final two years and permit State to begin use as soon as we can clear the debris, assuming the owner agrees."

Jason said, "I'll initiate the necessary actions, including checking with the owner, when I return home."

"That would be satisfactory and now I need to ask about the financial arrangements," Johnson rolled his chair back and reached to pull a folder from the top of his desk "Have you both received payments as promised?"

Almost in unison, Jason and Helga responded in the affirmative. Jason added. "It's worked well and no one within the university is aware of those payments. And all the invoices for expenditures have been submitted to your accounting people."

Walcott asked, "Any other concerns before we wrap this up?"

"Yes," Jason said. "I hate to sound like a broken record, but I have a continuing worry about information leakage from somewhere in the federal system. Reporters seem to know more than they should given the secrecy involved. I hope you will continue to look for that source before we're all embarrassed and placed on the defensive in the public eye. And you know better than I, those deaths will only provide additional incentive."

"We've had investigators looking into the problem," Johnson said, "but thus far they've discovered no suspects or even a lead toward one."

Jason pushed his point. "Those men who died knew we had an alarm and cut it off before they began their rampage. There had to be a tip from somewhere. Look at the people who might know about that installation."

Ignoring Jason's comment, Johnson glanced at his wrist watch, then stood. "Dr. Spradlin and Dr. Grimes, I thank both of you for a job well done. Maybe we can call on you again in the future."

Walcott, recognizing the movement of Johnson signaled the meeting had concluded, stood and led Jason and Helga into the outer suite, asking as they walked, "Would you be interested in lunch in the cafeteria before the agents ferry you back to the airport?"

They nodded and Jason said, "That'd be nice. It's been a long time since breakfast. And a stop in the rest room is in order."

Ten minutes later they were in the cafeteria line with Walcott pointing out the daily specials, putting the bill on his tab and leading them to a corner table. He continued to eye Helga as she removed her utensils from a folded napkin.

Then he said, "Helga, I didn't want to broach the subject in Johnson's presence, but have you thought about returning to the Agency? I believe I could clear the way in the next few months."

"That'd be good of you," Helga smiled at her former colleague, "but with Dr. Spradlin's help, I've found a temporary position at State university for the next year and there's the potential for it becoming a permanent appointment. I've truly liked living in a university town and the freedom of information exchange I'd never enjoyed within the Agency."

Walcott picked at his salad, spilling lettuce leaves onto the table. "Rumors are pretty persistent that Johnson will be replaced within the next month if that influences your decision."

"You must know I couldn't return if he were here, but even so, I've found the different environment to be quite stimulating and I look forward to the future." She told him about the temporary appointment in Biology and her hope it would turn into a permanent slot for her. She was already accumulating background material for a possible grant application and reading through the text she would use in the fall term for General Biology. And she'd notified the tenant in her northern Virginia condo that she intended to place it on the market.

The conversation turned to the upcoming election and the changing role of several agencies within Homeland Security under a new administration and likely a new Secretary.

The Friday beer group assembled with thoughts of Riley permeating their minds. Townsend and Pierson arrived together and secured a table in one corner of the crowded place. Within five minutes Harris appeared accompanied by a woman they'd seen him with previously. She was attractive, but not beautiful, with neatly combed brown hair framing an oval face, brown eyes, medium height with a good figure outlined by a knee length gray skirt and white blouse. A light scar across one cheek marred her features a bit, although she'd used make-up to mask it reasonably well.

Standing next to the table and holding her hand, Harris said, "I'd like you to meet Janet Webster. I brought her along to meet you guys and to join us for today, if it's okay."

Townsend and Pierson stood to shake Janet's hand. Harris dragged another chair to the table and held it for her.

Settled into his chair and having placed orders for beer, Harris said, "I assume you have been talking about Riley."

"We had just begun when you arrived," Townsend said," but Riley has been on my mind since the report in the papers about his death. I was surprised he failed to understand the potential consequences of messing with hazardous materials. All the signs around that facility should have been sufficient warning, especially to someone trained in the biological sciences."

Pierson sipped his beer then continued the line. "I agree. I walked around the outside of that lab three days after the break in and there are warning signs everywhere. Riley couldn't have missed those."

Janet spoke up. "I didn't know Riley but I've heard of him and his stalking Kathryn Helweg. It could be he was never at the lab and depended on his cohorts to do the damage. And we still don't know what really killed those men in that car."

Townsend fiddled with his pipe, maybe wondering if it would be okay to fire it up with a female present. "We know Spradlin and his colleague were working on some dangerous substance, maybe an infectious disease, or those signs wouldn't have been posted. I'd bet those idiots who destroyed that facility took some of the substance and didn't know how to handle it. As a result, all were killed."

Pierson chimed in. "And we know from the relevant literature certain toxins disappear within minutes when exposed to the atmosphere. That could explain why the authorities haven't found anything."

Harris asked. "And what do you think of Spradlin's becoming a candidate for the dean's position?"

"Some in my department," Janet said, "believe he's too young for such a responsibility. He's only been a department head for three years."

"If anyone asked for my advice," Townsend said, as he put a lighter to his pipe. "I'd support him without question. He's been a great head for us and I expect he'd do the same for the entire college. It's true he's fairly young, but he's level headed and more importantly, has a vision for what makes an academic unit stand out above the rest. In that regard, he might cause some tremors in certain departments, but he will do it fairly." He puffed at his pipe and continued, "Remember, everyone thought he was too young and inexperienced when he became head of Biology and look how that has gone. We've moved from an average department to an excellent one and getting better each year."

Harris stood and placed his hand on Janet's shoulder. "Janet and I are getting married the week after commencement. We'd invite you, but it's going to be a quiet family ceremony at her home in Kansas."

"Congratulations," Townsend said. "But does this mean you're dropping out of our little group."

"Not by any means. And if you're agreeable, Janet will join us to provide a different perspective on the academic world, including the upcoming selection of the next dean."

"We may have to curtail or modify some of our stories, but let's look forward to Janet's presence."

When the pair disappeared through the outer door, Pierson asked, "Does this mean Harris is done with his chasing of females?"

Townsend puffed at his pipe. "Maybe for the short term, but I doubt it will last very long. And Janet shouldn't be surprised. He was hitting on her while still married."

Chapter 26

Continuing to be concerned about a replacement for Lillian Carter as the end of the school year approached and the time of Carter's planned leaving became more imminent, Kathryn made several contacts with social service and related agencies that coordinated the placement of household workers, maids, and baby-sitters with interested families. She had sought advice from Mrs. Carter, colleagues and other families who required assistance with young children. For a while she believed she'd reached a dead end as no one seemed to have a good recommendation. A couple of names had been mentioned, but the source had been lukewarm or worse about the potential nanny.

A Thursday night telephone call from a stranger became helpful. When Kathryn answered, an unknown woman said, "I understand you're looking for a live-in nanny. A mutual friend told me about your situation and suggested I call because we have utilized this woman for two years, but no longer require her services. I thought she might be the answer to your search."

"Can you tell me a bit about her?" Kathryn asked.

"Her name is Maria Castile. She's from Guatemala and has lived in this country for three years. She's in her late-forties, has a green card and is applying for permanent citizenship. She lives with an adult daughter and her family but I believe she would be amenable to moving out of that household. On a couple of occasions she's mentioned in passing that the house was very crowded."

"I assume you've been satisfied with her work?"

"Very much so. She's been wonderful with our two small children. Our arrangement has been for her to arrive around eight and stay until either my husband or I get home from work. She drives an old car so transportation hasn't been an issue and she's always on time."

Kathryn said, "My husband and I would like to meet her. May I call her at your home or do you have a number for her?"

"Please feel free to call here." She recited the number and reminded Kathryn of the hours Maria would be there. Kathryn phoned for Maria the very next afternoon and arranged for her to meet with Jason and her.

They'd scheduled Maria's to visit on Saturday afternoon, a free day for her. After introductions Maria sat on the edge of a chair in the living room, nervous about this prospective couple who could become her employers. A mature woman with pleasant facial features, stocky build, dark complexion, black hair and eyes, white teeth that gleamed when she smiled. She spoke with a dialect characteristic of the Spanish, but readily understandable.

Jason and Kathryn sat on the couch across from her. Jason explained the arrangement they'd had with Lillian Carter, including a small apartment in the basement, their expectation she would assist Kathryn with the new twins as needed, prepare the dinner meal for the entire family, and run errands as required to maintain the household. If needed she could utilize the car they had for Carter. She would not be responsible for breakfast but should be available to help get the kids off to school, especially during those times when Jason was out of town.

Kathryn added, "And with twins coming, we're not certain of other duties that may become necessary, so you need to be flexible."

"I understand about small children," Maria responded, seeming to relax a bit and leaning back in the chair.

Kathryn led her through the apartment and the house, then they returned to the living room to meet Jennifer and Tony. Maria asked each about their age, year in school, and the kind of activities they liked. At one point she reached to hold their hands for a moment.

After the children returned to their rooms, Maria said, "I would like to work for you and use the apartment. When do you wish me to start?"

Kathryn looked at Jason who nodded, then said, "When the school term begins in September or if you could start the first of August, that would give us time to get settled before the new babies arrive in mid-month."

Maria agreed to the earlier start and both Kathryn and Jason felt they'd found a reliable replacement, but would miss the good humor of Carter. But time would tell how the kids reacted to Maria and how she performed in a household getting ready for a dramatic change.

Jason's hope the firestorm around the secret lab and the death of the five vandals would wither away was dashed when President Snyder called on Tuesday morning and asked that Jason come to his office as soon as possible. With Bridget's help, he rescheduled two appointments and left the office, walking across the busy campus on a bright spring morning to the administrative building. His thoughts wandered from the upcoming session with Snyder whose call contained a sense of urgency to Kathryn's appointment with her physician to confirm the initial diagnosis that twins were on the horizon.

Snyder seemed to be waiting for him. He was ushered in without delay to find the President pacing the floor behind his desk. His demeanor appeared edgy as he tugged at his coat sleeve. His usual smile was absent.

Snyder said, "Thanks for coming so quickly, but I promised the Governor I'd get back to him this morning. As you'd guess, it's about the demise of those five men who apparently vandalized your lab."

He led Jason to the semi-circle of soft chairs and continued. "The Governor called just after eight. As you learned from your earlier confrontation, he'd heard through some source the lab was conducting research on biological weapons and insisted, actually demanded is the more accurate term, he be brought up to date on the specifics. Again I tried to stress the work was classified secret by Homeland Security but that didn't deter him for wanting to be in on the details. I promised I'd talk with you and get back to him by noon."

"This is the second time he's raised the issue. And at an earlier meeting with him, I outlined the general concept of the work without revealing the core mission. At the time that seemed to be sufficient. Has he learned something new?"

"He seemed to know more than I would have thought given the classification of the research."

"If he truly knows, my speculation about a mole in the system is correct. Those vandals knew more about the work than you'd guess, although they paid little attention to the warnings. I've requested on at least three occasions that the Agency security people be charged with finding this leak, but thus far, they have not been successful." He paused, looking at Snyder, than added, "If, in fact, those D.C. officials took my request seriously." He remembered Johnson's dismissal of his concern when he'd broached it the first time.

Snyder focused on his immediate problem. "So what may I tell the Governor?"

Jason delayed his response as he tried to think about some positive information he could safely reveal to the chief executive of the state without compromising his vow to secrecy. "First he should know we took this task on because of some pressure from the Agency. I caved in thinking it would be a service to the nation and be useful in our fight against these terrorists groups. I understood from the outset the research and the product were to be secret. Part of the rationale of maintaining secrecy was to keep the development out of sight of those enemy groups. And I still feel obliged to do so."

"You know, Dr. Spradlin, that will not be a satisfactory response."

"I suggest then two possible contacts who might provide him more information than I feel comfortable doing. First, he can contact the Secretary of Homeland Security. Secondly, he might discuss his concerns with Congressman Wilke, the Chair of the House Oversight Committee for Science and Technology. Then the Governor must understand the consequences of releasing to the media anything that characterizes the product. The entire effort would become a waste of resources and potentially place certain people, including myself, in danger of retaliation by these groups who resist any project by the Federal government."

Snyder had watched Jason for any sign of compromise. Seeing none, he said, "I'll suggest he call both of those sources and trust he will be placated enough to move forward."

Jason said, "I hope the media will soon lose interest in this event, but if the Governor makes a big deal of it, that will only spur them to greater efforts to disclose the entire work. He, of all people, should understand that. And I don't know if he's immune from the Federal agencies if they hold him responsible for leaks that will jeopardize the goal."

Snyder stood. As they moved to the door, he asked, "And how's the Dean's job going? I haven't heard rumors of rebellion." A smile broke across his face, seeming to relieve the tension associated with the previous issue.

"Okay, I think, but I've been so caught up in this lab vandalism, I've gotten behind in some things."

"I'll let you know the Governor's response."

Kathryn's face betrayed her news when they met for lunch at a small restaurant near the campus. As soon as they met outside the door, she blurted, "It's twins and in mid- August." Her face broke into a huge grin.

Jason pulled her close and held her for a moment. "Did she give any advice about your physical condition?" He'd pushed her to discuss her activities that he suspected were too strenuous for someone moving toward the end of the second trimester.

"I raised the question and told her about the exercises I did. She asked about my feelings after the work out, then suggested I reduce the jogging to walking but she doesn't perceive any problems as long as I feel good. In fact, she encouraged me to continue unless I felt pangs of any sort."

He told her about Snyder's call and visit then added, "You know each day I hope this focus on the vandals will pass, but it seems to linger, even gain momentum as time passes. This sounds paranoid, but I suspect someone is stirring the pot so to speak, in hopes of bringing the research into the open and perhaps sabotaging the weapon system. Or maybe they want nothing more than to make Homeland Security look bad to the public. "

"What can you do about it?" She stirred her soup and took an initial taste.

"Not much as best I can fathom."

"Why don't you call Congressman Wilke again? He seemed to have quieted the Governor previously and maybe he can get the feds to search more thoroughly for this suspected leak."

Jason watched her for a bit. "I'm going to do that. Good idea. I know I married you for your brains and insights into problems."

"And all this time I've thought it was because of my looks."

He reached to touch her hand. "Well, that played a part."

President Snyder was on the phone when Jason walked into the office following lunch. Trusting he had good news, Jason grabbed the phone.

Snyder started, his tone somber. "Governor Brewster was not too pleased with our recommendations. He wants both of us to come to the capitol on Friday morning for a conference with him and a couple of other officials. I tried to convey the fact that you felt obliged to keep the matter confidential between those federal people and yourself, but that didn't get anywhere. He's determined to know the details."

"If we must do this, shall we travel together?"

"My office will make the arrangements," Snyder concluded, "and will let you know."

Jason called Wilke's office, knowing he'd end up either waiting for a protracted length of time or leaving a message for Wilke to call him back. The female associate who answered the phone suggested he leave a message and, if Wilke required clarification, someone would get back to him.

Jason explained Governor Brewster's demand that he know details of the biological weapon and seemed determined to push Jason and President Snyder to cave in or be threatened with dismissal from their positions. He wanted the Congressman to call the Governor to head off this confrontation scheduled for Friday morning or if he felt he couldn't do that, call the Director of Homeland Security and ask that he talk with the Governor. He had the woman confirm her understanding of his request.

Then Jason said, "If he cannot do either of those things, please let me know as soon as possible."

Feeling he'd communicated the importance of doing something, he replaced the receiver and wondered if he'd overreacted about the firings. The Governor likely could make a big to-do about Jason's refusal to reveal the information, but Jason doubted he could outright fire him because of protection against political interference under the tenure guidelines. But Snyder was more vulnerable and Brewster could pressure the Board of Trustees, a majority of whom had been appointed by the Governor, to replace Snyder citing insubordination or some other trumped up rationale.

He tried to concentrate on a set of routine issues important to the college, but he struggled to maintain any focus on the problem at hand. When a break in the schedule permitted he walked to Quincy and went into his research lab where the post-docs and graduate assistants were busy with projects. He talked with a couple of them, asking about their progress, before he realized he was interfering with the actual experimentations. For the first time in years, Jason felt like a fish out of water, disoriented for the short term.

He returned to his office and read through the stack of afternoon mail. One item, the draft of the position announcement for the dean's job, reminded him of his temporary status. The accompanying note had asked for feedback to the search committee chaired by Vice-President Hayes and composed of six faculty from various precincts in the college, the Dean of Engineering, the Dean of the Graduate School, a research specialist from chemistry, and a secretary from Psychology.

Jason scanned the announcement. Nothing amiss jumped out at him. He used a blank folder to start a new file and for a brief moment thought about his own decision regarding the vacancy. He E-mailed the Vice-President to indicate his acknowledgment of the announcement with no recommendations for change. But the Governor could erase any notions he had of applying for a high level administrative position.

At four a secretary in Snyder's office phoned to tell him about arrangements for travel to the capitol on Friday morning for their eleven o'clock appointment with the Governor. They would use the university plane, leave the local airport at eight-thirty and plan to return by mid-afternoon. That assumed the Governor and his aides maintained some semblance of a schedule.

During the forty-five minute flight Jason and Snyder reviewed their strategy and the possible scenarios Brewster might raise. Jason appreciated Snyder's backing, knowing he was placing his presidency in jeopardy if he rebelled against the Governor. And his hope that either Wilke or the Secretary had intervened had gone down the drain. He'd been disappointed he'd not heard back from Wilke but pressing the issue with the Congressman by calling again seemed out of bounds.

From the private terminal for non-commercial flights they took a cab to the capitol building surrounded by its outlying structures required to accommodate growing government, more bureaucrats living off the public dole. Passing through an identification check at the front entrance, they took the elevator to the third floor and immediately entered the huge suite of the Governor and his aides. The office was thriving with secretaries staring into computer terminals, telephones ringing, and pages rushing about with memos to be delivered. Portraits of former state officials adorned the walls. Deep carpet softened their footsteps as they were greeted by a receptionist who smiled and pointed to a rear office door.

Brewster and Throckmorton were waiting as they were escorted into the suite. Brewster came around his massive desk to shake their hands and lead them to a small conference room to the right of the desk. They settled around a small rectangular table with coffee service at one end.

Brewster started immediately, skipping past any preliminaries about the university, the weather or their private lives. "Dr. Spradlin, I have continued to be concerned about the research you've been conducting under a secret agreement with the federal government. The death of those five individuals has served to raise the public awareness of the work, although no one seems to know precisely what the goal is. You've told me before you feel compelled to refrain from divulging any part of the effort. But now I must insist you let me in on the secret. I believe as the chief executive of the state I have the right to know that." He looked stern and expectant as though knowing Jason would now come forth with the desired information.

Jason glanced at Snyder who nodded, confirming between the two of them their intended approach. Jason said, "Governor Brewster, while I understand your interest, even your need to communicate with the media about the catastrophe that occurred around the research lab, I promised federal officials I would not reveal the mission of the research. It is classified secret and only a limited number of people truly understand the implications or the intent of the work. I can tell you it's a piece of our national effort to defend against terrorists and their plans to wreak havoc in our society." He knew he'd revealed enough that the Governor could put the pieces together and reach a logical conclusion.

"But I cannot legally tell you more. It was stressed from the very beginning that the fewer who knew, the more effective the outcome could be. I'm sure you can understand any communication in the public arena will nullify all our efforts and set the defense against the terrorists back."

Brewster's round face took on a ruddy complexion. He leaned forward and said, "Dr. Spradlin, you should know you could be placing your professional position at State University in jeopardy. I don't for one second buy this crap about this outdated concept of tenure protection."

At that moment an aide entered through a side door and said, "Governor, there's a telephone call you must take. And it'll be better if you have the conversation at your desk."

Brewster looked at Throckmorton who shrugged. Then he rose and quickly left the room. For a moment they could overhear him, then the aide closed the door.

Throckmorton refilled their coffee cups and they waited in silence for five minutes. Then the aide returned and motioned to Throckmorton to come.

Another three minutes passed with Snyder and Jason wondering what emergency had occurred within the state.

Throckmorton returned, his face shadowed in gray, his hand shaking as he rubbed his forehead. "Governor Brewster will not return to this meeting. You are free to leave."

Snyder wouldn't be so easily turned away and asked, "Does he intend to pursue this matter with Dr. Spradlin further? You understand we'd like to reach closure as soon as possible."

Throckmorton stared at the portrait of the last governor for several seconds, then looked at them, still seated at the table. "I believe it is safe to tell you that you will not hear about this issue again."

With that he left the room. Snyder and Jason weren't quite certain about what to do, but then Snyder said, "Let's take him at his word." He led Jason out of the suite and into the hall.

As they waited for the elevator, Snyder said, "That's one of the strangest things I've ever experienced. What happened?"

"I can only speculate," Jason said. "That phone call could only mean someone convinced Brewster to cease his actions to find out about the lab and the outcome of our work. I called Congressman Wilke's office yesterday, but I didn't talk with him, only left a message about the Governor's demands."

"So you think Wilke called during our visit and headed Brewster off?"

"Who else would intervene and cause the Governor to change course so abruptly?"

Chapter 27

From their arrival at the Spencerville airport Jason rushed directly to his office, planning to call Wilke. He wanted to determine if somehow Wilke had put the brakes on the Governor's demands to know about the weapon. Or, if he hadn't, perhaps he would have some notion of what had dissuaded the Chief Executive of the state. Wilke came on the line after a five minute delay and after Jason had pressed an aide it was important that he speak to the Congressman as soon as possible. Apparently the assistant broke into a meeting to call him to the phone or fortunately the meeting ended.

"Dr. Spradlin, good to hear from you. I've learned of your success with the toxic aerosol. Congratulations on a job well done."

"Thanks, Congressman but I called about my Governor's continued interest in the project and wondered if you'd contacted him."

"I received your message but didn't call him. However, I contacted the Secretary of Homeland Security and asked that he speak to Governor Brewster. I thought he might have more influence than I."

Jason told him about the aborted session with Brewster, then added, "I assume the Secretary was the one who headed him off."

"That's likely," Wilke said. "He was upset about Brewster's insistence and would have threatened him with legal action if he persisted. From what you've said about his response to a phone call, he laid down a stern directive to cease and desist or face charges of meddling in top secret activities."

Jason said, "Well, whatever he did worked and thanks for your help."

Wilke continued, "On another topic I've discussed the problem of information leakage with the Agency Director and he's increased their efforts to locate the problem. I suspect they'll be successful soon, but it all may be too late now."

"I hope so, but the media are still nosing around looking for a cause of those deaths. And one reporter hinted he had an inside source."

"I'll speak to the Agency again and recommend they double their efforts before real damage is done, such as information about the weapon itself getting into the public domain."

Jason said, "Thanks again for intervening. I was concerned Governor Brewster would fire both President Snyder and me."

"I'd be surprised he'd go that far, but when big egos are bruised, you can never predict."

Jason trusted Wilke's influence would result in the Agency getting more serious about the leak but he didn't know the personalities involved. Then he called Snyder's office to inform him about the likely reason for the mysterious actions of the Governor.

Snyder took a moment to digest the news, then laughed. "I'm glad someone can get through to Brewster."

Jason had been impressed with Snyder's demeanor throughout the conflict with Brewster, but had never heard him express any reluctance to stand firm. Now he decided to ask. "Were you concerned at all about your position in this conflict with Brewster?"

Snyder laughed. "It crossed my mind he could fire me rather easily, but you have to take stands at times and let the consequences fall where they may. But there's an old expression that goes something like 'you must choose the hill to die on.' You can't die on every one."

"I'll remember that," Jason said, as they ended the conversation.

Jason's hopes the issues around the lab would subside were dashed two days later. A call came to Jason at home just after eight o'clock. He and Kathryn had just finished reading stories to the kids who were climbing into their respective beds when the call came.

A female voice asking for Dr. Spradlin. She started without delay after identifying herself as Betsy, the next door neighbor of Helga Grimes. "I'm calling to ask if you'd seen Helga this afternoon?"

"No, I haven't talked to her in three or four days." He knew Helga was finalizing a deal to sell her D.C. area condo and moving the remainder of her furnishings to Spencerville. He hadn't expected to see her for several days.

Her voice, shaky with obvious trembling, Betsy said, "I'm worried about her. She and I were planning to attend a concert at the university tonight and she didn't show. There was no answer when I called her home number. After several attempts I thought the phone might be out of service so I walked next door and knocked on her door. There was no response and the place is dark. We've gone to several events together and she's always been prompt."

Jason asked, "Has she indicated any problems, someone following her, crank calls, things like that?"

"No, but she's pretty close mouthed about personal things. When I asked about those men who were killed after ransacking her lab, she didn't volunteer any information I hadn't seen in the papers."

"Is her car in the lot?"

"I'm not certain I'd know the car since I usually drove when we went out. She did mention around noon she needed to go out to the lab soon to collect personal items that she'd left there before the clean up begins. But I don't know if she actually did that today."

Jason thought about possibilities but he didn't know much about Helga's life and activities after work. He said, "The phone has been disconnected at the lab but tell you what I can do. I'll take a quick run out to the lab and see if she's there and just forgot the concert."

He scribbled Betsy's number on the pad kept by the phone and told Kathryn where he was going. "Be back in thirty minutes or less."

He eased into the lot by the lab, dark and abandoned except for Helga's car parked near the front entrance. He knew immediately something had gone wrong. He thought about calling the police but decided to take a quick look inside and not look foolish if nothing had occurred to require the cops.

The street light provided sufficient light for him to open the front door with the key that in some ways surprised him that it still functioned. The heavy door opened smoothly when he pushed.

Inside the facility it was difficult to see anything. None of the lights worked when he flipped switches. Then he remembered the power had been cut after the vandals had ransacked the place. He hurried back to his car and retrieved a flashlight from the car pocket.

Picking his way around debris left from the vandalism, he entered the office and called out to Helga. There was no response. But the beam of the hand-held light showed she'd been there. Books and notebooks were stacked neatly on a desk. Her briefcase and purse rested near on a chair.

Now certain something had gone wrong, he pushed into the first lab. Helga's body stretched along one of the aisles between the chemistry benches. No movement was evident. Blood had dried across her cheek and forehead. Her left arm was bent in an abnormal position and he suspected it had been broken. Her sweater and slacks were wrinkled and twisted but intact. Her glasses rested three feet away on the floor.

Kneeling near her and peering closely, he could detect no movement of her chest. Her eyes were closed. He placed his fingers along her neck and searched for a pulse. After a few probes, he discovered a faint beat.

Using his cell phone, he called 911. "A woman has been injured severely in the building at 864 29th Street. Send an ambulance now. And the police."

After confirming the location and the condition of the victim with the operator, Jason waited close to Helga, hoping she would show some sign of coming around. He didn't want to move anything near Helga as he thought it might constitute evidence that would help identify the attackers. When she'd hadn't stirred for a couple of minutes, he returned to the entrance.

Five minutes later an ambulance roared to a stop at the front door.

Its flashing lights evoked an eerie scene as the beams poured across the parking lot and through the windows. Jason met them at the door and led the two men with a stretcher to Helga's body. They bent over her, checking pulse, listening to a stethoscope placed on her chest, opening one eye to peer at it, shaking their heads and mumbling to each other. They lifted her gently onto the stretcher and hastened to the ambulance.

One of the emergency crew said, "We'll take her to Spencerville General. She's been injured severely, probably internal damage we can't detect here."

"I'll follow and provide any information I know to admissions," Jason said. He called Kathryn to let her know his destination. He remembered to have her call Betsy to inform her about Helga's status.

As the ambulance roared off, a police cruiser pulled in. Two officers from the Spencerville force listened to Jason's description of the scene. They entered the building and using electric torches scanned the lab where the body had been.

The senior officer said, "It's difficult to see much without lights. We'll get forensics and detectives out in the morning."

"I'm going to retrieve her purse and glasses, if it's okay."

"Sure," the officer said. "If you don't move them, someone will step on the glasses."

They departed the premises. Jason locked the outside door as soon as they left and drove to the hospital.

Two hours later he made it home, feeling as tired as he ever had in his life. Kathryn forced him to sit on the couch and she brought him a drink. "You look terrible. Are you okay?"

"It's been a long day, but I'm fine." He told her about Helga. The emergency ward physicians confirmed she had a broken arm which should mend okay. She'd been slammed across the head with some heavy object and either hit or kicked in the mid-section. In addition to a concussion, he suspected her kidneys had been badly bruised and perhaps her liver was damaged. But with time she should recover. Her pulse had improved since being admitted but she was not yet conscious when I left."

"Who would do that?" Kathryn asked, her hand on Jason's arm as she sat close to him.

"I have an idea it was connected with the earlier vandalism and the death of those men, but it's a guess. No one else has paid much attention to the lab or to us. The police may have clues after they've looked over the scene in the morning. And Helga may be able to tell us something after she's awake and alert."

"If your suspicion is correct, should we be worried?" Her dark eyes bored into his face, concern creeping across her features as she contemplated the implications of her question.

"Maybe. I'll talk to O'Hare tomorrow. He'll know how we should respond."

"Jason, when will all this end? We go from one threat to another."

"I'm sorry I got into this. I should have known better than to get tangled up with all this secrect stuff, but I had no idea of the resistance we'd run into."

The next morning, utilizing a break from his busy schedule in the office, Jason drove to the hospital and found his way to Helga's room. Monitors ran from her arms and an intravenous tube dripped nutrients and medications into her veins. A temporary cast covered the other arm. Her eyes were closed, although the nurse on duty had indicated she'd been awake earlier and talking.

Torn between disturbing her rest and his need to understand what had occurred, he moved near her bed and whispered, "Helga, it's Jason. Can you talk a couple of minutes?"

Her eyes blinked then opened fully as she recognized him. "Dr. Spradlin, they told me you found me last night. I could have died had you not come when you did. I couldn't move enough to get to my car or my cell phone. And I kept passing out each time I tried to get to my feet."

"Can you tell me what happened?"

"I'll try, but things are still vague." She squirmed around in the bed and brushed a hand across her face. "I'd completed getting my personal things together and was preparing to leave the building when two men crashed into the office. One of them pointed some sort of rod toward me and screamed, "She's one of them who killed my son with all this stuff around this place."

"I tried to explain his son had been trespassing and tell him I was sorry his son had died, but they were yelling so loudly they didn't give heed to anything I said. I knew they intended to harm me and I ran toward the lab, but they grabbed me. One hit me across the face with his fist and the other hit my head with some metal rod. I almost passed out, but then they kicked me in the mid-section. I collapsed onto the floor.

That's the last thing I remember until I woke up here."

"Had you seen them before?"

She nodded her head, then winced. "They were near my car earlier yesterday when I came out of the corner grocery store. I didn't give them much attention as I thought they were waiting for someone in the store. Other than that, I don't recall seeing them."

"Did they say anything in the lot?"

"No, but they were looking around. In retrospect, I believe they would have attacked me in the parking lot but there were too many others near."

"You could be right."

Her voice becoming weaker, she mumbled, "Be careful. They'll come after you next." Her eyes closed and she rubbed her hand across her face.

Jason watched her for a moment then eased out of the room. The nurse nodded to him as he passed on the way to the exit.

From his office he called O'Hare. He explained the event involving Helga then said, "From what she remembers, it seems likely one of the men was the father of the younger man in the car. But the reason I called is I'd like some sort of protection for Kathryn and my children if it's at all possible. I am concerned these nuts will take out their anger on them."

O'Hare remained silent for several seconds, then said, "The Spencerville police are looking for those men but you're correct. They could evade the cops for days since there wasn't a clear description of them. Grimes wasn't able to respond to questions, but perhaps she'll remember more as she gains strength. Let me review my duty roster and call you back. We're always short-handed but I'll do what I can do. And maybe the city can assist."

"If one of the attackers is really the father of the young person, that should give a lead."

"You're correct, but I don't know if we could identify him at the time. I'll check."

Still thinking about the safety of his family, Jason asked. "Should I obtain private security?"

"Give me a few minutes to do some juggling of assignments. I'll try to provide someone to escort your kids to and from school and another person to tag along with Kathryn. But what about you? You're the primary target."

"I'm willing to take my chances. Unless they come after me with a weapon other than a metal rod, I'll be okay. They'd seemed more intent on hurting Helga rather than killing her."

O'Hare hesitated for a bit. "That may not be too smart, but be careful. You know the game—stay in crowds, stay alert to strange guys approaching you regardless of the number of people around, avoid isolated places where they could get at you alone. You're likely okay on campus but away from there, you could put yourself in danger."

An hour later O'Hare confirmed the arrangement to protect Kathryn and the children with an immediate start. Jason thanked him and tried to focus on the mound of papers on his desk. But his brain continued to mull over the potential for a confrontation with the angry, and probably irrational in their rage to revenge the son, men. They would know his name from all the press and could easily find his home address. He prepared himself for a lengthy period of being constantly alert and questioned his rationale for asking O'Hare to put priority on his family. He tried to think about the potential places he could be vulnerable and wondered if the assailants knew his schedule in any detail. Or would they tail him until an opportunity jumped out. And he suspected they'd not give up until they'd accomplished their revenge. He recalled Kathryn's question about the continuation of the threats, but had no answer. He knew he had to be on the alert until it ended.

But the confrontation came much sooner than he'd ever considered.

Chapter 28

At seven-thirty the next morning a uniformed patrolman appeared in time to escort Jennifer and Tony to school. After some reluctance about the cop, a gun on his hip and other contraptions fastened to his belt, the kids came around to think it was more than cool to ride in the back of the patrol car and wave at their schoolmates they passed on the street near the school. A uniformed woman came to the front door to identify herself and in an unmarked sedan followed Kathryn's Buick to her parking lot and watched as she entered the Medical School building. Jason drove to his normal spot on campus and walked into the building without seeing suspicious men around. The escorts appeared again to make certain the children and Kathryn arrived home without incident.

After working hours, Kathryn and Jason visited Helga in the hospital. She was sitting up with a book on her lap. Her eyes were closed when they entered but fluttered open when she realized she had visitors.

Jason asked, "Helga, how're you doing?" They moved closer to her bed. Jason touched her hand.

She shook her head. "Not very well. Still have lots of pain across my abdomen. The physician thinks perhaps they may operate to determine the damage. He thought I would be gaining strength and having less pain than I have. I'm on medication all the time."

"I'm sorry," Kathryn said. "We wanted to see you, but maybe we should let you rest as much as possible."

A faint smile creased her face as she responded. "That's all I've done for days now. But I've thought about Jason and worried the same guys would come after him next."

"We're taking precautions and have escorts to and from work and school."

An orderly appeared with the next dosage of meds and began to rearrange the bedding and alter the back rest so Helga could be more comfortable. Jason and Kathryn eased out.

The following morning Jason left the house at his usual six-fifteen time for his morning jog through the park, the trail beginning only two blocks from his residence. At Kathryn's insistence, he carried a container of Mace in one hand. Nothing appeared out of the ordinary as he entered the park and picked up his pace in the spring coolness. He passed two other joggers whom he saw most mornings. They waved and kept moving.

Nearing a place on the trail where it paralleled a busy street for two hundred yards, he saw two figures leave a car and crash through shrubs to stand near the trail. Still twenty-five yards away, Jason suspected they were planning to attack him. He slowed to a walk as they took positions to block his path. Both were taller than he and appeared to be much bulkier. Both had long tools in their hands and took cautious steps toward him.

Suddenly one screamed, his features contorted with rage. "You're the bastard who killed my son. Now we're going to repay you."

They came at him with a rush, the metal rods raised to strike. Jason sprayed the Mace at them. The leader was hit full in the face and dropped his weapon to grab at his eyes. The second one stopped then leaned over his companion.

Jason's inclination was to grab the rod, attack them and take his chances, then he accepted that to be a foolish notion. Instead he veered off the asphalt trail and cut into the woods. Small paths had been made by walkers who wandered through the woods looking for birds or just exploring the vegetation. He took one of those and increased his pace as the trail broadened, reasonably sure he could outrun them if nothing else. After a couple of minutes, he stopped to listen. Footsteps and noise of movement through the brush alerted him to their effort to follow. He cut along another path and headed for the main trail, trusting his instincts to lead him in the right direction.

He stopped again to hear the men yelling to each other about his whereabouts. They weren't far behind him in spite of his steady pace.

Jason found the asphalt path and raced toward the spot they'd initially confronted him. He left the trail, cut through the shrubs bordering the park, and jogged along the street until he found the car they'd driven to the spot. He noted the license plate and then crossed the large avenue and crouched behind shrubs in a residential yard. He wanted to be sure they wouldn't go to his house and wait for him there. And he needed to confirm he'd correctly identified the vehicle.

Ten minutes later his potential assailants returned to the vehicle, still looking around the area and no doubt frustrated they'd failed. Standing near the car, one said, "We've lost him this time. We showed ourselves too soon."

"Yeah, we should have waited and jumped him from the bush. Next time we'll get the bastard."

"Yeah before he could shoot that junk into my face. Hurt like hell. Couldn't see for minutes." They tossed their weapons into the rear compartment. The metal rods clanked together.

As they drove away, Jason left his hiding place and retreated along the trail and the street until he'd neared his home. He slowed to a walk, surveying the surroundings for the huge blue mid-nineties model Chevrolet sedan. Rather than go directly to his house, he circled a block and came from the opposite direction. He passed his house and walked another block to be certain they were not parked and waiting. Satisfied they were not lurking, he returned home, but now he accepted they knew where he lived and had a handle on his habits. They would track him until the right opportunity for revenge presented itself. Next time they would give no warning.

During the breakfast period with the children scrambling to get their things together for school, Jason remained silent about the confrontation in the park. He didn't wish to worry Kathryn more than she now exhibited, her face drawn and tiny lines appearing below her eyes.

At the office he called O'Hare. "Tom, I encountered those attackers this morning in the city park. Fortunately, I escaped them but I got the license number of their car." He read off the number—YTM-449, then repeated it.

"I'll run a check and then follow through. Maybe this is what we need to bring an end to your problems."

"Let's hope so. I don't like being on the watch continuously."

Two hours later, O'Hare phoned. The secretary interrupted a meeting with an experienced department head wanting more resources for his unit as they'd run out of funds for the year. Jason wanted to help, but inside he wanted to chew the head out for failure to manage the unit's funds. Finally, he promised some small relief, letting them flounder for the next three months when the allocations for the coming fiscal year would be made. He wondered if Hawthorne had consistently bailed out the department and made a note to check with the accountants.

O'Hare started immediately. "Jason, no luck. The plate number you gave me is out of date. Most of these thugs have old plates they put on when they're on unlawful missions or they don't bother to renew and take a chance the police won't spot the old plate."

"So we're back to square one?"

"Let's do one more thing today if you can work it in. Come to the station and look through our mug books. These types usually have a record."

He called Kathryn to cancel their lunch date and turned back to the stack of papers on his desk.

After grabbing a hamburger at McDonalds for lunch, Jason went to the security office. The dispatcher had arranged the mug books for him and he spent thirty minutes turning the pages depicting unsavory characters. But he couldn't identify the ones who threatened him and returned the books to the desk.

He knocked on O'Hare's door and waited for Tom to complete a phone call. "No luck. But I didn't get a good look at them in the rush of the moment."

"They are probably locals who haven't been charged with a serious crime in the past, but we'll maintain our arrangement for a few days. They'll do something soon."

"Thanks for your help. We'll stay alert."

Mid-afternoon Ben Ramsey, a faculty member in Biology, came by the office. After discussing mundane matters for a couple of minutes, Ben said, "You likely haven't paid attention but I'm on the search committee for the dean position. We met this morning in preparation for sending out the announcement to other universities and placing copies in prominent journals. I wanted to make sure you're thinking about applying."

"Frankly Ben, I've not thought much about it. I've been too busy with other matters."

"I hope you'll become a candidate. And several others hope you will also. If members of the search committee are a good representation of the college, you'll have solid support. They've liked your approach." Jason smiled to himself thinking no one had been called in on the carpet and pushed to do a better job.

Ben stood, adding, "I've delivered our message and won't take more of your time, but I'd like you to become a candidate. The deadline is in mid-July, so don't let it creep past."

Jason walked toward the door with Ben. "I'll let you know one way or the other well before the cut off. And Ben, thanks."

Jason returned to his desk and stared at the wall for a bit. He'd reached a definite turning point in his career and had to come to grips about his future. He could either commit fully to an administrative role or return to Biology as a faculty member. Uprooting his friend, Pamela Sturgis, was not an option he wished to exercise. Returning to the department had numerous attractions. He'd enjoyed the role of a faculty member, teaching his classes and doing research. But he wasn't certain he could compete for grants with the younger people now and he didn't wish to become a drag on Biology like others who had failed to maintain currency with their field and spent most of their time thinking about retirement while they went through the motions of their work. Neither did he want to become one of those administrators who returned to an academic unit and spent most of his time second-guessing a department head and his or her colleagues.

He'd learned as a department head that administrative positions had their plusses. He could probably make a positive difference in an entire college, a collection of twelve departments and three hundred and fifty or more faculty with varying degrees of national recognition and commitment to become better. The down side was confronting the daily mixture of problems and issues coming from central administration, department heads, and faculty, each of whom had their own agendas, often not in harmony with the goals of the entire unit. And there was the ever-present issue of scrounging resources from state budgets that seemed to become tighter each year. Then he recalled President's

Snyder's gentle urging him to assume increasing leadership roles within the university.

He found the folder containing the position announcement and dropped it into his briefcase. He wanted to talk with Kathryn about the future. Then he smiled as he thought perhaps he could apply and be passed over, thus reaching an outcome regardless of his personal ambitions.

Before leaving the office Jason called the hospital to check on Helga. A nurse in the critical care section responded. "Her physician, Dr. Mansfield, plans to do exploratory surgery tomorrow morning to try to determine the underlying problem. She continues to be in pain and gross exams and the usual tests haven't revealed the basic problem."

She paused and continued, "I'm glad you called. She's listed you as her immediate contact in case of an emergency."

"She doesn't have close family in this country but I'll try to locate the family of her late husband. She has some ties to them."

"Dr. Grimes listed two individuals when she updated the information given at check in, if you'd like to see her notes."

"I'll come by tonight. Having those names would save a lot of searching."

After dinner Jason and Kathryn attempted to visit Helga in the hospital, but she had been heavily sedated in preparation for the operation the following morning. She couldn't participate in a conversation as she dropped off again and again. After ten minutes, they gave up and left her room.

But they were able to locate in her admission records the name of Jim Grimes' married sister, Martha Ratcliff, who lived in Canton, Ohio. Jason decided to wait until after the surgery to contact her when he could provide a more definitive update of Helga's prognosis. And he trusted the news would be positive.

Just before noon the next day, the hospital called Jason at his office. A nurse from the operating room staff was on the line. "Dr. Spradlin, you requested we let you know the condition of Dr. Grimes after her surgery." She continued as though she must complete one more task in her daily routine. "She came through the operation okay. The surgeon found a small vessel leaking blood into her abdomen and was able to stop that. He believes she will recover with no further complications, although one kidney was bruised badly from an external blow. Two ribs had been cracked, but those should mend on their own."

"May she have visitors?"

"She'll be moved to a private room in the morning and visitation is permitted."

"Thanks for letting me know," Jason said, completing the conversation.

He then called Helga's sister-in law to communicate the news.

Jason had not seen the potential assailants since his encounter on the park trail, but he doubted they'd given up their mission of causing damage to either him or a member of his family. After a week had passed with no further encounters, O'Hare called to let him know they needed to stop the escort duties. "We're pressed to do other things and although this hasn't required much time, it does disrupt other responsibilities."

"I understand," Jason said. "Maybe they've given up, but I am still wary and concerned they're waiting for the right moment."

"Stay alert," O'Hare said, "but most of these guys lose their desire to exact revenge after the heat of the immediate time has passed. Their more rational senses take control and they suspect they'll be caught in the act and confront the law."

"Thanks for your support," Jason said. "I know it takes its toll after a time and you need to move on."

He replaced the receiver and stared at the opposite wall for a few minutes, thinking about what precautions they should take to maintain the safety of his family and himself should the assailants appear again. He was primarily worried about Kathryn as the thugs would perceive her as the easier target. And they wouldn't give a warning. They'd just be there when least expected and neither he nor Kathryn would be prepared. He decided an easy precaution would be for them to drive in tandem to and from work, using one car whenever possible and if that couldn't work on a given day, he would trail her to her office and maintain sight until she was safely in her building. He was fairly certain an attack would not come on campus with other people around, but he didn't want to remove that possibility and would ask Kathryn to always be with other people as she moved across the campus from her office to Quincy or to the library. She would regard that as an imposition, but something she must do until the danger passed.

He'd also discuss the situation with Mrs. Carter who dropped the kids at school to make certain she would be on the alert if a strange car followed her from home or from school. His advice was to drive quickly to the Spencerville police station and don't stop for any reason, even if they banged into her vehicle.

The buzzing intercom interrupted his thoughts about constructing other pieces of his plan.

For another week they went about their daily routines without an appearance of the revenge-minded thugs. But Jason had continued to follow Kathryn to work and then again follow her home after hours or they went together and he dropped her off near the door of her building. And he met her for lunch each day as they utilized either the faculty club or one of the restaurants near the campus where throngs of people would present an obstacle to the attackers..

They were running late on Wednesday morning because Tony couldn't locate his homework assignment they'd critiqued the evening before. After a frantic search and with the missing paper found under a sofa cushion, Kathryn hustled to her car and pulled out of the drive a few seconds before Jason left the side door. But as he backed out of the private drive, he saw the blue Chevrolet pull in behind her and heard the motor being gunned to keep up with her. The assailants were on her trail.

Chapter 29

Jason watched the villains' car turn the corner as he waited for a passing car to clear his drive. He backed into the street and charged after Kathryn and her tail. Ignoring his usual habit of never using his cell phone while driving, he punched in O'Hare's number. Luckily Tom responded on the second ring and Jason blurted out his message. "Tom, those guys are chasing Kathryn toward her office. I'm following but send officers if at all possible. Medical School lot. Quick."

"We're on it." The line went dead.

Jason jammed the accelerator down, speeding along the city streets, passing other cars when the least opportunity arose, taking chances he'd not dream about under normal circumstances, trusting a patrolman wouldn't nab him for speeding and reckless driving. He dialed Kathryn's cell and waited for her to pick up as he visualized her searching through her purse for the instrument while trying to navigate a busy street and wondering what idiot was calling.

Finally after seven or eight rings, she responded. Jason ignored her question about what he wanted and blurted. "Where are you?"

A brief hesitation as she determined her location, then, "I just turned onto Ninth Street, three blocks from campus. Why?"

"Those hoodlums are behind you. Park where you usually do, but don't get out of the car. Lock the doors and wait for the cops. And don't stop for anything. They may ram your car, but keep going."

He could visualize her being slammed in the rear by the nuts and stopping to see what had happened, then getting conked across the head. "I'm coming fast."

Thirty seconds later Jason wheeled into the lot by the Medical School. Still not eight o'clock, there were only a few cars in the large space. The Chevrolet had stopped behind Kathryn's car and two men were scrambling out, prepared to attack as soon she exited. Without a plan in mind other than divert their attention from Kathryn, he rammed into the side of the big Chevy, backed away and turned toward the man trying to yank open Kathryn's door. He steered toward him, easing up as he neared the man who had no idea he was a target. Jason didn't wish to maim the person, but intended in the rush of the moment to steer his attention away from Kathryn. Moving forward he realized he was shoving the guy between the front side fender of her car and his front bumper, pinning him across his lower mid-section between the two cars. The burly man's arms flew upward as he fought to escape. A steady stream of profanity spewed from his mouth, like lava from an erupting volcano. In his flailing and cursing he dropped his weapon which bounced off the hood of Jason's car and skidded cross the pavement. Seeing that his buddy was in trouble, the second assailant raced around from the passenger side of Kathryn's vehicle and, waving a tire iron, came toward Jason who recognized him as the one he'd maced in the park.

The tall middle-age man, his face contorted with rage and frustration, slammed the iron into the driver's side window, cracking the shatter-resistant glass and sending fragments in all directions. Jason scurried across the seat, his arms raised to protect his face from flying shards. The thug continued to pound at the glass, trying to remove the remaining pieces, then reached in to unlock the door. He fumbled for the handle, his eyes boring into Jason's face. Jason prepared to exit on the passenger side as soon as the thug opened the driver's door or tried to swing at him from inside the car.

Just as the man jerked open the door and Jason slipped out the opposite side, sirens and squealing tires announced the arrival of two police cars. They screamed to stops near the scene. Four uniformed campus policemen emerged from the cruisers and hustled toward the thug wielding the iron and reaching into Jason's car. Guns raised, one shouted, "Stop. Drop the iron. Get on the ground. Now."

Confused by the sudden appearance and commands of the police, he hesitated. The cop yelled again. "On your knees. Now." His pistol drawn, he edged toward the man, watching for any aggressive action. The cop yelled, "Drop the rod. On your knees."

When the man continued to stare in defiance, a second officer rushed in from behind. Jerking his arms together, the two cops shoved him to the ground and pulled his arms behind his back. In the meantime, the guy pinned was screaming and struggling to escape from his trap. On a signal from the officer, Jason backed his car away to release the man. Officers grabbed his arms, yanked them to his back, and cuffed him.

O'Hare arrived and took charge, directing the troopers to take the prisoners to the station. They hustled the two attackers into the rear seats of their cruisers.

Jason went to Kathryn, now coming out of her car and watching her pursuers being led away and jammed into the rear of the trooper's cars. He took her hand and stared into her face. "Are you okay?"

Still looking at the scene and the cruisers, their lights flashing, people stopping to look, she nodded. "Just shook up a bit by all the hullabaloo. I'll be okay when I can regain my senses and get to my office." She rubbed her hand across her face as though trying to clear the scene around her.

O'Hare came closer. "Are you both okay?"

"We're good," Jason spoke for both. "But that was too close. If I hadn't seen them following Kathryn, she could have been badly hurt, or worse. And thanks to the quick response of the Campus police we avoided being damaged." Visions of Helga stretched across the floor of the lab flashed through his mind.

O'Hare touched Jason's arm. "That was good thinking, pinning the one between the cars."

Jason shrugged and grinned. "I had no idea, no plan on what to do, except divert their attention, and hope you showed soon. Fortunately, it worked out." He took a couple of steps. "I knew I shouldn't try to attack those hoodlums with their weapons. That was what they wanted."

O'Hare said, "Sometimes the unusual approach works best. You never know."

The detective continued, "We'll hold them at the station and work with the City Attorney in charging them. We won't release them until we're certain they pose no further danger to you or others."

"Make sure there are no additional accomplices," Jason said. "I have no idea if these guys are family, members of the same group as Westlake and his cronies, or . . . ."

"We'll check it all out." O'Hare turned toward his vehicle to follow the police sedans, easing out of the lot in the mass parade of faculty and staff arriving for work.

Still holding Kathryn's hand, Jason scanned her face. The shock of the rapid events and the potential consequences had begun to sink into her consciousness, Her face was whiter than usual. Jason could detect tremors in her fingers. And his were not the epitome of calmness.

He waited while she retrieved her briefcase and purse from her car and walked with her toward the building.

At the door, she said, "I'm okay. I'll take it easy in the office for a few minutes before I meet my class at ten. But you need to take your car to the shop. You can't drive with the window missing."

"I'll call 'Biff's' Garage. They'll tow it in and do the repairs, but I may have to bum a ride with you home tonight." He had relied on 'Biff' Jamison for several years to do minor repairs, conduct the mandatory state inspections, and do routine maintenance of his vehicle. He had confidence in them to do whatever needed doing without an exorbitant charge.

Turning away, Jason said, "I'll meet you here and we can walk to the Faculty Club for lunch."

Kathryn smiled at his concern. "I'll meet you there. No need to spend another ten minutes of your morning coming here."

"I don't mind. I need to get out of the office and the walk will do me good." He turned toward his own vehicle to retrieve his briefcase.

He looked back at her. "Plus, I like to spend time with you."

In his office, Jason called 'Biff', explained the circumstances, and asked that they pick up his car from the parking lot. He tried to focus on the upcoming tasks he needed to accomplish but events of the chase and arrests were hard to tamp down. Visions of Kathryn being hit by one of those metal rods continued to thread into his concentration.

An hour later, O'Hare phoned. "Jason, we've booked these two men and are charging them on three counts of assault with a deadly weapon. They're not yet willing to reveal anything about others, but I suspect they're the only ones bent on revenge."

"We need to determine Helga Grimes' prognosis before we finalize those charges. If she dies, it could be murder."

"I'll find out before we go much further. At this point in the interrogation we haven't pinned them down to the assault on Grimes. We've learned their addresses and will get a warrant to search their places. I'll let you know what we find, if anything."

"Each time the older of the two assailants, the one with the beard, has yelled about revenge for his son's death."

"We did confirm he is the father of the younger man killed in the car with Westlake. The second one is an uncle."

"So somehow they're all related or have known each other for some time."

"We'll check all possible connections in the next few hours."

Kathryn was waiting in the foyer of the Medical Building when

Jason arrived near the lunch hour. She smiled and came to take his arm and lead him toward the outside door adjacent to the parking lot. Jason recognized immediately his car had been towed or driven away. 'Biff' had done his job as promised.

Jason asked, 'So how was your morning after all the excitement?"

"It was difficult to focus for a while, then I forced it aside in order to teach class. Afterward, I managed to work on a paper King and I are doing. So a reasonably productive time."

He watched her face, devoid of expression, her eyes on his face. He stopped walking, then said, "I'm sorry I got you into the middle of this. Now let's hope this is the last encounter with these guys. This has been going on for months in one form or another. We've had enough. It's time to find closure."

She squeezed his hand, understanding his frustration, as they continued the five-minute walk to the Faculty Club in the bright mid-day sun with the trees greening and the bulbs reaching full flower. Students were hurrying from class to their lunch. A few sat on the benches along the walks, waiting for friends or just enjoying a few minutes of relief from assignments. Two men jogged past and waved.

Kathryn said, "This is a beautiful campus. We're lucky to work here."

"You're right, but it's easy to miss the beauty and appreciate it during busy work days and all the other things that grab your attention."

Just after four in the afternoon, O'Hare phoned again. "Jason, I wanted to update you on the situation with the assailants. We searched the houses of these two and found numerous documents and pamphlets berating the federal government for almost any thing you can imagine. And we found a list of their buddies along with telephone numbers and E-mail addresses. All of those who died in the car, except Riley, were listed."

"So they were a gang or sect out to wreck havoc where they could."

"Right, and for some reason focused their efforts on that lab and the work you people were doing. We found a computer holding a horde of messages to and from unknown names but we're continuing to unravel the communications."

"It might be worthwhile having Feller and Sparks review those messages. See if they recognize anyone from the D.C. offices."

"Good idea. We'll do that."

The next week went rapidly as faculty focused on the end of the academic year, students crammed for exams, and traffic in the town increased as parents came to pick up their children. Students and parents lugged belongings from dorms to cars, tossing some things into the dumpsters provided nearby. Adding to the congestion, the University Commencement ceremonies attracted extended families of those receiving degrees. Grandparents, aunts, uncles, cousins and others came to see their kin complete his or her education and finally be on their own. Motels and hotels within two hours driving distance from Spencerville were overrun, although the rates had been raised to take advantage of commencement attendees.

Jason focused on his responsibilities as the interim Dean, thinking he might never have to do this again. One task he'd not thought about until the last moment was his need to preside at the college level commencement ceremony. Fortunately a commencement committee of faculty had arranged the details and led key players through a rehearsal. The chair, Dr. Rose Murphy, a long-time professor in chemistry, gave him an outline of the parts he was responsible for, even with suggestions about his comments to the graduates and their kin. Then on Saturday morning, he stood before five thousand in the huge gymnasium, congratulated the graduates, wished them well and shook each hand as they passed across the stage, a precious diploma clutched tightly.

His children were looking forward to summer break and a brief vacation period with Jason and Kathryn. As they reviewed brochures of possible sites, Jason insisted they not stray far from home as the termination of Kathryn's pregnancy approached. He didn't want an early delivery while away from her physician and other medical facilities available in Spencerville.

On Tuesday after the university commencement, O'Hare telephoned Jason to update him on the investigation. "We've confirmed the two who chased Kathryn were associated with Westlake who acted as the leader of this band of local men who tried to upset several projects supported by the federal government. They picketed a dam site for weeks a couple of years ago and even attempted to blow up the trailers used by the workers.

"Feller and Sparks followed through by tracking messages

between Westlake and his contact in D. C. After days of searching computer records and questioning suspects, they focused on an accountant, a long-time federal employee named Brent Hogge, a member of a group who maintained all the records associated with the weapons project. Hogge reviewed the original contract between the Agency and you. He recorded all the expense vouchers and made certain those were handled correctly.

"Then he went beyond his normal responsibilities. From his home computer he sent Westlake a steady stream of information about the 29th Street lab and the renovations going on there. Somehow he figured out the research was not on a common disease, but in fact was an effort to develop a toxic weapon."

"Maybe he knew enough about the equipment and supplies to know or at least to cause him to speculate about the actual mission." Jason figured an intelligent person with an inquiring mind could readily determine the project was not what had been in the original contract between the Agency and Jason. Then bringing Helga Grimes on board with her history of weapons development may have been another important clue.

O'Hare continued, "Sparks discovered that Hogge was living with one of the secretaries in Johnson's office. He likely used her to discover even more about the actual work. We can't prove that she knowingly aided him, but more likely in their routine conversation about work, information was passed that supported his suspicions."

"And," Jason said, "she would have overheard conversations within Johnson's office, perhaps between Johnson and me. Having

Walcott come into those meetings would have served as another indicator of the true focus. She also would have been aware of the telephone calls back and forth between us."

"Sparks and Feller believe she was an unwitting instrument used by Hogge and have recommended no charges be placed against her. But they're working with the legal team to bring Brent Hogge up on charges of sabotaging a federal project."

Jason said, 'That seems to bring closure to the mysterious mole, but a lot of damage was done, not to mention serious injury to a valuable scientist. I hope he can be put away for a long time."

"How is Dr. Grimes?" O'Hare asked.

"She's been home for several days. Her neighbor looks in on her and helps her with shopping and other chores. She came by my office a couple of days ago. She looks a lot better, but is still weak from the surgery and aftereffects of the injury."

O'Hare said, "I'll let you know if anything changes, but it looks like those two who confronted you and Kathryn will plead to some lesser charge rather than go through a trial, but nevertheless will end up serving some time in a state institution. Their lawyer is trying to convince the Prosecutor they intended only to scare Kathryn and, indirectly, get to you. But that's a hard sell after their assault on Dr. Grimes."

Jason said, "That seems to wrap it up and I'm glad it's behind us." Then he added, "Just so you know in case you need to contact me I'll be away for ten days starting next weekend," Jason said. "My family is going to a quiet resort in the Ozarks for some down time. Then we're back here getting ready for twins changing our household."

"Good luck. Twins will be exciting, but I don't envy you the turmoil they will bring."

Chapter 30

Preparing to leave for the day, Jason arranged folders in his briefcase and started for the door. The building had gone quiet and the outer office had become dark as the staff had departed thirty minutes earlier. Then his phone rang.

Tempted to keep walking and let the caller try again in the morning, he decided the message could be important or the person wouldn't try after hours and he turned back to pick up the receiver, placing his briefcase on the corner of his desk.

"Dr. Spradlin, it's Beverly in Deputy Director Johnson's office. I'm sorry to bother you after working hours, but he insisted I try both your office and home numbers." Jason recalled the forty-plus year old brunette at her desk outside of Johnson's office, constantly shuffling papers and dialing numbers. She'd been the only one in that office to demonstrate any signs of recognition or friendliness during his several visits.

"You almost missed me here, but what's up?"

"He would like for you and Dr. Grimes to come to D. C. day after tomorrow. He needs to complete the final review of the contract you had with the Agency."

Jason flipped two pages of his desk calendar. Nothing that couldn't be rearranged appeared in the listings, an appointment with two faculty complaining about their raises for last year, and another with Roy

Blount about the Redlake project. And the daily paperwork would pile up to be taken care of when he got to it. Into the receiver, he said, "I can do that and I'd guess Dr. Grimes can also." Helga was not engaged in any activity at the moment as she continued to recover from the confrontation with the hooligans.

"We were hoping it would be okay and have made reservations on the usual flight for the two of you. Either Sparks or Feller will meet you at the gate and escort you here."

"Do we need to bring anything?" They'd given Johnson and Walcott a summary of their tests to develop a toxic weapon. And he wondered if this meeting was essential as they'd communicated everything on the previous visit.

"He wasn't specific but you'll know what he and Dr. Walcott might be interested in reviewing and confirming."

"We'll take a guess and see you on Thursday morning." Jason left a note for Bridgett to rearrange his schedule and exited into the quiet hall. With no students around immediately after the end of the spring term, most faculty had taken time off and those with academic year appointments with no teaching or research assignment for the summer session had gone on holidays. Most would come in to check their mail at random times. Others would be in their office most days working on a manuscript or a book. Those with research projects would toil away in labs overjoyed to work on their venture without interference.

From home he called Helga to alert her. After telling about the request from Johnson, he said, "I hope you're okay to travel. If not, I'll let Johnson's office know tomorrow."

"I should be okay. My physician has told me to take it easy for the next few weeks, but hasn't placed any restrictions on my movements. Traveling to D. C. shouldn't be too strenuous."

"We're on the early flight into Reagan. I'll come by for you at five-thirty." The seven-fifteen flight was usually filled but they wouldn't have to worry about luggage and security would be easy at the early morning hour.

As scheduled, Sparks was waiting for them at the gate when they emerged from the gangway at eight-thirty. He wore his usual brown sports jacket and lighter colored slacks.

He grinned and came to shake their hands. "Good to see you both. You know the routine. I'm parked in the usual spot. Unless you need the restroom, we can be on our way." They started weaving their way through the crowded terminal.

An hour later they arrived at the now familiar suburban building and parked in the rear. Sparks led them on the usual route through the front door, down one floor, and into Johnson's suite. The place hummed with three secretaries working on computer terminals or on the telephone. Beverly, dressed in a light blue dress that matched her eyes, stood as they approached. "He's waiting for you but let me ring Dr. Walcott's office and you can enter together." She dialed the interoffice phone as she talked.

Sparks said, "I'll come back for you after the session." He nodded to Beverly to confirm their signals.

Johnson and Walcott shook their hands and pointed them to chairs around the conference table in one corner of Johnson's office. Beverly brought in coffee and the usual condiments.

Johnson started without any preliminary questions about flights or their well-being. "You may have heard I'm leaving this position in the next two weeks to take a slot with the Secretary of the Interior. It's somewhat different than this job, but my experience here will be useful. But before I depart, I wanted to review the work you accomplished under the contract, tie up any loose ends, and discuss how we might have done it better. You may not know, but this is routine with any contract we have with an outside organization or scientist."

Jason chimed in to say. "You will recall that we provided a summary of our experiments before. But we can respond to any questions that may have arisen during your review."

Johnson nodded. "Anything we should have done differently?"

"As for the actual work in the lab, we were satisfied," Jason said. "A different arrangement for security may have saved us several headaches and a serious injury to Dr. Grimes. I understood the intent was to not advertise the nature of the project by having a host of federal people around the facility, but somewhere in between that and almost no security may have been the better approach. We likely could have saved money we spent for repairs after those break ins, not to mention some lost time. "

Johnson nodded. "Of course, that's hindsight. We could not have predicted the interest the project generated in the community nor could we have foreseen the upheaval caused by the information leakage."

Walcott shifted in his chair. "What about the science phase?"

Helga looked at Jason before responding. "We had sufficient information and background about the organism we were using and the equipment was top-notch. As you know, we struggled some but that was expected. After all, we were trying something new and I think innovative."

Walcott continued. "This was our initial attempt to farm out a major project to a university based scientist on or near a campus and I'm pleased the way it worked out. I'm disappointed we lost all of that valuable equipment to those hoodlums, but the outcome of the project was a success. Actually, it exceeded our expectations. I want to share something with you that undergirds my statement about success."

He opened a folder, pulled out a news clipping, and handed it to Helga. She placed it so both she and Jason could read.

The headline, apparently from an inside page of newspaper with neither a date nor an identification of the paper showing, grabbed their attention: **Strange Deaths in Isolated House.**

Walcott waited for them to scan the five paragraph article. "As you might guess, we utilized the toxin you developed to stop a terrorist cell from doing significant damage in one of our major cities. This group led by a well-know radical was using the house on the outskirts of the metropolitan area as a meeting site and for the collection and storage of materials to be utilized in a bomb or bombs."

Walcott paused, seemed to collect his thoughts. "We had suspicions because of their purchases of commonly used ingredients for bomb making. Luckily we were able to infiltrate the group and figured out their time schedule for placing bombs in an airport terminal and a downtown bus station. In fact, we recovered the bombs after the toxin had disappeared from the premises. As the article stresses, everyone is puzzled as to the cause of death in seemingly healthy men. And of course, we're not revealing anything. The local Medical examiner ruled the deaths as a pulmonary malfunction without going into details. I suspect he really didn't understand what had happened and there was no pressure to explore in any depth the cause of death further."

Johnson added, "This worked perfectly and will no doubt get the attention of these guys planning on doing damage to the U. S."

Helga said, "So it's obvious you were able to replicate our toxin."

Walcott nodded, his grin revealing his pleasure at their success. "It turned out to be an easy process after the usual trials and errors. We did improve the delivery system so it's reasonably safe and easy for an operative to drop the container into a place and escape without placing himself in imminent danger. "

"So," Johnson said, "you did a fine piece of work and have aided us in adding another instrument that can be employed against these terrorists. The Agency appreciates your efforts." He paused, reached for a folder and asked, "We're ready to officially close out the project and give up our lease of the lab in Spencerville."

Jason said, "State University has agreed to pick up the lease and perhaps at the appropriate time, purchase the building. I've cleared this through our Research Office and the Vice-President for Administration. I'm authorized to sign for the University if the documents are ready today." Jason had spent several hours talking with university officials and had given them a tour of the 29th Street lab. He had stressed the advantages of the facility to those who knew little about laboratory based research. The administrators saw the building as another way to relieve crowding in the research labs across the institution. Jason hadn't tipped his hand during the discussions, but he anticipated taking the building for another research lab for Biology.

Johnson pulled another paper from the folder. "Here is the paperwork to pass the lease from the Agency to State University effective immediately." He pushed the papers to Jason. Jason signed the multiple copies and removed the one marked for State University.

Walcott said, "If you are interested in another project down the road, we'd be open to discuss our needs. We're always looking for better products and improved methods of utilizing those. And our requirements change as the enemies alter their approaches."

Jason was pleased he and Helga had discussed the possibility on the plane. "We might be at some point if we can be assured there will be no release of information about the work. Neither of us wish to confront groups intent on sabotaging the effort."

Walcott nodded his understanding. "Of course, any future contract must be approved by Deputy Johnson's replacement, the Agency Review Board, the Secretary of Homeland Security, and Congressional Oversight committees. We may get in touch with you in a few months." Jason and Helga understood a new administration may wish to continue producing biological weapons or they could decide to scrap the initiative.

Johnson shoved back his chair and stood. "I believe we've covered everything. I appreciate your work for the Agency. Now Dr. Walcott has arranged for lunch and your return to the airport." He reached to shake their hands.

In the outer office Jason shook Beverly's hand and thanked her for keeping all the logistics working.

Ten days later as summer established itself in the region, Jason, Kathryn and the two children found themselves at a small resort in the Ozarks, fifty miles from State. Huge trees surrounded the lake and provided shade and a feeling of privacy for each of the twenty cabins varying in size to accommodate families or couples. The grounds were well-groomed with walking paths, flowers and shrubs of every shape and size, all contributing to the ambience of beauty, rest and relaxation. The main building housed an excellent dining facility, a coffee shop for those looking for quick service, and other amenities including a spa, workout equipment, gift shops and other lures intended to earn money for the organization and keep the residents content.

Jennifer and Tony had explored every aspect of the grounds within the first few hours, trying to satisfy an innate curiosity and searching for pastimes to keep them busy and challenged. Like children everywhere, they had made friends with others their ages. Jason and Kathryn were content to watch from the comfort of the front porch of their cabin, to consume the excellent food, read works of fiction and take strolls along the well-marked trails through the surrounding forest. But they were careful about any activity that could in the least way challenge the well-being of Kathryn, now into the early part of her eighth month of pregnancy.

The last night at the resort the family had dined in the restaurant, consuming more than they should, but enjoying the fine food. Jason was pleased with the manner in which the children had become comfortable, even adept, in using the correct utensil, avoiding spills, and apparently enjoying the experience. But he accepted they would rather utilize a fast-food establishment and wash down hamburgers and fries with soft drinks.

As the desserts were finished, Jason said, "Well guys, tomorrow we go home and things will soon be different. You know Mrs. Carter will be gone and her replacement, Ms. Castile, will start the next morning."

Jennifer jumped in. "And soon Kathryn will have twins."

Kathryn smiled and touched Jennifer's hand. "That's right, a girl and a boy if the tests are accurate. And you both will have to pitch in to help. Two babies will take a lot of effort on everybody's part."

"I don't think I can change diapers," Tony growled, his face contorted into a grimace.

Kathryn said, "You probably won't have to do that. Between Ms. Castile and myself, we can likely take care of those things. But you might enjoy rocking the babies and watching them fall asleep."

Jennifer piped up. "What are their names?"

"We're working on that," Kathryn said. "If you have ideas, let us know. But we may need to wait until we're absolutely certain they are a girl and boy."

A group of children came by and enticed Jennifer and Tony to join them for a last walk around the lake. As usual Jason warned them about keeping out of the water except in those areas patrolled by resort employees.

Watching them leave, Jason took Kathryn's hand. "Are we ready for this?"

She snuggled closer in the swing. "We have no choice, do we?"

His arm around her shoulders, Jason said, "We'll make the best of it and at the same time keep our careers going at State. You made the right decision to cut back to half-time, focus on the department seminar and your research."

"And you are again jumping into uncharted waters with this dean's search coming to a close by Thanksgiving. You worried about that at all?"

"It'll work out for the best. I have several options if I get passed over." Jason had submitted his application two days before the deadline. He had some confidence he would be successful because the President had encouraged him to make the jump to a college-level administrative slot. And he suspected Vice-President Hayes favored him but could not openly support him before the actual process approached decision time. Understanding the process, Jason realized that the top university administrators would influence the choice unless there was an outright rejection by the search committee. And his friend Ben Ramsey assured him that wouldn't happen.

"We've talked about those before but I want you to be happy."

"As long as I have you in my life, everything is rosy." He kissed her on the cheek and held her closer, thinking about the turmoil and challenges they had experienced together and knowing they could overcome almost any adverse condition the future might hold for them.

THE END

CPSIA information can be obtained at www.ICGtesting.com
Printed in the USA
BVOW021819021211

277147BV00005B/5/P